It's Raining Cats and Dogs

Geoffrey Doody

AuthorHouse™ UK Ltd.
500 Avebury Boulevard
Central Milton Keynes, MK9 2BE
www.authorhouse.co.uk
Phone: 08001974150

© 2010. Geoffrey Doody. All rights reserved

No part of this book may be reproduced, stored in
a retrieval system, or transmitted by any means
without the written permission of the author.

First published by AuthorHouse 12/28/2010

ISBN: 978-1-4567-7108-9

Any people depicted in stock imagery provided by Thinkstock are models,
and such images are being used for illustrative purposes only.
Certain stock imagery © Thinkstock.

This book is printed on acid-free paper.

Because of the dynamic nature of the Internet, any Web addresses or
links contained in this book may have changed since publication and
may no longer be valid. The views expressed in this work are solely those
of the author and do not necessarily reflect the views of the publisher,
and the publisher hereby disclaims any responsibility for them.

Humorous Adventures of a Boarding
Cattery and Kennels Proprietor
Dealing with the Animals
in his Care

Acknowledgement

For my incredible wife who has had the patience of a saint to work with me over the years it has taken me to publish this book. She painstakingly typed my awful long hand and helped to revamp it hundreds of times since, into this wonderful humorous collection of stories.

My sincere thanks go to Mickey Leighton, a golfing friend, who has drawn the caricatures giving the book its own personality.

I would also like to thank all my family, friends, customers and their pets, of which many are characters in my book.

Although all the stories are based on true facts, some names have been changed to protect identities.

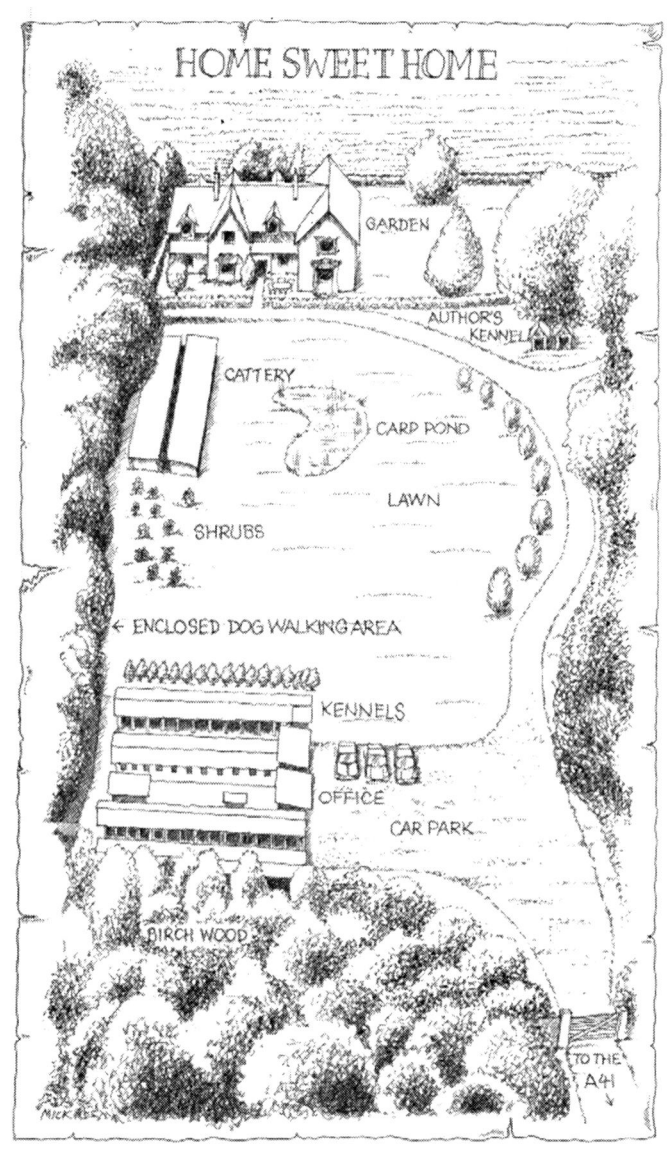

Contents

Acknowledgement	vi
Introduction	xi
Benson	1
Houdini Hounds	13
Sukie	41
The Idea	49
Planning Permission	61
Building	67
The Howling	79
Creating Interest	93
Pugs Came First	101
Chinese Take-Away	105
The Signs	115
The Sign Writer	133
Walking Diners	147
Indian Take-Away	155
The Love of My Life and the Lustful Lab	167
When Arthur Met Sally	181
Temperament!	187
Are Rotties Aggressive?	221
Are Cats More Dangerous Than Dogs?	227
Tiger, Tiger, Shining Not So Bright	249

The Escape Artist	257
Not the Sweetest of Smells	269
Percy Police Dog	275
Bath Time	285
Spots before Your Eyes	295
Filipino Take-Away	307
Mother	315

Introduction

It is a February day here in Spain where I live with my wife Kathy. I am sitting enjoying my retirement with Moet our Maine Coon pussycat, he is doing his best to try and take up more space on my easy chair than me. No golf today because the rain is coming down like cats and dogs, (very appropriate for the title of this book), which has prompted me to start writing. It is nearly six years since we sold our cattery and kennels business in Shropshire, England and I have spun a lot of humorous yarns about our experiences working with cats, dogs and people, making our friends burst into hysterical laughter. For years they have always said I should write a book, so I will stop procrastinating, release my guilt in hoarding these stories to myself and entertain you.

Benson

I just couldn't resist whetting your appetite with this first story, about a doggy character called *Benson*. The other players in this story are Kathy, her sister Ann, who lived with us at the time and of course me.

In the early days when I was still on my own, business took off rapidly and it wasn't long before I had twenty dogs and fourteen cats to look after, for one person a heck of a lot of work. Kathy and I always knew we would soon need an assistant or two to help me run the cattery and kennels, but I needed to manage on my own as long as possible. This meant we didn't have to start paying staff wages while we were still repaying the small bank overdraft on the business. Kathy and Ann helped me any way they could. We all got up at five o'clock each morning to walk the dogs, before they went to their own work, and I was likely to receive any phone calls or customers.

In the evenings when the girls arrived home, we would walk the dogs again and as it was summertime, the long daylight hours were a bonus. In the beginning it was a novelty, we all thoroughly enjoyed it and when we had friends over for an evening, they also helped us to walk the dogs and it was great entertainment for everyone.

The three of us walked the dogs around a circuit in the beautiful surrounding woodland, which consisted of oak, ash, birch, and Scotch pine. The bracken had grown to about four feet high on either side of the pathway I had cut, so it appeared that when we were separated on the woodland path we were totally on our own in a lovely tranquil world. When we were halfway through dog walking, both in the mornings and the evenings, Ann went to the cattery to feed the cats which was about 300 yards away.

Now we come to my friend Benson, he belonged to Donna, a friend of Kathy's from work. They both worked in the same department in a bank in Cheshire. On most weekends Donna boarded my future doggy friend in our kennels. Donna lived quite close to the bank's premises, but as it was over fifty miles away from our kennels it made good sense for Kathy to bring Benson back with her on a Friday evening and then take him back on a Monday morning. Both Donna and Kathy also worked away in London a lot, so Benson had many seven-day stays with us.

Benson was a mongrel, they are often more intelligent than the purest breeds. And he certainly fitted into the intelligent category. He was a little bit smaller than a Labrador and a similar colour to a fox. He had a very appealing mischievous face and large black eyebrows that made him look more like a human being than a dog! He was just over a year old, absolutely full of life and energy, just as he should have been for a dog of that age. He became a real pal of mine and it was only natural that the three of us—Kathy, Ann, and I—wanted to walk our favourite dogs, so I always chose to walk him.

Benson was very friendly to other dogs, especially bitches and never showed any sign of aggression to any of the male dogs that boarded with us. All the dogs that came to our kennels had to be fully vaccinated, so it was never a problem to walk some of them together, providing they liked each other. Benson usually had the pleasure of walking with one of the lady dogs that was staying in the kennels. With him coming so frequently, he got to know the place and dogs really well, but more importantly, he knew the routine of dog walking.

Benson, as clever as he was, knew he was my favourite and when I was walking him he used to look up at me with his appealing, but mischievous big brown eyes, as if to say, "Come on Geoff, let me off the lead. I know this place like the back of my paws!"

My strict rule was we definitely *do not* let someone else's dog off a lead, unless you know you can outrun it. As fit and fast as I was at that time, I knew that there was absolutely no chance of me out running him. Although he wasn't my dog, as I saw him so often, I felt I was his owner, and I would like to believe that he thought the same. The three of us (Kathy, Ann and I)—not including Benson, because if he could have spoken he would have said yes—talked it over and agreed that it wouldn't be a problem to let him off his lead and as a bonus, it would save time.

The plan was that I would be able to take two other dogs on their leads while he was exercising and hopefully behaving himself. Anyway, Benson got his own way, so off the lead he went. This new idea worked successfully for many weeks. He thoroughly enjoyed himself and appeared to be completely trustworthy, always coming back to me when I called him. He had got into the habit of running around the circuit several times and looked to be running at a hundred miles an hour. Each time he passed me and the dogs I was walking, he appeared to grin and show off to them as if to say, "Look at me; I'm Benson. I'm Geoff's favourite and I'm fre-e-e-e-e."

Well, of course, the inevitable happened as it usually does. One sunny morning with the birds singing, I didn't have a care in the world and I was really enjoying life. Benson had done about

four of his usual twenty laps, when he suddenly disappeared. After about five minutes of not seeing him, it dawned on me. *Where is the little devil?* It usually took him about two and a half minutes to do his circuit, while grinning at all the dogs on their leads. After another five minutes of not seeing him, I shouted to Kathy, "Have you seen Benson?"
She shouted back across the high bracken, "He went past me about five minutes ago like a bat out of hell. I thought he was with you."

I was not unduly worried and thought he would probably turn up in a few minutes, but of course he didn't, did he! By then he had been missing for over ten minutes and the speeds he could achieve meant he could be miles away. I thought, *No, no, no, not my Benson. You wouldn't do this to me, surely you wouldn't you little devil!* (At that time I could have used words much stronger than that, believe me.) Oh yes he would, and he damn well had! My so called friend Benson had been conning me all the time, making me believe I could trust him.

When he disappeared that morning, I was walking two black Labradors, which were sisters. I decided to keep them with me because I knew he liked the two good-looking young ladies! Hopefully, when I called him he would come running back to see me and, of course, them. *Good plan,* I thought.

Walking from the woodland back into our grounds with the two black beauties on their leads, I spotted him. He was in a world of his own, running from the kennels to the cattery. His nose was down to the ground sniffing all the new smells that doggies like, with his tail wagging high in the air. I could see he was really enjoying himself, totally oblivious of me and obviously couldn't give a "monkey's" where I was.

"Benson, Benson" I called as sweetly as possible, although by then my temper was rapidly rising. I didn't want him to sense that I was getting very, very damn well annoyed and frustrated with him. Hearing me calling him, he lifted his nose from his sniffing, looked me straight in the eye, wagged his tail and then totally ignored me. I might as well have been bloody invisible. With that he proceeded at high speed—not toward me—but away from me in the opposite direction, disappearing into our garden. Oh, I can tell you, I was absolutely seething with anger. I still couldn't let it show, or he would have sensed my anger and I would never have gotten anywhere near the little sod. Believe me, with my mounting frustration, I could have used a word to describe Benson a damn sight stronger than *little sod!*

Our garden was all fenced in, as was all the property. I thought, *No problem; I'll corner him.* But no, Benson had different ideas. He thought it was fun running round with Geoff and the two

Labradors chasing after him. He showed not the slightest bit of interest in the two gorgeous black beauties, so I obviously stood no chance of enticing him back with them. I was only ten yards away from the cattery where Ann, unaware of my situation, was inside feeding the cats. Whilst trying to hide my mounting frustrations and rising blood pressure. I shouted rather abruptly, "Ann! Come out here and hold these two Labs!" She immediately came out and after taking one look at my purple face, knowing me well she never said a word and took them straight from me. Being free of the Labradors I was quite confident that this would enable me to catch the flying Benson. I thought, *Okay, mate. Here I come. Your freedom is coming to an abrupt end!"*

Benson obviously had other ideas. To him his fun was only just starting! My temper was rising by the second as I ran him around our house and garden at least eight times imagining what it would feel like to get my hands around his throat! Then he just vanished into thin air.

Exhausted, I ran to the garden gate and as fit as I was I flopped onto it for support, gasping for breath. I looked up a moment later and the sight that greeted me was way, way beyond my comprehension. There was my friend Benson in serious love mode! Can you believe he was mounted on top of one of the Labradors Ann was holding! At the same time, the little sod was gazing straight at me! His ears were pricked up and his tongue was lolling. I am sure by the expression on his face he was saying, "Hey Geoff, is this good fun or what?" I felt like killing him.

Ann hadn't even realised that he was on top of one of the dogs she was patiently holding. He had shot behind her so quickly and quietly while she had been looking toward the garden for me—and of course, the lunatic Benson!

"For Christ sake, Ann, stop him!" I shouted.
She looked down in amazement and finally saw what the sneaky Benson was up to. But by then he was well into the swing of things, so to speak. His backside was going ten to the dozen, not unlike a fiddlers elbow! I angrily rushed over to Ann with her two black companions and the naughty Benson. I can tell you at that moment in time I was in some sort of a temper and I am afraid I upset Ann with my colourful language. She, in turn, stormed off away from the farce back toward the cattery, leaving me holding the two black Labradors with Benson still in full love mode!

While holding the two Labrador's leads in my left hand, I made a grab for him with my right and completely missed him, as he jumped off his doggy friend who didn't seem to have a clue what was going on. Then the unthinkable happened, as Ann entered the cattery Benson quickly shot in behind her. I just couldn't believe what I had witnessed . . . *a dog loose in a cattery, my cattery, oh my God!* So that was when the fun really started. The intrepid Benson let loose in pussy paradise! In all his wildest dreams, he must never have thought he would get a day like this. What a lucky dog, for certain, no other dog in the world would get a similar chance!

Ann stood at the cattery door sobbing and as I went by her I stuffed the leads of the two Labradors into her hand and screamed, "Hold these." I stormed in after the nutter. I knew he couldn't get to any of the cats as they were all locked away in their separate runs, but he certainly could have frightened some of them—especially if they were not used to dogs. He was running at breakneck speed and almost heeled over on his two right legs as he ran in a clockwise direction around the pathway. All the cat runs were on his left side and the occupants were hissing, spitting, meowing and flying everywhere. As he passed each cat, he barked at them in his mounting excitement.

The noise in the cattery was increasing all the time; Benson's fun was increasing all the time; Ann's sobbing was increasing all the time, and Geoff's blood pressure, frustration, and temper were increasing all the time! God knows what customers might have thought if they could have heard the racket erupting from the cattery that morning. It was a good job we didn't allow customers on the premises at six o'clock in the morning; that's for sure!

Benson seemed to be increasing his speed even more and was absolutely bemused by so many cats, which had started to ricochet from their side panels and doorways! As I gave chase, he kept trying to outrun me, while at the same time having a good look at each cat as he flew past. He kept looking back at me with his mischievous grin on his face as if saying, "Hey Geoff. Catch me if you can, you're a bit slow."

After at least six circuits, I eventually made a flying rugger tackle and caught him as he tried to get past me and then there was a warm and wet feeling on my legs as I slid along the tiles holding Benson next to my body. He started licking my face and looked into my eyes, as if saying, "Please forgive me, Geoff. I was only having a bit of fun."

I can assure you I most certainly didn't think this episode had been fun at all, especially when I looked down at my once clean jeans in disgust to see that they were covered in runny dog excrement! By then I wanted to kill the little sod—not kiss him—but how could I be annoyed with such a lovely character! So I put him on a lead and walked him calmly over to the kennels, trying to keep my disgusting looking jeans from clinging to my legs. I must have looked a

sorrowful sight! Through gritted teeth I said, "Well young lad, there is more chance of hell freezing over than you ever being let off the bloody lead again!"
He looked up at me wagging his tail, as if to say, "Every dog has his day, and I have certainly had mine, mate!"

To end Benson's story, which I think will still have been the most exciting day in all of his life, the black Labrador bitch could never have got pregnant as she was not in season. None of the cats were harmed in any way at all. In fact, when I returned to them, I must point out, wearing a second pair of clean jeans, they were all very calm and happy . . . eating their breakfasts as if nothing had ever happened. Ann eventually forgave me for shouting at her, and we laughed together about the eventful fun hour we had just spent. Did I say fun hour?

Kathy had carried on with the dog walking, wondering where the mischievous Benson and I were. And I am sure Benson just felt as if it had been a normal day for him. He stayed many, many times after that day, but was never trusted again to be walked off the lead. No more repeat performances for me, thank you very much! Mind you, I suppose you can't beat a bit of early morning exercise, can you!

Well I hope you enjoyed Benson's little story. There are plenty more like him to follow.

Geoffrey Doody

Houdini Hounds

It was most certainly a lot easier for dogs to escape than cats, quite simply because we exercised the dogs around the woodland. And yes, we did have some escapists out of the kennels, just like my friend Benson! But fortunately, after a lot of excitement, effort, trauma, frustration, and whatever else you can think of, we eventually got them back. Very few cats, if any, would come back to a stranger's call, but dogs normally did—especially if you have a treat of some sort in your hand. If any dogs slipped their leads when we were exercising, they usually came trotting back. But I must say we did have fun with some of them, believe you me. Did I say the word *FUN?* It would have been more appropriate to have used the words, *downright traumatic*! The fun experiences we had (and I certainly had a few), could increase the rate of your heartbeat for sure.

It was an early winter's evening and the night was pitch black. Ann was outside finishing feeding the few cats boarding with us at that quiet time, while Kathy and I were in the house. The curtains were drawn making the house all cosy and warm. I was sitting in front of the fire watching the television and Kathy was in the kitchen preparing our evening meal. The smells were tantalising my taste buds and my ravenous tummy was starting to rumble, suddenly Kathy came running into the lounge and said, "Geoff, quick! Turn the television down. I can hear strange noises outside."

I grabbed the remote and pressed mute, killing the sound instantly. We listened and there was a terrible noise outside, it sounded like a woman screaming. Kathy exclaimed, "Oh my God! Ann's still outside!"

I immediately shot out of my armchair and ran into the hallway to open the front door. I whipped it wide open, not knowing what I was going to find. Looking down the pathway through the gate, I could see Ann's red Fiesta parked by the side of my green Daihatsu four by four. The strange thing was, the interior light of the Daihatsu was on and it was more than odd to see Ann sitting in the passenger seat, looking directly away from me. I ran down the path and grabbed hold of the driver's door; it was locked, so I banged on the window. Ann screamed and jumped in the shock of hearing me outside the door and looked toward me, I could see the relief flooding over her face at seeing me there and sadly she had tears streaming down her face. I ran around to the passenger door almost in a panic to find out what on earth was wrong with her. I opened the passenger door (there wasn't central locking in those days) and asked her, "Why are you sitting in here? What's wrong? What has happened? Why are you crying?" The questions were rolling off my tongue so quickly that I didn't even give her time to answer.

Ann shouted back hysterically, "I've been attacked!"

I was thinking in the terms of a sex maniac. "I'll kill him! Where has he gone? Has he hurt you?"

Through her sobs, she managed to get out in a shocked voice. "No, it wasn't a man; it was an animal."

"What do you mean an animal? Are you alright? What kind of animal?"

"I don't know. It was just big, hairy, and heavy. It came from behind and jumped onto my shoulders, nearly knocking me over."

Ann is five feet three inches tall, so the thing—whatever it was—must have been quite big to have landed on her shoulders.

She spluttered through her sobs, "When I screamed it ran off, I ran to your vehicle because it was the closest thing to me. Thank God the passenger door was unlocked. I have been screaming and blowing the horn for ages. Why didn't you come out before?"

"I had the TV on and Kathy was in the kitchen. I didn't hear you until Kathy came running in to say she could hear strange noises outside."

I eventually managed to persuade Ann to get out of the Daihatsu and go with me to the safety of the house. I said, "I'll get you a brandy to calm your nerves." I knew that would persuade her, she has never been known to turn down a brandy as our Ann. I thought, *Don't be so cruel Geoff; that wasn't called for.* When I saw Ann's eyes light up, I didn't need to feel too guilty for my thoughts.

Once Ann was safely inside the house with a brandy in her hand, I could see she was a little calmer after her stressful ordeal. I said, "I'm going outside, to find out what's going on around here."
"Aren't you taking your gun with you?" Kathy asked in alarm.
"Surely you're not serious?" I replied.
"Of course I am. You don't know what's out there, do you?" Kathy asked.
Ann then piped up, "I'm not kidding you, Geoff. Whatever it was, it was enormous!"
I could tell Ann was still under severe shock. I thought, *What can it be? I mean there aren't any grizzly bears around here, are there? We live in England, not Canada!*
Kathy in her wisdom said, "Well, at least take a stick with you. Surely you need some sort of protection, if that thing is as big as Ann said it is."

To put them both at rest, I decided to take one of my walking sticks with me, the type that has a 'V' in the top. I also took my rechargeable torch that was as powerful as cars headlights, which I often used to scan the grounds. Off I bravely went with I must say just a little bit of trepidation, I was careful to hide my cautious feelings from the two sisters. I went into the blackness of the night and flashed the torch around; I saw nothing and heard nothing. I decided to go down to check the kennels, even though it was as quiet as the grave. I hated to disturb the dogs at night, but I had to know that all our doggy boarders were okay. For all I knew they could have been attacked by the monster Ann had been described.

I went quietly into the office and looked through the window into the kennel block and carefully studied each run. I didn't want to turn any lights on which would have disturbed their doggy dreams, as I knew it would have been the end of a peaceful night. My eyes by then had adjusted to the darkness and I could see all the gates to the runs were closed. I couldn't see any dogs at all as they were hopefully sleeping or resting in their sleeping quarters. I thought, *Surely, they can't all be dead, could they?* Anyway, I was certain I would have heard the racket even from within the house. *Well if it is a big dog that has escaped, then at least it isn't from our kennels!*

I left the office and went back outside to make my way back to the house. A vixen (female fox) screamed out and that sound never fails to send shivers down my spine. You always seem to hear the same noise in horror films, don't you? Anyway, I was quite determined nothing, but nothing was going to frighten me out there that night. I turned the flashlight on again and scanned the grounds all around me, nothing stirred at all. Well that was it, there was nothing out there and whatever it was must have gone.

I headed back to the house to get my much-needed dinner, I was absolutely starving. My stomach started to rumble and with all the excitement I had forgotten just how hungry I was. As I was going through the gateway to our house I heard heavy breathing right behind me. I half turned just as something big and furry came into view and it hit me with considerable force between my shoulder blades. "Jesus Christ, what on earth is that?" I shouted out.
Spinning around with my stick at the ready, at that moment in time I wished I had my gun with me. My heart rate must have gone right off the Richter scale. To my surprise, standing in front of me was a monstrous long-haired German Shepherd dog, and thank God, it was wagging its tail. With relief I softly called, "Come here boy. Good dog."

The large dog jumped toward me, its tail thrashing from side to side like a scythe. Then in its excitement it launched its two front paws right onto my chest. Its hot breath was all over me and it was doing its best to lick my face. I could see it had a collar on, so I grabbed it and pulled the dog down off my chest back onto its four legs. All it wanted to do was play and I must say, it was rather boisterous to say the least. No wonder it had almost frightened poor Ann to death!

I thought, *Where the devil is it from? I don't recognise it as being one of our dogs.* I hung onto its collar with great difficulty. The dog must have thought we were playing some sort of game, as it playfully bounced about. I managed to drag it by its collar and banged on the window of the house. I shouted, "Kathy. Quick, get me a dog lead. And tell Ann I've got something to show her."

Kathy passed me the lead through the window and I managed to secure it to its collar as it still kept bouncing all over the place. I said to her, "I've never seen this dog before. It's not from here!"
"Oh yes he is. He came in just before we closed and his name is Rory."

Ann arrived at the front door as I laughed and said, "Let me introduce you to cuddly Rory, your little attacker. He's as friendly as they come."
"It's not bloody funny Geoff, he really frightened me you know," Ann retorted back. Ann still wasn't seeing the funny side of it but I was sure she would do soon.
I thought, *I'll give her another brandy after dinner and she'll be happy then!"* After my jesting I felt sorry for Ann and said, "I can understand why he frightened you, he just did the same to me."

Anyway, back to the serious stuff. (Or was that serious?) We had no idea how Rory could have possibly got out. As far as we knew the only way out of his kennel was through the gate of his run and then he would have had to get out through the main door of the kennel block. I asked Kathy, "Where about in the kennel block is he from?"
She replied, "He's down on the right hand side, in the end kennel."
"I'll take him back and find out how on earth he's got out," I said.

A very playfully Rory and I walked back down to the kennels to install him once again, hopefully for good that time. Unfortunately, I had to turn on all the lights and this disturbed the sleeping dogs, which made them erupt into excited barking and I knew it was going to get even worse, when Rory and I walked in. I also knew they would be thinking they were going out for an extra evening walk!

"Quiet, You Lot."
I bellowed at the top of my voice as I walked into the kennel block with the still playful bouncing Rory. Fortunately, most of the dogs quickly quietened down after my loud command. I walked Rory to his run at the far end of the kennel block and his gate was securely locked, obviously that couldn't have been his escape route. So how on earth had the big lad got out?

It's Raining Cats and Dogs

As I opened the gate to his run to lead him in I looked around and then up at the roof on the woodland side, I knew there was a small gap in between the mesh and the roof. It was no more than twelve inches deep and over six feet high from the ground. I would never have believed that a big dog like Rory could possibly scale a six-feet-high barrier, let alone squeeze through such a small gap. But Rory, the little devil had achieved that amazing feat. Did I say little because he was absolutely enormous! I locked Rory in his sleeping quarters for the night because I decided I would do the repair job in daylight the following day. I was sure he would attempt to scramble through and escape yet again if I had left him in the run.

Early the following morning, while my mate Rory supervised, I took some spare wire mesh to fill in the gap. It only took me about thirty minutes to complete the job, so my big furry friend wasn't inconvenienced for too long. I hoped he had enjoyed his fun night out on the tiles because I was absolutely sure it was going to be his last—on our premises anyway! And, I am certain Ann would reiterate those last few words! So, that is how I met Rory the dog 'Houdini'!

Over the years we had a large variety of dogs boarding with us and you would be amazed, just how many of them were able to scramble over a height of six feet. The amount of times we saw dogs climbing the high sides of the steel mesh was unbelievable. The most agile of them all was a dog called *Ozzie*. With a name like that you would think he was an Australian outback hound of some sort, but no, he was a beautiful three-year-old black and white Border Collie with a mischievous glint in his eye.

On Ozzie's first visit after his initial walk, I personally put him in kennel number three and then I went to get his water. When I came back, he wasn't there. I just couldn't believe my eyes. I scratched my head in deep thought as I walked down the row of kennels and there was Ozzie in kennel number five. I was absolutely bewildered. Had I put him in the wrong kennel? Was I going mad or what? I put him back in kennel number three and never thought anymore of it. Later that day one of the girls went into the kennel block to find young Ozzie sitting with an apparent big grin on his face in kennel number twelve! I knew damn well I hadn't lost my mind earlier. I had put him in the correct kennel that morning. We would put Ozzie back in his kennel and as soon as we had turned our back he would be down at the other end, standing there proudly panting. Most times he would hurdle all the way back again to where he had started. Thank God, at that time we had no aggressive dogs in as it could have been disastrous if one had attacked him as he intruded into their run. Fortunately, he couldn't escape out of the block, as the end had been secured by me because of Rory's previous antics. Ozzie was

It's Raining Cats and Dogs

absolutely incredible; he made Olympic hurdlers look like beginners! And Ozzie's hurdles were over six feet high! So, what do you think of that, all you Olympic hurdlers? I suppose the one other thing Ozzie had in common with Colin Jackson, the famous British Olympic hurdler, was they were both Welsh! A member of the S.A.S. would never have been able to get over the barriers half as fast as Ozzie!

Young Ozzie really created a lot of work for me because the gap I had filled in at the top of Rory's run was duplicated all the way down the kennel block and I had to spend more money getting some steel mesh. I measured up how much mesh I would need for one gap and then multiplied it for the twenty-two runs. I completed the work in two days and on reflection he had done me a big favour because if one dog like Ozzie could hurdle from one kennel to another, then sooner or later, other agile little devils could do the same and no doubt run into big, big trouble. Trouble could have materialised in the form of a large bad-tempered guest who wouldn't have been too happy in sharing his or her run with an uninvited visitor. There could have been blood and bits of dog everywhere! It doesn't bare thinking about. How do you explain to Joe Public all the stitches that are holding their pooch together is because they were able to climb into another dog's territory! I couldn't really have said, "Well it was their own fault because they went to visit big Bruno in the far kennel." Would they believe me? Somehow, I don't think so.

We had another escape artist that I nicknamed *Mole*. After Ozzie did me that great favour, although with more expense, of pointing out the twenty-two gaps, I thought that all the escape routes were sealed off and escape from our kennels was impossible. WRONG! I suppose you think just because I have nicknamed this next escape artist Mole, that she escaped by digging her way out. Well, you are wrong again because it was impossible; all the floors were solid reinforced concrete. The little devil was a black and white Cocker Spaniel bitch called *Pru*, which was short for Prudence. A Cocker Spaniel is a bit like a Springer Spaniel but smaller. From now on I think it will be more appropriate to call Pru Mole because of the trick she accomplished in this story.

Mole was small but very strong for her size, she could push and squeeze through gaps just like a mole in its tunnel; hence, the name I gave her. She had been a guest of ours in August the year before and had been no trouble at all, so we eagerly looked forward to having her back. Little did I know how different things were going to be with her second stay. If I had known what that little dog was going to do to my stress level I would most certainly have thought twice about boarding her again.

Eleven days into Mole's two-week stay disaster finally struck—and I really mean disaster. Within five minutes of the staff arriving at the usual time of eight o'clock in the morning, the Manageress rang me from the connection in the office to the house and said in a distressed tone, "Geoff, the little Cocker Spaniel has gone."
"What do you mean gone?"
"Gone . . . like disappeared . . . vanished!" she exclaimed.

Do you ever have a feeling you have had this conversation before and you know it is going to be a bad day? I sprinted down to the kennels at a speed that seemed close to 100 miles an hour and ran straight into the kennel block. I don't mean I literally hit the kennel block. I meant I went inside the kennel block to where I knew Mole should have been. Alas, it was true. The little devil had vanished right off the face of the planet for sure. The mystery was how and where the hell had she gone? I couldn't understand why on earth she wanted to escape anyway. She had been quite happy staying with us for the previous eleven days. The bad news was she was due to be collected in two days time. I angrily thought, *You naughty, naughty little doggy you.* I can assure you, you don't want to know what I was really thinking.

I could see from bits of loose hair that Mole had managed to squeeze under the framework at the front of her run, I found it unbelievable because there was only a four-inch gap. She had then squeezed down a waste water gully under the outside framework that led to the walk in the wood. I immediately shouted to one of the girls, "Run down the drive and shut the gate. She might still be loose in the grounds." My hope was that she hadn't gone through the gate in the short time since the girls had arrived for work. I knew once it was closed the grounds would have been fully secured. The wire-mesh fencing around the perimeter served two purposes; first to keep any loose dogs in and second to keep the large population of rabbits out. It was four feet high, so the little Cocker Spaniel wouldn't have been able or I hoped, had the initiative to climb over it. Rabbits quite often found a way of burrowing under the netting, even though it was buried and turned outward at the bottom. I checked every square inch of the perimeter fence and there were no tunnels anywhere.

We fruitlessly searched the grounds but to no avail. I had that horrible déjà vu feeling I had been down that road before. I thought, *Oh no! Not again!*

I checked the netting on the five-bar gate which I had securely covered and it even had a plastic skirt attached to the bottom that dragged on the floor. I had really tried to copy Fort Knox with all

my security. When I saw the bottom of the gate my heart sank.
"Oh, no, no, bloody no!" I shouted in frustration.

I knew for sure she was no longer in our grounds. The gate had been her escape route. I could see where she had squeezed through at the bottom, up against the gate post. There was a tiny gap of maybe four inches and the proof was a little tuft of hair exactly the same colour as Mole's.

I uttered under my breath, "Oh stuffing hell!" I knew for sure this dog was going to be flattened on the main road at the bottom of the drive. In my frustration I had a horrible sick thought, *Well at least if she has been flattened by a lorry she will now be able to fit through a gap an inch wide!*

I ran for my vehicle that was parked by the house 150 yards away. All this running was keeping me wonderfully fit. Don't ask what the stress factor was doing to me! I jumped in and had to be careful not to speed too fast down the drive in case I ran over our little friend Mole. She could have been coming back after her night out on the tiles and by that time she should have been hungry.

After driving down the drive and seeing no sign of her I parked at the bottom and climbed out of my Daihatsu. With some tasty doggy treats

in my hand I searched all around the area while calling in a friendly tone, "Pru, Pru; come here, good girl."
There was just no sign of her at all. In utter despair I jumped back into my vehicle and slowly drove down the busy main road for two miles in one direction and then the same distance in the opposite direction—but nothing, absolutely nothing! There wasn't a flattened Cocker Spaniel anywhere in sight, which made me feel a little relieved. I supposed at least that was some good news that dreadful morning.

I drove back to the house and phoned the police, hoping that someone could have handed her in or reported her running along the road. And guess what? Nothing! What on earth could I do? Nothing—nothing but wait to hear from the police. Hopefully some kind soul would save Mole's life and take her to the nearest police station and with my rising stress level, save my life as well. The day progressed sadly into night and there was still no news.

The next morning I felt absolutely drained having had little sleep with the worry of telling Mole's owners we had lost their dog. Just before I was about to leave the house to continue my searching the phone rang, jolting me out of my gloomy thoughts. It was our vet who asked, "Have you lost a dog?"

I thought, *Have we lost a dog? You bet we have mate and I've lost a bloody good night's sleep as well!*

I replied, "Yes we lost one yesterday and I have searched high and low. I have also notified the police and they have heard nothing."

The vet continued, "Well I have a bit of news for you. I was driving along the A41 when I saw a Cocker Spaniel trotting along the grass verge near the end of your drive. I stopped my car and as I got out it ran off into the wood."

I thanked him for his trouble slammed down the phone and rushed off to do a repeat performance of the day before. Well at least she was still alive. I was sure it wouldn't be for long if she tried to cross that road with the enormous juggernauts thundering along. I searched for hours again but alas nothing. Where the hell was she hiding? Didn't she realise what she was doing to my nervous system! I returned back to the kennels with my 'tail between my legs'. An appropriate saying for the way I felt at the time.

Later that day we had four more phone calls from people reporting they had seen a Cocker Spaniel on the verge of the main road, at the end of our drive. Well, where else would she be? I thought, *Why is everybody else seeing this damn dog and not me?* After each phone call I went down to search for her but found nothing. Every time I went down I stayed a little longer and waited for her to hopefully come out of her hiding place. I was sure Mole was nearby and could probably see me—very likely even watching me! I called out her name time and time again and then waited for hours sitting in my vehicle, each time to no avail. I realised I was going to have to face another night of worry and no sleep. I ironically thought, *Marvellous, bloody marvellous. I'm not making enough money for all this stress and they are meant to be collecting the little sod tomorrow!*

I woke up from a disturbed sleep with the realisation that the dreaded morning of Mole's supposed collection had arrived, with no lovable little Mole anywhere to be seen, or should I say no Pru anywhere. I was absolutely dreading telling her owners the bad news. I mean, everybody's dog is virtually a member of the family and there Mole was as of yesterday wondering round the woodland as free as a bird.

Can you imagine coming back off a wonderful holiday having gotten rid of all the stress, which you accumulated throughout your working year, to be told that some idiot kennel proprietor has lost your dog! My sarcastic thoughts were, *Oh, I'm so sorry, but I've lost your lovable little pooch. She has run off into the wood and we can't catch her. She was seen several times yesterday playing amongst the lorries on the main road!*

Oh my God, surely life can be better than this! I knew only a miracle could save me and of

It's Raining Cats and Dogs

course Mole. Well, at precisely eight fifteen on the morning of Pru's collection a miracle did happen, for who should pull onto our car park but our local vet. He got out of his car and to my considerable relief there was Mole by his side on a secure lead. I could have kissed Mole and even the vet as well. Frankly, Mole was better looking than the vet and at least she did have the advantage of being female. And she hadn't got a beard either! I just couldn't thank him enough. She looked incredibly fit and didn't appear to have lost any weight at all. Her coat was shining and as a bonus her stumpy tail was wagging like mad. I thought, *I must start going to church again, my prayers have been answered. Thank you God, you've saved my skin this time.*

Mole's owners came to collect her later that day and I couldn't wait to tell them all about their little doggie's adventures! *I don't think so*! They had absolutely no idea what had happened to her over the last three days and as far as I was concerned, that's the way it was going to stay. The manageress brought Mole—sorry, I mean Prudence—out of the kennels to be received by her owners. They thought she looked wonderful and exclaimed, "Oh she looks so happy and she's even put on weight as well!"
I thought, *Must have been all the rabbits she has eaten!* Well, I looked happy and unsurprisingly I had lost weight as well! I wonder why! My manageress and I gave each other a knowing

look and told Pru's owners how good she had been and how she had been no trouble at all! Were we bloody joking, or what?

Now we come to the final mind-blowing adventure of the last Houdini escape artist and his name was *Skip*. He was a black Mongrel with a strong strain of Border Collie running through his blood. His owner was an extremely nice gentleman who couldn't praise us up enough with all the good reports he had heard about our kennels. *I hoped it wasn't for losing dogs*! He had been recommended to us, which was always the best way of expanding our business.

After his inspection Skip's owner said, "I really like the look of your premises and I shall have no hesitation in recommending you to everyone I know." And that was even before Skip had stayed with us. Hearing comments like that from any customer was always an excellent boost to my ego. With that information buzzing in my head, I most certainly had to make doubly sure he was going to be more than happy with good old Skip when he eventually collected him.
Skip's owner said, "Sometimes Skip is very clever at slipping his lead."
I thought, *Uh, uh, here we go again*. I replied jokingly, "Don't worry; we have GLEAD's here."
"I have never heard of that. Is that some kind of special dog lead you have?" he enquired.

"Oh, no, it's not some special kind of lead. It's just my description of what we do here. We are the GREATEST LIVING EXPERTS AT DOG walking. GLEAD's."
He laughed at my corny joke.
I continued, "I will walk Skip for you personally. He looks like my sort of dog and there is no way he will slip his lead with me on the other end. I can assure you of that." *Famous last words!*

Skip's owner handed me the lead with his best doggy friend safely secured to the other end, returned to his car and drove off down our drive. Skip and I turned around the corner of the kennel block building and headed for the woodland.

I looked down at him and he wagged his fluffy tail as he looked back up at me. I said in my friendliest voice, "I can see you aren't going to be any trouble at all. Are you Skip?'
He wagged his tail even more as I stroked his back. Then in a flash he suddenly pulled backward, just like his owner had told me he could. To my horror and astonishment his collar slipped over his head, it was like watching it happen in slow motion. Skip had skipped!

"Oh, my God!" I shouted out aloud.
Goodbye, thought Skip.

Skip bolted toward the car park in the direction from where we just came, I shot after him but giving him as wide a berth as possible, I didn't want to chase and possibly frighten him. I needed to get past him to get to the five-bar gate before he did. I would then be able to close it and stop him making his escape down the drive. It was imperative I beat him to that damn gate. I felt I had gone from zero to 100 miles an hour in less than a second. Believe you me, I could really run in those days and at that moment I ran like the wind. Skip had never been on the premises before so he wouldn't know his way around and hopefully not find his way out. Or would he? But to my dismay as I rounded the corner of the kennel block, he was fifty yards in front of me, disappearing around the corner of the wood at the end of the car park. He was heading straight down the drive toward the main road.

I cut through the wood trying to head him off and get to the gate before he did. An Olympic hurdler would have had nothing on my turn of my speed through that 100-yard sprint as I hurdled over briars and thorn bushes in the birch wood. Alas, I was too late. He had beaten me to it by about five yards. I pleaded in a scream, "Come back, please, please Skip. Come back, Skip, Skip-p-p-p-p-p.....'

No chance. He was off down the drive like a bullet. I thought, *There goes another suicidal maniac about to get himself flattened on the main road.* I immediately about turned and sprinted off to get my vehicle, which was parked outside our house

It's Raining Cats and Dogs

150 yards away. I was running so fast I must have scorched the grass as I sped over it. I always left the keys in the ignition during the day and often at night. Thankfully, that day was no exception.

My old faithful Daihatsu started at the first turn of the key and I reversed fifty yards flat out to turn around with wheels spinning, trying to get traction on the tarmac. I slammed her into first gear and away she lurched. It was the fastest three-point turn I had ever done in my life. I had never driven down our drive so fast and as I did and I prayed no one else was coming up the drive because if they were they were going to get a big, big shock, especially when they saw a large green blur, representing my Daihatsu four by four, filling their windscreen.

At that time of the day, if anyone could have been coming up the drive, it was more than likely to have been the postman and I knew he drove like an absolute maniac as well. I had asked him on many occasions to slow down, but he never seemed to listen to my requests. Luckily, I didn't kill or even run into the postman or meet any other vehicle. At least something had gone my way, but could I save Skip's life?

When I reached the end of the drive I did an emergency stop. With the tyres screeching and smoking, I looked quickly left and right. Which way had he gone? I looked left again and to my horror there he was about 250 yards away, just a dot in the distance, running flat out down the middle of the A41 main road!

I shouted out, "Oh, my God, no, no, no! This idiot's going to die for sure!"

Pressing the accelerator to the floor, the four by four shot out the of the drive entrance. It was just like Batman's Batmobile rocketing out of his secret cave. With incredible luck for Skip and for my preservation as well, there wasn't a car or lorry in sight—an incredibly rare occurrence. Believe you me that was an absolute miracle on that road. At the speed Skip had run down our drive it was a wonder his owner hadn't seen him running behind his car through the rear view mirror.

I knew there was no way Skip was going to outrun my green rocket! I had my headlights on and my hazard lights were flashing. I was travelling down the centre of the road, with the wheels on either side of the white line. All I needed was a siren and blue flashing light!

I finally overtook Skip on the wrong side of the road. He appeared to be oblivious of me and was transfixed, just like a greyhound chasing a hare. I passed by him by about fifty yards and skidded from sixty miles an hour into an emergency stop with tyres smoking and squealing. I parked astride the centre white lines and looked to see a juggernaut 100 yards in front of me, heading straight toward me at speed. It looked enormous. I had not even seen it coming toward me in the opposite direction. I had been too engrossed in watching what Skip was doing in the rear view mirror. The lorry driver hit his horn, brakes, and flashers all at the same time. I leapt out of my vehicle totally ignoring it as it slowed and rolled toward me. Within a split second, I was round the back of the Daihatsu and Skip was by then only five yards away from me and looked to be tiring. He was swaying with exhaustion and his tongue was lolling from side to side, it wasn't surprising as he had run flat out for over a mile. He still jinked and tried to dodge past me. I screamed out at the top of my voice, "Sit down. NOW............!"

Skip was so shocked with the loud sound of my screaming voice. His backside immediately hit the tarmac, sitting him down so fast it was a wonder he didn't burn it! I always knew I was a damn good dog trainer! Lunging forward, I grabbed him by the scruff of his neck before he had time to bat an eyelid. With one swift movement I lifted him clean off his feet, opened the back door of the Daihatsu with my other hand and catapulted him safely inside, slamming the door behind him. I looked behind in the direction from where I had come. There were six cars parked up with their hazard lights flashing. I had been totally oblivious to any of the vehicles on the road. I waved a quick embarrassing thank you, jumped back into my Daihatsu and waved another big thank you to the driver of the enormous juggernaut, which was then parked very close to the front of my vehicle with his hazard lights still flashing. Behind the juggernaut I could see a long stream of traffic, patiently waiting for the roadblock to clear. The memorable event, which had taken place in the middle of the busy main road, had taken no more than twenty seconds in duration. But to me, I can assure you, it felt more like a lifetime! It was a memorable event I will never ever forget for as long as I live! Skip was safely stowed in the back of my Daihatsu, thankfully no accidents had occurred and fortunately I was still in one piece!

Skip had no idea how lucky he or should I say, *we* had been. After that escapade I nicknamed him *Skip the Slip*. Do you know he never slipped his lead again! "Why do you think that was?" Because I put a choke chain on him every time I walked him, that's why! Now that cured the problem. I am sure you can guess what went on his card outside his run in large red writing: MUST ALWAYS BE WALKED ON A CHOKE CHAIN CAN SLIP HIS COLLAR. I would sooner have taken the slightest risk of strangling the little devil with a choke chain, rather than let him get flattened by an enormous juggernaut! Skip came to us many times after that first traumatic experience and I never told the happy owner about Skip's adventures. Are you surprised? And as far as I am aware Skip didn't tell his dad either. Anyway, it was me that was traumatised, not the dog!

Skip was only the second dog and fortunately the last one to ever escape outside our boundary fence. There were quite a few we chased around our enclosed premises and that was because I had sprinted and got to that five-bar gate before they did!

Skip went down in doggy history with us, but what about the hero who had undoubtedly saved his life? Well, he had many more adventures to come. The question was: Was he up to it? Of course I was damn well up to it! There was plenty more life left in this old dog for future adventures and I was getting wiser and wiser but unfortunately aging by the minute!

Geoffrey Doody

Sukie

Now after those doggy adventures let's move onto a pussycat.

In the early days when I was still working alone, answering the phone was a bit of a problem. We had an answering machine but I really didn't trust people to leave a message. Not only did a lot of people dislike using an answering machine in those days, they might also have thought that we weren't even on the premises and the animals in our care would have been left unattended. On the occasions when customers did leave a message it was often difficult to decipher what their names and telephone numbers were and impossible to phone them back. I decided to purchase a mobile phone and at that time they were a lot larger and more cumbersome than our modern state of the art mobiles.

I bought a Swiss-made telephone which had two handsets with the radio base situated in the office. I carried the large handset in a pocket of my shirt, where it fitted snuggly. If I didn't have a pocket I carried it in my hand, no way would it fit into my jean's pocket like the tiny modern phones of today!

We had a lady customer whose name was Mrs. Jones. She owned a Siamese cat called *Sukie* that used to come and stay with us on a regular basis. We got to know each other really well and being very affectionate toward me she loved to be picked up and cuddled. In fact, she always insisted on it. I do mean the cat and not Mrs. Jones!

One day, as previously arranged, Mrs. Jones turned up with Sukie in her carrying cage. Her vaccination certificate was checked, which we routinely did every time, no matter how frequent the pets visited us. In the latter years this wasn't necessary as we tuned into modern times and became computerized. All owners appreciated how strict we were, as it ensured the safety of their pets against any infections or diseases. Mrs. Jones handed the wire carrying cage to me containing her Siamese pussycat. Sukie immediately looked up at me and lovingly pressed her head against the mesh at the top of her cage. Mrs. Jones said, "Sukie obviously can't wait to get out to you." The good lady didn't realise just how true her words were going to be! Mrs. Jones usually came down with me to the cattery to make sure Sukie was contented and installed okay before she left, she had been many times before so on this particular day she decided to trust me to do it alone.

Mrs. Jones drove down the drive and I carried Sukie down to the cattery with one hand and her soft sleeping bed in the other. I went in through the outer door of the cattery, which was made of steel mesh and walked halfway along the left hand side to install her into her run, closing the door behind us. I was locked in the run with my friend Sukie and as I looked down at her in her cage she began to purr loudly, begging me to let her out. I bent down and slid the fastener across that opened the mesh top. She immediately jumped out and that is when the fun started for Sukie, but certainly not for me! The handset that was in my shirt pocket started ringing. I could see it had startled Sukie slightly, but I had to answer it. On the other end of the line was a new customer who wanted to come and inspect the cattery before she made her booking. We always encouraged an inspection, not only because we were proud of our premises, but also because everyone who saw our facilities was very impressed and we knew they would tell their friends about us, even before their pet had stayed at our cattery and kennels.

I was totally engrossed in full sales mode with the potentially new customer. In the meantime, Sukie had jumped onto the top of her sleeping quarters, which were at chest height to me. I watched her as she lovingly looked at me and she couldn't understand why I wasn't taking any notice of her. Her meowing and purring became louder as if she was asking, "Why haven't you picked me up for my usual welcoming cuddle?"

I mentioned to the lady on the phone that I was actually in the cattery installing a regular pussycat guest called Sukie. At that precise moment Sukie lost all her patience with me and decided it was time for her usual cuddle. She suddenly launched herself toward me, leaping three feet through the air and landed on my chest as if I was a tree. But I wasn't a tree. I was a soft vulnerable human being! Her front feet landed on the top of my chest and her back feet landed on the upper part of my stomach. All her claws were naturally out and hooked into me through my thin shirt to stop herself sliding down the tree, (sorry I mean my body)! I gasped with pain! With my free hand I grabbed her by the loose fur at the back of her neck to try and support her weight, trying desperately to stop her slipping and ripping down my chest with her claws and prevent them digging deeper and deeper into my body! I knew I wasn't hurting her, but I can assure you, she was truly hurting me!

Sukie started purring down the phone contentedly, but I was in absolute bloody agony! I only just managed to stop myself letting out a yell as the lady on the other end of the line said, "Yes, I can tell you are in the cattery. It sounds like a happy cat is purring right by you."
I thought, *I know you can. This cat is also torturing me to death and trying to become part of my body! All I want to do is SCREEEEEEAM!*

It's Raining Cats and Dogs

I was doing my utmost to keep the tension and pain out of my voice as I pleasantly replied, "Oh yes, I am just giving Sukie her usual welcome cuddle." But the cuddle Sukie was giving me wasn't exactly a welcoming one at all! Sukie kept on purring; the lady kept on talking; I kept on hurting; the claws kept on digging in and going in deeper and deeper all the time! I kept thinking, *Please, please! For Christ's sake, get off this damn phone. I'm bleeding to death here!*

The customer said, "With all that purring going on you obviously have got some happy cats in there. I haven't any need to see your premises. I will make the booking with you now." I thought, *There should be a lot of screaming going on in here, as well as the purring*! The last thing I needed at that moment in time was a long telephone conversation, which taking details for a booking could do. Although I had a pen and paper with me I told a little white lie to terminate the conversation and more importantly my pain by saying, "I now have your number on my phone. Can I please phone you back? I haven't a pen and paper with me to take your details."

She thanked me for my time, which to me seemed like a lifetime, it felt like the longest phone call I had ever taken. Sukie was purring away even louder than ever and I was still hanging onto the scruff of her neck, trying to support her weight. As I gently unhooked each of her four sets of claws with my free hand she jumped back onto the top of her sleeping quarters opposite me and looked at me as if nothing had ever happened.

I vacated Sukie's run and let out an enormous yell of relief, "EEEEEEE.........ARGH!" I was sure it could have been heard miles away. To my utter surprise I heard a voice from the outer mesh door of the cattery say, "Are you having trouble in there?"
I thought, *Oh hell, who on earth is that?* Looking down the cattery I saw a lady peering through the mesh door at the end of the building. I was totally embarrassed and wondered what she must have been thinking when she heard my yell; perhaps she thought I had got a tiger in with me! I certainly felt like I had been mauled by one! My mind raced and I quickly replied, "I'll be with you in a minute; I'm just installing a cat called Sukie and I've just banged my ankle on her door as I closed it." It was amazing what little white lies I could come up with in the heat of the moment! I hurriedly turned away from the lady, I just couldn't wait to look down the inside of my shirt and scrutinize my chest and stomach to find out just how many pints of blood I had lost! Surprisingly, there were only four sets of claw marks with pin pricks of blood oozing out of my chest and stomach. Luckily the blood never even came through my shirt. Turning to the lady, I smiled and asked, "How can I help you?"

"I have heard good reports about your cattery. If you don't mind I would like to have a look around," she replied.

I walked up to her and opened the outer mesh door to let her in. "Please come in and meet my friend Sukie. She comes to us so often she virtually lives here." (Good sales talk!) I went into Sukie's run picked her up to cuddle her and she purred even louder than before.

"Oh, how nice. Sukie obviously loves you. I can tell you are definitely a cat lover."

I thought, *If you had seen me three minutes earlier in pain from her claws, you might have thought differently!*

She continued, "Your cattery is so beautiful and clean. I will have no hesitation in you looking after my two cats."

"Oh, thank you very much," I proudly replied.

She joked, "Do you know, for a moment when I was standing at the outside door and heard you cry in pain, I thought you were keeping lions and tigers in here!"

"Oh no; we only accept cuddly cats like my friend Sukie here," I replied laughing.

Geoffrey Doody

The Idea

Having read the first few chapters, perhaps some of you readers would like a similar business of your own or maybe not!

Ok this is how things got going. Kathy and I were living in Keepers Cottage. I was a self-employed gamekeeper and Kathy worked for a bank. For nine years I worked from home and looked after almost 2,000 acres of farm and woodland in the surrounding area. For sure, if I had my life again I would certainly never miss out on being a gamekeeper.

From a very early age I was interested in birds and animals. By the age of ten I knew virtually all the British birds and eggs in the book and I had an impressive egg collection, as did all my country friends. Today this is strictly illegal and I am now a staunch conservationist. Like most boys who lived in the countryside by the age of twelve I moved on from catapults and fishing rods to air rifles. At fourteen I progressed to shotguns, with adult guidance of course. I left school at fifteen to work in the family fish, fruit, and vegetable shop and after three months of that work I was craving to be a gamekeeper. My father thought I was crazy. His words were, "You will never make any money by being a gamekeeper."

My father reluctantly let me work for an Irishman on his mushroom farm. His name was Mr. Wilson, who sold his mushrooms to our shop. You might wonder what mushrooms have to do with gamekeeping. Well, Mr. Wilson's rented farm was smack bang in the middle of a country estate, inundated with pheasants and an old part-time gamekeeper living next door. I thought I had hit the jackpot! I was able to bike there and back, it was only two miles from the market town of Newport, Shropshire, where I lived. As a fit fifteen year old cycling was a piece of cake for me. My plan was to pick mushrooms all day and in my lunch hour roam the private countryside. Little did I realise that there is a lot more to mushroom farming than just picking the damn things!

Mr. Wilson was a hard task master but to his credit he would never set me a task he wouldn't do himself. After one week of working with him there wasn't any room left on my hands for any new blisters, both my arms felt six inches longer! In the initial weeks I pushed heavy six-feet-long flat wheelbarrows loaded with four galvanized tubs of peat and limestone twenty-five yards up steep ramps!

After three months of working with Mr. Wilson I was totally gob smacked when he informed

It's Raining Cats and Dogs

me I had been late for work for a total of thirty minutes. He had been adding up the odd thirty seconds for three months! Can you believe it . . . the occasional thirty seconds! He absolutely amazed me when he said in his soft Irish brogue, "Do you want me to deduct the half hour from your wages or would you rather wash my car?"

I thought, *Is this man for real or what?* By the way, my wages were only £4 7s 6d a week! Unfortunately, I think this could be giving my age away. For you young readers that happens to be £4.37½p, no such things as a ½ these days! So, I washed his new Vauxhall Velox. Valuable lesson learned I was never late again! After that episode I always made sure I was five minutes early.

After a year of hard labour in Siberia—sorry, I mean the mushroom farm—I went swimming with my mates. They looked at my previously skinny body in amazement and thought I had been on a body-building course! But my ruse had worked, during my lunch hours I had made contact with the gamekeepers on the surrounding country estate.

At sixteen my father talked me into going back to work with him in the new family fish and chip business. The tremendous advantage to me was that I worked five nights a week and in the days I could roam the country estate with my new game-keeping friends. For the next two years I was able to shoot and fish on the estate.

However, to my father's dismay, I still wanted to be a gamekeeper even more than ever.

At eighteen my father reluctantly let me go—this time I moved from my home in Shropshire to a job as an underkeeper on a Bedfordshire estate, owned by Sir Francis Pym. I was only there for three months before my father persuaded me to go back to the fish and chip business in Shropshire, where I worked for a further six years. Unfortunately, time proved my father and I to be incompatible, so after eight years I left and became a successful double glazing salesman. The advantage of this job was that working at night allowed me to shoot and fish in the day. I hated the job, even though I was earning as self-employed ninety pounds a week, which was incredible money in those days. I didn't know then that the selling experience would be extremely advantageous in the future cattery and kennels business.

At the age of twenty six I secured a single-handed gamekeepers post, with a tied cottage, only three miles from my home town of Newport. Bliss! I already knew the estate like the back of my hand because over previous years I had helped with the beating on shoot days. The old gamekeeper Eric was retiring and fortunately happened to be a good friend of mine, he kindly recommended me for the position. This is how I arrived at Keepers

Cottage, the future grounds for the cattery and kennels.

After four years of game keeping I met Kathy. Eight months later we got married. No, she wasn't pregnant. She just swept me off my feet and living together at Keepers Cottage was absolutely fantastic. I soon found out that being a single-handed gamekeeper was enjoyable but very hard work. It was rewarding most of the time, although not financially secure, as my fathers words rang true. Father's wise words usually do ring true. Don't they?

A year after we got married we were able to buy, as an investment but not to live in, a cottage in the nearby village of Tibberton, with a preferential staff loan from Kathy's bank. After I renovated and extended the cottage, as well as doing a successful gamekeeper's job, we sold it for a very nice profit. Thank you very much. After eight years of being a gamekeeper, it was coming out of my blood and I had been bitten by the bug to make money. I also had been bitten by another bug, which was building.

In my last year of game keeping, which made a total of nine years altogether, a pretty sandstone cottage with a woodland backdrop came up for auction half a mile down the road on the same estate as Keepers Cottage. With a friend Gordon, we formed a partnership and were able to purchase the cottage as another investment. It virtually needed gutting as no one had lived there for over thirty years.

Kathy's mother and father, Isabelle and Ronnie, who lived in Cheshire, came over for the weekend. They couldn't wait to see our new project. They walked into the dilapidated cottage and Ronnie walked out much quicker, muttering and not mincing his words as usual, "You must be stark staring bloody mad!"
To be honest, when I found out how hard the work was, I often thought Ronnie was right.

Another exciting thing happened during the purchasing of Little Croft, as it was known. I asked the country estate agent, "I don't suppose Keepers Cottage will ever come on the market?"
"How much do you want to offer?" he replied.
I was so taken aback I could have dropped through the floor. Rumours had always been that one of the trustees of the estate would keep Keepers Cottage for themselves. By describing the setting of Keepers Cottage I will explain the reasoning behind the rumour. It was situated in a beautiful spot, up against a 100-acre wood with panoramic views of rolling farmland behind. There was a quarter of a mile private driveway through the woodland and the nearest neighbour was half a mile away. I asked the agent, "Can you give me any idea of a figure?"

"We are looking in the region of 40,000 pounds," he answered.

"I'll let you know within a week," I replied.

Kathy and I could not believe our luck. We knew we had found paradise and had a chance of buying it as well. I had only half-heartedly mentioned to the agent and received the best information I could ever have wished to get in my lifetime!

During the following week Kathy and I made a few discreet enquiries. I spoke to Ron an estate agent friend of mine who informed me, "At that price they are not doing you any favours but cottages like that are becoming rare. If you can afford it, then buy it."

And we did! We ended up owning the two cottages at the same time. So it was a good job I had a partner with the Little Croft project, which after a year gave us a very nice profit. As a bonus, John and Cath, who purchased Little Croft, became two of our very best friends. In fact, in later years it was John and Cath who influenced us to move to Spain, but that is another story.

During the last year of my game keeping life David, the head of the shoot syndicate, wanted to cut costs. It didn't help that my wages were increasing each year, so I helped the situation and gave him a year's notice. On my part, game keeping held no more challenges for me and I felt it was time I made the move and look for a new career. But I still didn't know what I was going to do.

Kathy had a good career with the bank and she had been appointed senior manager over her department. She was earning at least ten times my salary as a gamekeeper and I felt I was living off Kathy's moral earnings. Maybe there could be a pun there somewhere! Everyday we were racking our brains for my future career.

One day while walking in the nearby wood called Shutts Wood, gun under my arm, as gamekeepers do, my Springer Spaniel Sally at my heel, I heard the woodman Dave working with his noisy chainsaw. I always took the chance to talk to woodmen because they are very observant people and it's amazing how much information one could glean from them. The conversation moved away from trees, pheasants, foxes, badgers and country life to holidays. I knew he had just been away and he owned two German Shepherd dogs, I was interested to know where he had taken them. I asked, "Who looked after your dogs, Dave?"
"I took them to a boarding kennels and it cost me an arm and a leg."
"How much would that be?"
"Forty five quid!"
"Jesus, they must be raking it in," I said in amazement.
Dave and I were talking on the edge of the wood and 500 yards away, standing in all its glory was

It's Raining Cats and Dogs

Keepers Cottage. Dave looked hard at me and said, "I can hear your brain working. Are you thinking what I'm thinking?"

"I've been way in front of you for the last few minutes mate."

According to Dave I had pound signs in my eyes and they were rolling like a one-armed bandit. So on that day the idea of a boarding cattery and kennels was born.

On my walk back to Keepers Cottage my mind was racing. I thought, *Where do we go from here?* I couldn't wait for Kathy to arrive home from work so that I could explain my fantastic new idea. The idea of a cattery and kennels sounded right up my street. I had been very successful at training gundogs all my life, now I had a chance of working with dogs again and getting paid for it as well! And yes, what about cats? My mind was in a whirl. I had already made my first million before Kathy had started her long journey home from the bank. My brain was in overdrive and at seven o'clock when I heard Kathy's car coming down our drive, I opened the front door with a big smile on my face and proudly proclaimed, "Geoff's got a new career.

Kathy's face was very puzzled as she asked, "Doing what?"

"I'm going to open a boarding cattery and kennels."

"What a brilliant idea," she replied.

All night long we discussed how we should go about it. My brain was racing away with anticipation and I said, "It won't take me long to knock up some kennels and runs with a bit of concrete, wood, and wire. But little did I know it wasn't going to be that simple. It never is, is it? At the end of all our discussions and planning we had decided primarily, we would need to do a lot of research for the new and exciting idea.

The first thing we did was to look up boarding cattery and kennels in the local Yellow Pages. Good God, there appeared to be hundreds of them! In fact, there were in excess of seventy and being so many made us just a little bit despondent. I thought, *How on earth can we make a living out of this with so much competition?*

Not being the type of people who give up easily, the following weekend trying not to be too downhearted, we decided to go and look at some of the cattery and kennels advertised. Enter, *'Geoff Bond 008',* the new spy on the block. With his accomplice Kathy, who was a darn sight better looking than *Moneypenny!* We entered into the world of industrial espionage. We pretended we had a cat and dog to board. What cat? We didn't even have one! We visited several cattery and kennels in the surrounding area to do our spying bit. No sorry, I mean inspect them for our dog and make-believe cat's stay. When we did the rounds we were amazed and sometimes shocked with what we saw. Their standards and cleanliness were generally poor and a lot of the buildings were very old, dirty and draughty. In some cases the area each dog was given was so small that the large dogs could only turn around if they got up onto their hind legs. Some even sat in their own excrement and their stressful barking was horrendous. Cats were even boarded in the same buildings as noisy dogs! We found the noise unbearable and a lot of people don't realise that a cat's hearing is thirty times greater than humans. Unfortunately, the stressed-out cats couldn't put their paws over their ears to block out the noise! We met people who were running their businesses single handedly. In fact, one lady said she was really struggling to cope and had already suffered with two nervous breakdowns! Nervous breakdowns! This worried me more than a bit coming from the tranquility of game keeping, the last thing I needed in my life was a n-n-n-n-nervous breakdown!

After a few weekends of this type of spying, (sorry, research), we came to the conclusion that only a few establishments could give us serious opposition in the future. By then we had made up our minds. We were definitely going to become the very best around. Gone was my idea of doing it the cheap way with wood and wire, we needed bricks, mortar, and steel. I was determined we were going to build a palace, which would be fit for a King or Queen! We for sure, were going to have a five-star hotel for cats and dogs!

Geoffrey Doody

Planning Permission

Yes, I am afraid like any building a cattery and kennels requires planning permission. Initially, I needed an architect to draw up professional plans from my own drawings and designs. Finding one was no problem. I just got out the good old Yellow Pages and within a short period of time we had professional plans to submit to the council for approval and permission.

With all my research I found out there were two main requirements. Number one was the noise level, which could be a nuisance factor to the surrounding area. Let's face it, a whole building full of dogs could have possibly made quite a row! Noise can travel a long way, especially on the wind. Noise of any type can annoy neighbours. Lucky for us our nearest neighbour was over half a mile away and we were mainly surrounded by woodland. I hoped the noise factor wouldn't be a problem. Little did I know what the council would come up with!

Number two was access. Our quarter of a mile drive, at that moment in time, was a bumpy potholed stone track, which accessed to the main A41 trunk road. This particular stretch of the A41 was dead straight, where traffic could break the speed limit and easily do over 100 miles an hour. I thought the fast stretch of road could possibly be a concern, with traffic entering or leaving our drive entrance. We could only wait and see with bated breath while the council considered our planning application.

Kathy and I nervously waited six weeks to find out the result of the council's decision. They seemed to be the longest six weeks in our lives. It's a good job I've never been into nail biting because I'm sure I would have bitten my nails right up to my armpits! During the six-week-period we had to post a notice of our intentions to build a cattery and kennels at the end of our drive and also in the local newspaper to give people the opportunity to object to our plans. And yes you guessed it, sure enough, an objection was raised. You always get one awkward sod, don't you! The objection was raised by the proprietor of our nearest boarding cattery and kennels who could have become one of our future rivals. He was claiming there was already an adequate number of boarding cattery and kennels in the surrounding area and why would it be necessary for another one. Well he would do. Wouldn't he? We were flabbergasted! Of course we knew his real reason for objecting was obviously the fear of us taking some of his business away. I don't suppose you could blame him—especially when he could see a very modern posh establishment was going to be built only four miles down the road.

After the objection, the next step was a meeting with our architect and the council to prove our case that another boarding establishment was needed. To my extreme surprise, the council person turned out to be someone from my past. She had been an old classmate of mine from junior school and her name was Catherine. I knew she had liked me at school or even fancied me. Hey, I've always been a vain boy. So I thought I would have a nice friendly chat with her.

We spoke of our fun days at school and I don't mean kissing behind the bicycle shed either! Give me a break, I was only ten! The conversation was about our classmates . . . what they were doing and where they were living. But Catherine soon clicked on and was having none of my creeping! After a short while I thought, *Be careful here Geoff lad. This lady could turn out to be a right dragon.*

Catherine proved to do her job fairly and thoroughly. I had asked—and in fact, almost challenged her—to check out as many cattery and kennels as she possibly could. My opinion was most of them were still in the 'dark ages' and in reality shouldn't even have been granted a license.

After recalling 'Geoff Bond 008' reconnaissances, Catherine was convinced that a modern establishment was very much needed. In the future, maybe even she would bring her dog to stay with us. And that is exactly what she did. Her dog's name was Henry and over the future years he had many happy stays with us. Catherine left the meeting saying she would recommend that the objection should be overruled. I could have dropped through the floor! I had just made my first sale in my new career. Hey, perhaps Catherine did fancy me at school after all!

We were also visited by another council member who arrived at Keepers Cottage with our plans tucked under his arm. He had no objection to the cattery building, which would be well away from the kennels, but he was concerned with the noise level the dogs could possibly produce. I was absolutely gob smacked! When I eventually got my thoughts together, I retorted, "But we live in the middle of nowhere with woods all around us!"
"Yes but noise can travel miles across country," he replied.
His suggestion was that I should use expensive sound-damping materials in the building of the kennels. I thought, *What a shame it isn't you paying for the bill mate!* My fears were rising that this new venture was going to cost us 'an arm and a leg' and take forever to build. Have you ever noticed how council officials never seem to

mind how much of your money they can spend for you. This was frightening me to death! So I hit him hard, not with my fists, but with the idea. If the dogs couldn't see each other on the opposite sides of the aisles that separated them, they wouldn't bark. I had already designed the kennels that if a dog wanted to see his or her neighbour on the right or the left, the dog would have to stand on its hind legs, which would make it impossible for the smaller varieties. Oh, by the way, it is true dogs can stand on their hind legs, but not for a long period of time. The council official could see my point of view and my mind was racing away trying to think of ideas. Suddenly I thought I had got the perfect answer. I suggested the possibility of rigging up a big curtain that would hang down the centre aisle. It would be made from a plastic tarpaulin, which could be hosed and disinfected when necessary and it would also act as a sound baffle. The council official thought all my ideas were more than acceptable to control the noise level. Perfect, he wasn't a bad old stick after all!

In total it was eight weeks before we heard from the council. Hip, hip, hooray! We got the planning permission and license. It was for twenty two dog kennels with runs and thirty cat houses with runs. It made my dream become a reality. *Hooray! Hooray! Geoff lad, you are now in business!*

Geoffrey Doody

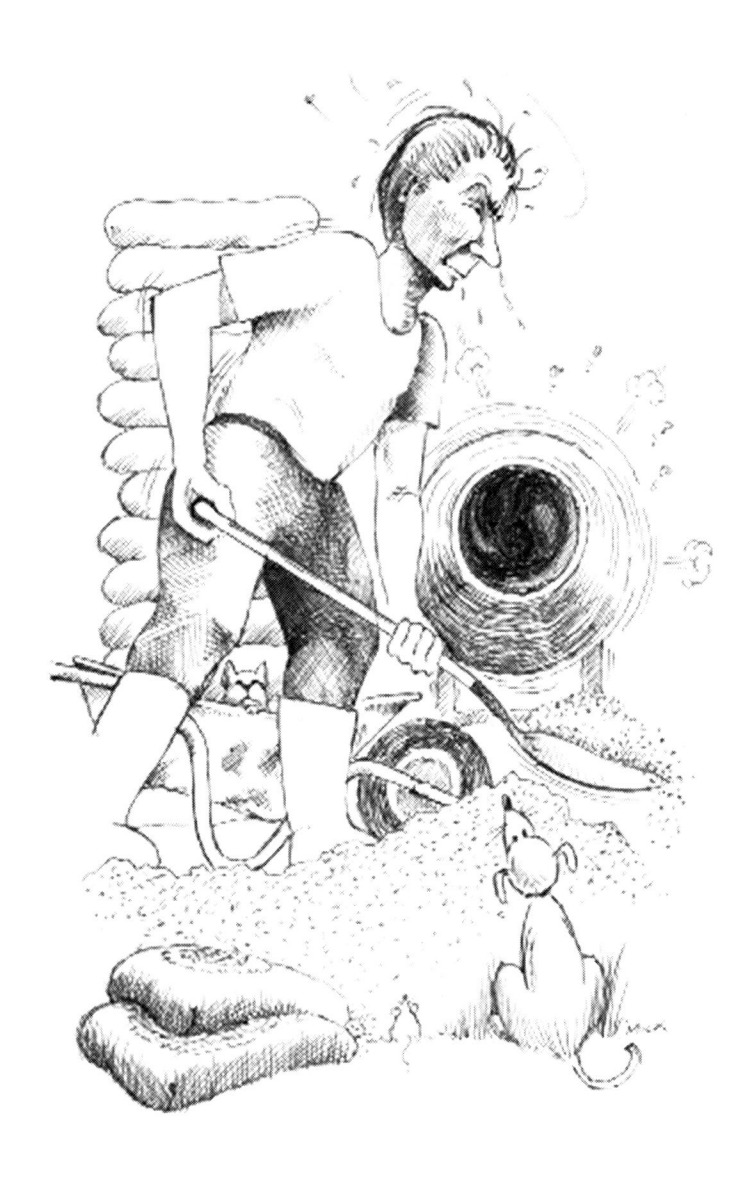

Building

I have always liked building having done house renovations, extensions, built garages and sheds. I have never had any problems with the labouring side of the building trade. In fact, I thoroughly enjoyed it. For the skilled labour, like bricklaying and plastering, I would always use a sub contractor. The ground work, like concreting, which only needed muscle, I could do myself.

Initially I needed to clear and level the ground. To do this I needed a powerful machine, such as a JCB. So I looked in the Yellow Pages and found the nearest contractor who happened to be just down the road in Newport. An appointment was made with the company director George, who I already knew. George turned up at the time agreed to check out the ground and decide which type of machine was required to do the work. He decided a four-wheel drive JCB would be more than adequate. The machine and driver were booked for a week later.

Things were now starting to get really exciting and my main concern was the weather. The last thing we needed while the machine was working was rain. With rain and the heavy machine the area could easily have turned into a quagmire. I intensely watched every weather forecast during the coming week and prayed that it would stay dry. Let's face it, the United Kingdom is not exactly one of the driest countries in the world! Remember Michael Fish saying, "What Hurricane!"

The week had painstakingly passed by and at seven thirty on Monday morning when I heard the roar of the machine, as it came up our drive, my heart was thumping with excitement. The driver jumped down from his cab and I knew him as well. His name was Frank and we had attended the same school in Newport. After working as a lonesome gamekeeper I hadn't been in my new career three minutes and I had already met two school pals. Frank described how he was going to do the job and then climbed back into his cab. The powerful machine roared into action. I found it fascinating watching those large machines work and the skill that the drivers have. I couldn't take my eyes off it, the sheer power and accuracy was awesome. I had marked out the plan of the buildings with powdered lime and after three hours the machine had moved the top soil away quicker than fifty men could do by hand in a day.

After two days the ground was level, the foundations were dug out and ready for the next stage. A local farmer friend Selwyn came with a tractor and trailer to take away the rich top soil for one of the nearby fields. We were left with two building sites—one for the cattery and the other for the kennels, office and car park.

Stage two is where I came in for the concreting. It is very hard physical work but I always found it extremely satisfying. The look of recently laid concrete is fantastic when you have just completed a long run and it is still wet and shiny. I started with the cattery, which consisted of two strips of thirty yards by three yards. First, I had to peg down the shuttering and it all had to be level, with a slight fall running toward the centre. This took three complete days and as we all know, the preparation of any job always seems to take longer than the actual job.

I purchased a second-hand electric cement mixer and decided to mix the concrete myself, opposed to Ready-mix. **Big, big mistake**! The local builder's merchants delivered the sand, gravel, and cement. I just couldn't wait to get started. The following day at eight o'clock I had the cement mixer going and I started the arduous task of mixing the concrete. I was so keen and enthusiastic as I barrowed the heavy concrete to the proposed runs and then levelled it.

The first morning I worked like a dog. Is that a pun, considering the business I was going into? Kathy had taken time off from work for her family to come over for lunch. My God, there were a tribe of them, consisting of Kathy's grandmother, who was nearly ninety, her mother, Isabelle, and Kathy's two sisters, Audrey and Carole. They were all interested to see what we were up to, or should I say what I was up to (or were they just being nosey)! They will kill me when they read this! I would just like to say in my defence, I do get on very well with all of them and perhaps this last sentence will save my life!

I thought I was making good progress and a couple of hours later when I looked at how much I had achieved, I began to realise I should have used Ready-mix concrete. It was a hot day and I could hear laughter coming from the garden with wine glasses clinking. Kathy and her family were obviously having a good time and I was wishing I was with them. If only I had ordered Ready-mix concrete, I would have completely finished the job and be in the garden too.

I struggled on throughout the afternoon and by the evening I was absolutely shattered. I had only completed three quarters of the first run. After finishing off the first stretch of concrete the next day I decided the second run would be done with Ready-mix. That afternoon I made a phone call for a load of concrete to be delivered the following day. Early the next morning a large concrete lorry arrived and within two hours I had levelled the lot. There is nothing like learning the hard way . . . and boy, I just had!

Stage three was the block work. This was going to be a lot more straightforward, especially for me, I was going to be the dumb labourer for my two bricklayer friends, Eric and John. An articulated lorry incorporating a crane turned up with an enormous load of blocks stacked on pallets. It only took the driver twenty minutes to unload them. But sadly, there was no crane to help poor old Geoff. So with the help of my trusty wheelbarrow, it took me eight hours—yes eight bloody hard hours—to stack them where Eric had instructed me to do so for his convenience. Another lorry arrived with the sand and twenty bags of cement, all I needed were the two "brickies" in the form of Eric and John and we were ready to rock and roll.

Eric and John arrived the next day at seven thirty. They had given me strict instructions on how to mix the sand and cement. I poured a little water into the mixer with a squirt of fairy liquid, followed by one shovel full of cement and four shovels of sand with more water added. The consistency had to be just right or they were not happy bunnies and boy, did they make sure I knew about it! It wasn't because of any unpleasant threats, like sticking me upside down into the cement mixer, it was more their tut, tuts and hard looks that rapidly made me an expert mixer! My God, could those lads lay blocks quickly. I could only just keep up with them! After five hard days of sweat and toil all the blocks were laid and after another two days they were all rendered in cement. We then had a skeleton of the cattery completed.

Stage four was to lay the floor tiles (by yours truly), this would make the cattery look very smart. This was yet another job I had never attempted before but after explicit instructions from Eric, I soon became quite proficient. What he didn't know about the building trade wasn't worth knowing. The tiling was backbreaking and even worse knee-breaking as I spent virtually all my time kneeling. Thank God, I had taken Eric's advice and purchased some strap-on knee pads. After three long weeks, even after wearing knee pads, my knees were red raw and I felt I had a humped back just like Quasimodo's.

Kathy and I had chosen a cream-coloured tile that would most certainly show up any dirt and also make each individual run very easy to keep clean and even more importantly germ free. But wow, those tiles did make it look exceptionally spacious and I have to say a little bit posh too. They looked absolutely fantastic. We were certain our cattery was going to be the best in the United Kingdom. And as far as I am concerned it was!

It eventually dawned on me that all the building materials were costing us 'an arm and a leg'. Kathy was driving to work over fifty miles each way, working seven days a week in a large department of the bank, bossing 350 people around and earning big money. The bonus I was getting from this was she didn't have time to boss me around! I felt very guilty. I wasn't earning any money at that time; I was spending the stuff instead! I decided to revisit my double glazing past and contact one of my friends whose name was Ivor. He informed me that he was now selling central heating systems. Hey, the good news was the company was looking for more salesmen. The wages were incredibly good and the work was in the evenings and weekends. These hours suited me down to the ground and as I had been so successful at selling before the company took me in with open arms.

Although I hated the job, we needed the money, so I laboured for myself in the day and went out selling in the evenings, sometimes coming back as late as two o'clock in the morning. The following morning, I would start work at eight o'clock. Talk about burning the candle at both ends! Again, I was absolutely shattered. I kept this up for a year, successfully selling the central heating systems and the much-needed money helped us big time.

Now back to my day time job. Stage five was to erect the steel framework, the doors and the see-through sneeze barriers, which were in between each cat run. Within five days I had erected and fitted the thirty cat runs—fifteen on each side, with a three-yard space in the middle for the pathways and an enclosed shrubbery. Shrubbery . . . you may well ask what the hell does he want a shrubbery in a cattery for? Don't worry, I will enlighten you later.

The space in the middle was to enable the cats to see each other but they were well apart. We now had the shape of the cattery to admire and my excitement was mounting every day. Stage six was the roof. I used green translucent corrugated fibreglass sheets; they let the light and warmth in. The sun shining through the roof gave the cattery a slight green glow. Apparently green is the most soothing colour for cat's eyes. I bet you didn't know that, did you? I'm a mind of wonderful information you know! I don't know who is paid to find these facts. I suppose you learn something new every day.

I also erected a steel mesh roof between the two sets of runs. This was the area that was going to be the shrubbery and would enable it to be watered naturally with rain falling through the mesh. Roofing was a job I had done before as I had built many sheds in my game keeping days, I sailed through fitting the fibreglass sheets and steel mesh in only two weeks.

Stage seven was, I must say, one of the simpler tasks, painting all the walls in white. I mean any idiot can do that, can't they, even me! I completed the painting in a couple of days. Not bad going for an ex-gamekeeper!

Stage eight was to erect thirty cat boxes; these would be the sleeping quarters for each of our boarders. They were made of melamine, which is the same used for some kitchens cupboards. I had ordered a cream-coloured melamine to match the floor tiles and it was cut to my specified measurements and design. They consisted of four sides, a lid and a bottom. I erected the cat boxes thirty inches off the floor in each of the separate runs to ensure that all of our guests wouldn't be in any draughts. My next task was to make thirty solid ladders out of wood for the cats to climb up into their sleeping quarters. I painted the ladders white to show up any dirt and make them easier to clean and disinfect. This turned out to be an annual job because most of the cats used the ladders as scratching posts, even though we had separate scratching posts for them. God only knows why the ungrateful pussycats wanted to vandalise my beautiful ladders.

The ninth and final stage was to create a shrubbery down the centre of the cattery between the two rows of cat runs. A shrubbery? What on earth does he want a shrubbery for? There you go again! Well, I said we were coming to this and here is the answer. The shrubbery was to soften the steel and concrete to stop it looking like a prison. Good idea, I thought. I purchased some beautiful dwarf shrubs from the local garden centre and planted them. I covered the soil in between the shrubs with Cotswold gravel, which is light brown in colour. This gave the cattery a lovely tranquil appearance. Alas, all of this work was another big mistake! I'm not infallible, you know! Although the shrubbery looked really nice it turned out to be a complete waste of time and money, which the next couple of years were to sadly prove. But in the meantime yes, yes, yes we had a fantastic cattery!

Next I started the mammoth task of building twenty-two kennels, an office, kitchen, and toilet. Don't worry; I will not bore you with another long building episode, the process was pretty much the same as the cattery. The only difference was the time of year, we were then well into the English wintertime. The roof was the biggest problem being four times as large as the cattery area and ten times as fiddly. It took me the whole of February to complete and it happened to be one of the coldest winters ever recorded. It was below zero every day with snowflakes in the air. Boy, was it cold on those roofs and not surprisingly there wasn't a 'Brass Monkey' to be seen anywhere! Just poor freezing Geoff!

At long last by the end of March virtually all the building work was finished and the biggest job left was the painting of the kennels. I wanted to catch the summer season and I was running out of time for me to complete the work on my own, so I hired a painting contractor. I was now getting more and more excited every day as we were getting very close to opening our new cattery and kennel business.

Geoffrey Doody

The Howling

It was a beautiful early spring morning in late March. The birds were singing, the sun was shining in a clear blue sky and there wasn't even one fluffy cloud in sight. It was the sort of day that made you feel light on your feet, almost as if you could fly with the birds. I felt I was going to have a brilliant day as I only had one small job to finish in the cattery. It would then be totally completed and ready for the first pussycat guests to arrive.

I was just about to leave our cottage and make my way to the cattery when the phone rang. Whilst talking to the person at the other end of the line, there was a strange sound coming from somewhere outside. The window was closed so I stretched over and opened it. Trying to concentrate on the conversation I looked up toward the new kennel block, the only thing I could see was Dave's car parked outside the office and he was walking into the kennel block. He was the contractor painting the inside of the kennels. Dave came and went as he pleased and it didn't matter what hours he kept, he had given me a price for the job and had promised it would be ready for the big opening day. Nothing unusual was going on up there. I closed the window and finished the phone conversation. As I placed the receiver down I immediately heard the strange sound again, this time it was a lot louder and it sounded really eerie. I ran outside to see if there was an animal in terrible pain and if it wasn't an animal, then I hoped it was a human making the strange sound, not an alien! The only animal to be seen was my faithful Springer Spaniel Sally. She looked very frightened with her tail between her legs and she was trembling. She wasn't hurt, but whatever the sound was, it had certainly terrified her and I knew she wasn't capable of making the strange sound anyway. I stood still, listened and could hear nothing except the faint sound of the painter's radio blaring away while he was working. I also noticed that the birds had stopped singing. Were they frightened as well? I felt a shiver go down my spine and thought, *For God's sake Geoff, pull yourself together and enjoy this lovely spring day.*

Wandering off to the cattery with Sally at my heel, I noticed she was walking much closer to me than normal. As we entered the cattery I heard a cock blackbird chirping away with his beautiful voice. I bent down and patted Sally gently on her head while saying, "Don't worry old girl. There is nothing to worry about. Listen, the birds are singing again."

It's Raining Cats and Dogs

I picked up my electric screwdriver to start my day's work, which was to continue erecting the joists to support hanging flower baskets that would bring some colour to the cattery later on in the year. As I squeezed the trigger to start the electric screwdriver there was a sound that will stay with me for the rest of my life. The hairs on the back of my neck actually stood up. Sally ran to my side and tried to force herself between my knees, so she could feel protected by my calves. I thought, *What the bloody hell was that?*

Sally and I bolted out through the cattery door together and as I ran I had great difficulty in picking up any speed because with every stride I almost tripped over her. The poor old girl was only trying to seek my protection by being so close. The only faint sound I could hear was the painter's radio in the distance and I noticed the birds were quiet again. What was going on and what on earth had made the awful screech? I hadn't a clue from which direction the blood-curdling sound had come from and didn't know which way to look. And I can tell you I wasn't too sure if I really wanted to find out.

In my time as a gamekeeper I had heard some frightening sounds, but never anything quite like the one made that day. Most of the unusual sounds were made at night, but they weren't strange to me as often I heard them while I was night-watching for poachers, making sure all the game was safe. To a 'townie', the sound of stags when they are in the rutting season could sound like a machine gun. The sound of a heron calling could sound like a dinosaur and owls give a ghostly screeching sound. In my opinion a vixen, female fox, shrieking from close range was probably the most terrifying sound of all. None of those sounds frightened me one little bit, nothing even came close in my mind to recognising what the hell the new sound was. I thought, *Nothing in this beautiful countryside that I love is going to frighten me. Come On. Pull yourself together Geoff.* At least the daylight gave me the advantage of being able to see what it was rather than searching around in the dark. I thought, *Where do I look? Where do I search?*

I wandered aimlessly around finding nothing, getting nowhere and getting no closer to finding out what it was or where the sound had come from. There was no more noise—nothing. I was just completely wasting my valuable time. Perhaps whatever it was had gone, at least I most certainly hoped so. I thought, *Whatever it is if it can make a sound like that, I don't fancy meeting it, even if it is in broad daylight!*

I went back down to the kennels to ask Dave the painter, if he had heard anything. He said he hadn't, of course he wouldn't have. His radio was so loud you couldn't even hear yourself think! Tina Turner was blasting away singing, 'Simply the

It's Raining Cats and Dogs

Best'. I suppose he needed it that loud as he was as deaf as a proverbial post. I didn't think he could have heard it, I was sure he would have come to me at the cattery to find out what the sound was. Off I strode back to the cattery to rescue what was left of my morning. I eagerly picked up my electric screwdriver and just as I squeezed the trigger, yes you guessed it, what fantastic timing. There was that awful sound again. I thought, *Someone out there is trying to take the pee out of me, that's for sure!* Suddenly another almighty shriek let rip yet again. Sally was trembling with fear. I wasn't the least bit frightened, I was getting really, really mad instead. I thought, *I'll get my gun and put whatever or whoever it is out of their misery!*

I decided the only way to find out what was going on out there was to stand outside and wait until the creature from hell or whatever it was, let rip again. If it made the sound again I would be able to pinpoint where it had come from. I had got to the stage where I didn't care how much of my valuable time was being lost. I was going to solve the puzzle if it killed me! I thought, *Perhaps whatever it is could kill me! Maybe I should fetch my gun from the house. Come on Geoff lad, calm down. There has to be a simple explanation to this.*

I crept around the premises within a 400-yard radius of Keepers Cottage for almost an hour, an hour I really couldn't spare. I heard nothing, I saw nothing and I gained nothing, except feeling a lot more peed-off than an hour earlier. After my hour of searching I thought, *It must have gone; thank goodness for that. Now for God's sake Geoff, get back to work and forget it.* As usual, it wasn't that simple because as soon as I entered the cattery, the almighty blood -curdling shriek erupted yet again. *Surely, Dave must have heard that shriek. It must have been heard miles away! Somebody is definitely playing a practical joke here and if I get hold of whoever it is I'll break their neck!* So yet again, off I marched back to the kennels with Sally clinging as close to my legs as possible. I opened the door to the kennel block and on entering, Dave was just behind on a stepladder. I could see I had made him jump.

"God, you frightened the hell out of me," he said.

"You're not the only one who is being surprised around here," I retorted back.

He looked at me rather blank and I could see he hadn't a clue what I was talking about. Trying to make myself heard over his blaring radio, which was really starting to get on my nerves, I shouted, "Have you heard any strange noises this morning Dave?"

"No, nothing unusual mate," he replied.

Dave went back to his painting and I left even more frustrated than ever. What a wasted morning it had been, I decided to walk back to

It's Raining Cats and Dogs

the house and have an early lunch. I was just going through the garden gate when the same eerie shriek erupted from somewhere behind me. I nearly jumped right out of my skin and Sally nearly jumped into my arms. I spun around expecting to see some sort of monster stalking me, but saw absolutely nothing, nothing. Dave was just walking away from his car and he gave me a cheeky wave as he walked back into the kennels carrying his lunch box.

It was him, I knew damn well it was him. He had obviously been doing it all the time and he had been taking the pee out of me all morning. I had no idea how he had been able to make the noise from such a long way away from me, but I knew damn well I was going to find out how and pronto.

Dave had certainly had a great laugh on me and I couldn't blame him, I am a practical joker myself. I had played a few jokes on him in the past whilst he had been doing previous work for me. I suppose, "What is good for the goose is good for the gander."

While I ate my lunch my mind was working overtime thinking of how I could get Dave back, even if it was the only thing I was going to achieve that day. After rushing down my lunch I had an idea, I opened my gun cabinet to retrieve my twelve-bore shotgun and grabbed a cartridge.

Carrying the shotgun I made my way quietly back to the kennels where Dave was working. I stood outside the kennels door, loaded the cartridge into the guns chamber, snapped it shut, and pointed the gun in the air over the kennel block. I released the safety catch and fired. *BANG!* The loud sound echoed around the kennel block and woodland. I quickly ran into my new office and hid behind the door. I didn't have to wait many seconds before Dave came bolting out of the kennel block, almost like his backside was on fire. He ran up to his car and looked around it to see if it had been damaged. I was doing my utmost to stifle my laughter and could see him scratching the top of his head in deep thought. He was obviously wondering what the bang had been and where it had come from. After hiding the gun behind the door, I came sauntering out of the office and innocently asked, "What's up, Dave? You look like you've seen a ghost?'

Within a split second of the words leaving my mouth, there was an ear piercing shriek. The dreadful noise had exploded from right behind me! If I had got a dickey ticker, I would have been dead before hitting the ground!
I shouted at Dave over the noise of his radio, "What on earth have you got in those kennels?"
"Oh that. That's only Jane."
"Who the hell is Jane?"
"She's me dog."
"It sounds more like a werewolf than a dog."

"Come and have a look at her mate."
I followed him into the kennels. It was almost as if Dave owned the place, not me! Halfway down the right-hand side of the kennels in one of the runs was *Jane*, standing there looking lovingly toward Dave. She was an incredibly large dog, not a Deerhound or a Wolfhound, I would say she definitely had a mixture of both.
"What sort of dog is that, Dave?"
"A Lurcher!"
"It's the biggest Lurcher I've ever seen in my life and I've seen a fair few in my time. I can tell you."
Dave made the statement, "You want to see her catch rabbits!"
"She must be as fast as a cheetah. Rabbits won't stand a cat in hell's chance against her!"
"You're dead right, they don't mate. Me missus and kids will never starve while me Jane's around."
"Have you got any neighbours near your house?"
"No, nobody lives within half a mile."
"I'm not surprised. Because if they did they wouldn't stick around for long if she makes that awful noise all the time. Anyway, why has she been making that blood-curdling shriek?"
"Oh, every time I walk out of the kennels to fetch summut or disappear out of her sight she misses me, so she just yells."
"But I suppose you don't really notice how loud it is as you're a little deaf, aren't you, Dave?"
"What'd ya say, mate?"

I suppose that answer confirmed it.

Everything from the morning's traumas were fitting into place, the jigsaw puzzle had been solved. The awesome sound only erupted when Dave was out of sight of his fearsome-looking hound Jane and by the way she was as soft as a brush with people, obviously not with bunny rabbits! I'm sure 'as eggs are eggs', I wouldn't like to be a rabbit when Jane was around.

Dave then gave out a mortifying statement, "You'll have to get used to this sort of noise once all these kennels are full mate."
I looked at him absolutely gob smacked and thought, *Oh my God, surely not. What on earth am I creating?*

My ambition was to have over 100 dogs on the premises; surely they wouldn't all make noises like Jane. Was I creating a monster or a business! Perhaps the council were right when they had made all their rules and regulations regarding noise levels. All those negative thoughts flashed through my mind, I tried to dismiss them as quickly as possible. I had to be positive about my new business. I thought, *Please God, surely there is only one dog on this planet that can make a noise like that and she is standing right here in front of me.* Her tail was wagging and her large mouth was open, looking almost as big as a crocodiles, her big red tongue flopped out of

the side. I was sure she would have been able to hold two rabbits in her mouth at once!
I curiously asked Dave, "Do you ever go on holiday?"
"No mate. I never have time. If I get any time, I go off with Jane and the kids, it gives me missus a break and keeps her happy. Anyway, it costs too much to take my tribe away."
I thought, *Thank God for that at least I wouldn't have to tell Dave any white lies that we were always going to be full, where his lovely Jane was concerned. That was one dog for sure I would never want in my kennels. I knew there was no way I would have been able to stand all that shrieking. The thought was too dreadful for me to comprehend.*
Dave brought me back to my senses again.
"Oh Geoff. Did you hear a loud bang just before? It sounded to me like a gun shot, but it was too loud for that."
"Never heard a thing mate. Well not above that terrible noise your Jane was making."
I winked at him as Sally and I turned away and walked back down to the cattery. Dave watched with his hands on his hips. At least Sally had met the awesome-looking hound called Jane, although she probably never realised that Jane had been making the fearful shrieking sound. Sally was going to have to get used to it, just like me and we would have to hope that Dave wouldn't leave the kennels too often while he was working there. Surprisingly, the difference

in their size didn't seem to stop Sally and Jane becoming the best of pals, even if Sally did look like a little toy dog against the big lolling Jane.

When Kathy arrived home from work that evening I told her all about my day and how the awful sound had initially frightened the hell out of Sally and me. Yes even me, and it was only coming from a dog! It just didn't seem possible.
Kathy said in a jesting tone, "I thought nothing could frighten you out there?"
"Oh we are funny, aren't we?" I said sarcastically. "Anyway, I think I'm going to buy Jane off Dave."
Kathy looked at me, as if I had lost my marbles.
I added, "That hound is a million dollars on legs. I'm going to record her voice and sell it as an alarm for burglars."
Kathy said with laughter, "You could be onto a winner there, Geoff."

It dawned on me that our first guest had been staying that day, even if it was the howling Jane. I for certain, was going to make sure it was her very last stay too. Hell would have to freeze over before she stayed with us again, even if she was only a non-paying guest while Dave was painting.

It was because of Dave's words and his howling dog Jane that I decided to have music in the kennels. When the kennels were up and running I went out and purchased a radio and hung it up halfway along the kennel block on a six-inch nail. There's nothing like being practical, is there? I thought if the dogs couldn't hear what was going on, especially outside like cars and people coming and going on our car park, they wouldn't be disturbed and start barking. Brilliant idea Geoff! Virtually everybody has music playing at home, so why shouldn't it make the dogs feel less stressful when they were with us. And why not cats as well? Out I went again to purchase a radio for the pussycats too and as we expanded there was a radio for each new kennel block.

It appeared the cats loved the music; the dogs loved the music; the staff loved the music; the customers loved the music and being a pop fan, Geoff thought it was absolutely fantastic. I often used to lie in bed with humorous thoughts picturing the cats and dogs having a rave up, boogieing the night away to the music. In later years with so many radios, it was like having surround sound. Have you ever heard of radios wearing out? Because over the years we wore them out big time, they were never ever turned off!

Geoffrey Doody

Creating Interest

In our exciting new business we had to create the pet owners' interest and there were various ways of doing it. We designed a large sign to advertise our boarding cattery and kennels that would be situated at the end of our drive. And would you believe we even had to get planning permission for that from our friendly Council, which was much harder than you could imagine. The sign had to be a certain size, the exact distance from the main road, the exact height from the ground and the exact size of lettering. The requirements appeared to be endless, but of course we did exactly as we were ordered.

The sign was finally erected to the exact Council requirements at the bottom of our drive on the verge of the A41 and it stood proud with the name of our business on it for everyone to see. So, hip, hip, hooray!

One night four weeks later, the local students were on the rampage and nicked all the signs along the A41, including ours! Arghhhhh! I wasn't the slightest bit amused. And for sure, I wasn't damn well having it! There was a definite cure for this. Good old Geoff fixed the next sign with large nuts and bolts, plastered with a tube of superglue to heavy steel scaffolding poles and concreted them deeply into the ground. After all these years when I drive past, I see the original sign is still standing.

The Yellow Pages were one of the best instruments we used for creating interest. I was very pleased with my own designed advert and I knew it was totally different to the dozens of others portrayed by our possible competitors. All the others were very much the same, describing what I thought amounted to be a stay in a high security prison! I described our new modern-designed cattery and kennels to be a luxurious place for your cats and dogs to come and have a holiday. Our cattery and kennels were in a beautiful tranquil setting, so that is exactly how I described it. The cats were going to be loved and pampered and the dogs were going to be walked on arrival and then twice daily in the surrounding woodland of oaks and birches, throughout their stay with us. Our establishment was described as a paradise for all our guests. We even had a logo of a dog and a cat sitting in a deckchair, holding a glass of wine. I can honestly say we did provide the odd deckchair, but not the glass of wine or champagne! It is a fact that many pet owners over the years did make the statement, "We will stay here and send our pets to where we should be going!"

Over the following years we advertised in Yellow Pages in four separate counties, which were Shropshire, Staffordshire, Cheshire, and West Midlands. We took a half-page in each of the Yellow Pages, which was initially larger than any of our competitors and it stood out superbly. Throughout all the years in the business we never changed that advertisement.

To Yellow Pages we were considered to be one of their largest customers, which when all said and done meant we spent a lot of money with them. They treated us like VIP's and we were always looked after by one of their senior managers. Unfortunately, each year a different manager would turn up in August, (well he would wouldn't he) just because it happened to be our busiest time of the year. I could never get them to come in November when I had plenty of time. As they say, 'When it rains it pours'. Each year the manager suggested we change our advert. But no, I stuck to my guns. I knew for sure it was a really good advert and I couldn't see how anyone could better it. One of the questions a manager asked was, "How many telephone enquiries do you get a week?"
"Oh, about thirty or forty a day and the majority of them book with us."
He nearly fell off his chair as he responded, "That's unbelievable. I expected you to say two or three a week!"

I have to boast that 95 percent of all enquires, wherever they came from, were converted into new customers, by Geoff the ex-double glazing salesman. I can assure you, selling boarding facilities for cats and dogs was a walk in the park compared to selling twin sheets of glass in window frames!

We found Yellow Pages to be an extremely good tool for our advertising and we gained more business through them than any other source. I know it sounds a bit like an advertising campaign for them! I can absolutely assure you it isn't. I am definitely not getting paid for promoting them in this book! But I sure wish I was.

The third way of generating business was through recommendations. We got literally hundreds, which proves if you provide a good service, whatever business you are in, then you will be recommended.

Another ploy I used annually was to ring around the other boarding cattery and kennels, pretending to be a new customer. 'Geoff Bond 008' was spying again. This was a double-sided enquiry. I was able to find out what their prices were going to be for the coming year and this enabled me to increase my prices accordingly. Secondly it was to see how our competitors treated their own new telephone enquiries. Well, often to my surprise, it took them two or three minutes to even answer my phone call. Their attitude was often offhand. They sounded miserable or sometimes even arrogant. This was another reason why we were so popular, always being very pleasant, friendly, and happy, whatever problem we might have been in the middle of at that time. My rule to our staff was to answer the phone within four rings and I had said to them jokingly, "Because if you don't, you'll get the sack!" I think they knew I was only joking; fortunately it never had to be tested.

The very first phone call I received for our new business was from the Yellow Pages advert. Ring! Ring! Only two rings you will note! I excitedly picked up the phone and explained who we were. In my full sales spiel, I explained to the person that she was actually speaking to the owner of probably the most prestigious pet boarding premises in the United Kingdom. Now, that got her really going, I can tell you.
"Have you got any vacancies in August for my dog?" she enquired.
Immediately, I realised that August would be the busiest month of the year. So I have to admit, I told her a little white lie. I opened up the blank pages in the diary at August and as I looked at the empty pages, I sucked in a deep intake of air and said, "Phew, we are pretty full. What dates do you require?"
"From the 7th to the 21st," she replied.

Another little white lie came from my lips, as I noisily fluttered the empty pages of the diary down the mouth piece of the phone. "Actually, we have had a cancellation for that period only this morning."

"I'll take it," she immediately replied with obvious panic in her voice.

I calmly asked, "Can you please give me your name and address so I can send you our booking form for you to complete and return with your deposit?"

"To make sure I don't lose that kennel space, I'll send you the deposit by first class post today and send the completed booking form later," she instantly replied.

After the conversation had finished, I placed the receiver down, punched my fist high in the air and shouted, "Yes! Yes! Yes!" I couldn't wait for Kathy to come home to tell her loud and clear, "We are in business. We have our first customer booked in!"

Geoffrey Doody

Pugs Came First

In late April of our first year, the very first customer to arrive at the kennels was a pleasant Scottish gentleman who had two little dogs, which were Pugs. Being on my own, the two little doggies, whose names were Henry and Timmy, were very easy to look after and they reminded me of the Pug dog in the *'Rupert the Bear Stories'*. If my gamekeeper friends could have seen me walking the two toy dogs through the woodland they would have keeled over laughing. It was certainly a big change from my normal macho Labrador and Springer Spaniel gundogs. Sally initially came on the walks as well, I'm sure at times even she was giving me some very strange looks.

The big thing was I was going to be paid for the special service and the other thing was this macho ex-gamekeeper has to admit, he actually enjoyed doing it. Henry and Timmy were two nice little characters and they really grew on me during their two-week stay, although I never went to the extremes of buying a pair!

The total for Henry and Timmy's two-week stay came to over 60 pounds and I was dreading handing the bill to the Scottish gentleman.

As most English people have heard, Scots do sometimes have a bit of a reputation where parting with money is concerned. My rule was going to be: You don't get your pets back until you have handed over your dosh mate! I cringed as I presented him with the bill, which I personally thought was massive and stared in amazement when he never even flinched as he looked at it and immediately wrote out the cheque. I looked at the cheque and thought, *My God. This is more than a week's wages when I was a gamekeeper!* With the cheque safely in my back pocket, I went into the kennels to put my mates, Henry and Timmy on their leads and brought them out to their owner. He was so taken aback with their happy appearance, their shining coats and also how they were making as much fuss of me as they were of him.

He said, "Well Geoff, you have done a fantastic job, here get yourself a drink."

To my utter amazement, he pressed a ten pound note in my hand.

Henry and Timmy came to us for many years and their Scottish owner was very happy with our service, he always gave the staff a generous tip.

So what is this nonsense, they say about the Scots and their money?

Geoffrey Doody

Chinese Take-Away

We decided to make a large lawn in between the cattery and kennels; it was going to be more like a small playing field! The lawn would be approximately one and a half acres in size. My farmer friend David from next door—well half a mile away actually—kindly offered me the use of one of his farm workers, whose name was Peter. He arrived driving a large four-wheel drive tractor with plough and it didn't take him long to plough up what was originally our paddock for Kathy's horse. He returned back to the farm to return with another machine on the back of the tractor, this was called a Rotearer. It broke up the rough ploughed soil and leveled it at the same time, the soil was very black when it was first worked and had a lovely earthy smell to it. Apparently, the soil was some of the finest in the county, as for many years it had been naturally fertilized when it used to be woodland. The soil was ideal for growing grass or corn and in our case it was going to be top quality grass.

Peter, with David's machinery had done a fantastic job and the area looked even bigger than before. It was now Geoff's turn, as he was going to be the one to sow the grass seed. I had previously been put in touch with a local seed merchant by my farmer friend David. The seed merchant advised me which was the best type of grass needed to cope with lots of people walking on it and it was apparently the same type used on cricket pitches. I picked up two, 100-weight bags of the special seed in my four-wheel drive vehicle and was ready for action. I decided to tip the seed into a bucket and scatter it out by hand, which was the same way I used to feed the pheasants with wheat corn in my gamekeeping past. It took me about one hour to scatter the grass seed and it was equivalent to feeding about 10,000 pheasants! I was quite pleased with the finished result, the seed seemed to have scattered very evenly.

Peter returned with the tractor and a set of chain harrows and did yet another good job of harrowing the grass seed into the rich soil. "That's it Geoff, finished."
"Hey Pete, don't you think we ought to roll it?"
"Only if you are intending to drive vehicles on it and I'm sure you haven't intended this lovely lawn to be used as a road. Have you?" he joked.
"Over my dead body!" I exclaimed laughing.

I had built the car park to cope with at least twenty cars, why on earth would anyone think of driving a car across my lovely lawn. The only vehicle I intended to go on the beautiful new

It's Raining Cats and Dogs

grass was going to be my brand new Wheelhorse tractor lawn mower.

The tractor mower was being delivered the following week from Craven Arms; it is on the other side of the county from where we lived. I had shopped around and they had given me the best price. I just couldn't wait for my red tractor to be delivered. We all know every little boy's dream is to own a red tractor! I did have a toy once when I was a little boy, but my new one was going to be a lot bigger! I had gone to great pains to find out which would be the best tractor mower for the job and had narrowed it down to a Honda, with automatic gearbox, or the tough Wheelhorse. The dealer whose name was Mr. Jones, (that sounds Welsh, doesn't it? Well, he did live on the Welsh side of Shropshire) had the dealership on both. When he showed me an old Wheelhorse it definitely made me decide which one to have.

He asked, "How old do you think this machine is?"

"About seven years," I replied.

"You are a little bit out. It's twenty-three years old and it's in for its annual service."

My mind was instantly made up; it had to be the Wheelhorse. Hey, by the way, I'm not getting paid for advertising Wheelhorse tractors either! The price was 4,600 pounds. It was a lot more money than I had intended to spend, but I really,

really wanted the red Wheelhorse. As luck would have it, the wintertime was approaching fast and Mr. Jones wanted to get rid of his stock. I ended up with a bargain and only paid 3,800 pounds for it.
Before we struck the deal Mr. Jones joked, "If you had carried on haggling I would have offered you twenty quid just to go away!"

The red tractor mower was delivered at the end of September on the back of a light lorry, by Mr. Jones personally. After he unloaded the gleaming machine he explained all the controls to me. It had a forty-two inch rotary cut with a high and a low ratio gear box, making eight gears in all. It was so powerful its front wheels would do a wheelie if you let the clutch out too quickly. It was like having an expensive toy. In fact, it was an expensive toy and I knew from that day I was going to have many enjoyable hours sitting on my lovely red tractor.

That evening, Kathy and her sister Ann, decided they would like to try out my new toy. Anyone would think it was a Ferrari! At least it was red! I explained to both of them, in great detail that they needed to release the clutch out very slowly, but did they listen, did they hell! They both did great big wheelies and squealed with fright as the front wheels lifted high in the air, once the wheels touched back down on terra firma they both had beaming faces as they drove around with growing confidence. Little did they know it was going to be their first and last ride on *my* tractor!

It takes about ten days for new grass shoots to appear and three weeks after it would need its first cut, I figured my new mower wasn't needed for at least four weeks. I was desperate to use my new toy and even thought about cutting some long grass on the neighboring woodland rides, I just had to be patient and wait for nature to take its course.

Hey, but what good timing! The day after the grass was sown we had rain and it came down steady all day long. It soaked the grass seed good and proper, therefore naturally settling the ground as well. It was absolutely perfect growing weather! I noticed the following day the rain had brought a lot of stones up to the surface and some were quite large. I decided they needed to be picked up and the only way was by hand. I enlisted the help of my two loyal helpers, Kathy and Ann. With their buckets in hand the two girls picked up the offending stones and I barrowed them off into a pithole in the wood. After a rewarding, but back-breaking hard day's work for all of us, there wasn't an offending stone to be seen anywhere.

The grass came up right on schedule and three weeks later, as planned, I was able to give my new lawn a light top cut and wow, give my new red tractor a real workout. After completing my exciting task I sat aside the little tractor, admiring the freshly cut grass, it looked so green and lush and set off the grounds beautifully.

When I used to cut the grass, a fond recollection of mine was of one my favourite birds, the swallow hawking and hunting flying insects the tractor had disturbed. The swallows flew so close to the tractor I felt I could almost touch them and look right down on them as they swooped past me, skimming incredibly low over the cut grass and almost touching it with their narrow streamlined wings. The sun shone on their backs and their dark blue feathers glinted in the suns rays. What a beautiful memory. Whenever I smell freshly cut grass, it always conjures the memory of those halcyon days, with those graceful jet-like birds, my swallows.

Sometimes on hot days, while I was mowing the big lawn, I was so relaxed and subdued with the warmth from the sun and my surrounding environment, I would briefly nod off. You could always tell when that had happened, as my normal precise straight lines would have the occasional kink in them.

What has all this boring rubbish got to do with the title of this story, "A Chinese Take-Away?" You might well ask! Hey, I'm on a build-up here! Well, if you can hang about, all will be revealed.

One day I was sitting in my office at the kennels doing some paperwork when a car drove onto the car park and out stepped an attractive Oriental lady, who I presumed to be Chinese. As she walked into the office I looked up and pleasantly asked, "How can I help you?"

She answered in perfect English, "Would it be possible to view your cattery please? I am going away for three weeks and need to board my two cats."
"No problem. If you would like to follow me down to the cattery I'll show you around," I replied.

She followed me out of the office and I assumed she was walking right behind me. The distance across our lovely new lawn from the office to the cattery was just over 100 yards. I was about halfway across when I realised I must have been walking a little too quickly, as I couldn't hear her following me. Oh, she was following me alright, in fact, twenty five yards behind me. To my absolute astonishment she was in her Mini—not mini skirt, but her Mini car! Can you believe it? She was driving on my new grass! Why hadn't I heard her car door shut? Why hadn't I heard her car engine start? Why hadn't I heard her car behind me?

Oh no, my poor grass. I just couldn't believe my eyes. I jumped up and down with my hands raised above my head making all sorts of gesticulations shouting, "Stop! Stop! Please go back!" My thoughts certainly contained much stronger words.

It finally dawned on her she shouldn't have been on my lovely new lawn. So what did she do then? Now believe this! Oh yes, she went back alright, instead of slowly reversing along the same tracks she had made, she took off at speed toward the car park with wheels spinning and grass flying everywhere. She did a great big 'U' turn, damaging yet more of my lovely new grass. I walked back toward the car park rather dejectedly and at the same time I was inspecting my mangled grass. I was thinking of all the hard work we had done and how it had been a complete waste of time.
"I am so sorry," she said.
In the traumatic circumstances in which I found myself, I smiled at her and said through gritted teeth in the most pleasant tone I could muster, "Oh don't worry. No harm done. It's no problem at all, it will soon grow again." But frustratingly I thought, *Argh! You ****** idiot!*

As we all know, the customer is always right and I didn't want to lose a new one by showing any anger at all. Believe me I seriously felt like strangling her at the time. The good news was she loved the cattery and booked her two cats in.

Fortunately, the car was only a Mini and it hadn't sunk into the lawn too deeply, most of the damage turned out to be bruised grass. There was no long-term damage inflicted and I have had many a laugh over that incident since.

Maybe you can guess what I had printed on a sign for all to see.
It read: PLEASE KEEP OFF THE GRASS.
With a bit of luck perhaps that sign would **stop** anymore, 'Chinese **Mini** Take-Aways', with the added wheel spin across my lovely lawn!

Geoffrey Doody

The Signs

If anyone had informed me how many signs needed to be displayed for our business, I would never have believed the figure. The first sign was erected at the end of our drive. Remember, it was the one that got nicked by the students and had to be replaced. Not only did it advertise the business, it also made it easier for people to find our concealed entrance. I am quite sure it saved numerous accidents people might have had, as they would have been driving slowly along a fast highway searching for our premises. So you mischievous students, perhaps you now realise removing signs is not a good idea. It can be very, very dangerous.

When we first started the business, we were literally open twenty four hours a day. Big, big ***mistake!*** We soon became quick learners and decided to have strict opening and closing times. The second sign simply read that we were closed and also gave information about our opening times. It was fixed onto a new five-bar gate, situated along our drive fifty yards before the turn into the car park.

Unfortunately, the word *closed* didn't mean *closed* to many people, they just ignored it and came through. So I fixed another sign with it that read in large bold red capitals, GUARD DOGS LOOSE. This seemed to do the trick and meant we were really, really closed. People didn't seem to like the idea of large vicious guard dogs running loose. Well that is the impression people seem to have of guard dogs, isn't it!

Good idea, Geoff thought. It wasn't a complete lie, we did have Sally, my friendly Springer Spaniel always loose and she preferred to lick people to death rather than show any aggression. I realise the wording seemed a bit dramatic, but when you have a business operated from home, you do have to have a break now and again. Some of the *Joe Public's* seemed to think we were there entirely for their convenience and whatever time they decide to drop in on us.

Can you believe a gentleman phoned us at three o'clock one Sunday morning? He wanted to book his two dogs in for the following year! He was slurring his words and it was a good job I wasn't slurring mine too. At least I managed to understand him as quite often on a Saturday night I could have had one too many as well! Now that could have been some sort of conversation that could have been well worth listening too! It was necessary to have the business line to the house so we could at least pick up out-of-hours calls.

It's Raining Cats and Dogs

But surely not at that time! Initially, we only had the one line; it could easily have been a private call from family at that time in the morning.

Only having one line was due to that well-known phone company that used to advertise on television how good they were with that famous "Yellow Budgie" named *Busby*. He could supposedly work wonders, except getting Geoff another much-needed telephone line!

Let me get back to the GUARD DOGS LOOSE sign. One beautiful summer evening I was sitting in the office sorting out some paperwork. Unfortunately, the business generated masses of the damn stuff, not my favourite pastime, that's for sure.

It was just before nine o'clock in the evening when I heard a car engine and two doors bang. I crept around my desk, slowly popped my head around the door and looked through the nearby spinney of silver birch, which was in between the office and the padlocked five-bar gate. To my utter surprise (and that is an understatement if ever I made one), there was a man and a woman climbing over our gate. They certainly didn't look like burglars, they looked more like customers! I just couldn't believe my eyes! They had totally ignored the two massive signs, GUARD DOGS LOOSE and CLOSED, which also stated very clearly, we closed at five o'clock. Perhaps it should have read: VERY DANGEROUS GUARD DOGS LOOSE, or even YOU WILL GET RIPPED TO SHREDS AND EATEN IF YOU CLIMB OVER THIS GATE!

The couple who looked to be in their mid-sixties were dressed very respectfully and were tiptoeing up the drive toward the car park. I could see they were obviously quite wary, probably because they were imagining a pack of guard dogs loose! I knew they wouldn't have been able to see the office clearly until they got to the beginning of the car park. I must say I was quite annoyed with what I was seeing. It was an evening of peaceful tranquility and I sure didn't want two cheeky people entering our premises at that late hour, which would have disturbed the dogs resting or sleeping in the kennels. What I really meant was I didn't want the noise and bedlam to erupt with over thirty dogs barking their bloody heads off. No way was I going to let anybody, or anything, disturb that silent night.

As it turned out I wasn't needed, without any interference from me, nature took its course. They were about to round the corner of the spinney when they hesitated and stopped, they were almost hidden from my view by the small elderberry bushes growing in between the birches. The man pointed at something and I looked to see in which direction he was pointing, to my amusement I saw Sally, the doggy love of my life, with her back to them, curled up fast asleep on the grass.

They were only fifty yards away from her and all they were able to see was a liver-coloured dog, they wouldn't have been able to tell that Sally was a harmless twelve-year-old Springer Spaniel. Sally suddenly stirred and raised her head; it was more than enough for the watching couple. They just turned and fled in apparent terror. The five bar-gate was no barrier to them whatsoever. They virtually vaulted it. Within seconds I heard their car engine start and the car roared off down the drive with tyres screeching.

I burst out laughing and could only imagine what type of fierce guard dog they must have thought my Sally could be. What made it so hilarious was that she was almost deaf and her sight wasn't too clever either! I beckoned to her to come over and she looked at me with her tail wagging. She must have surely wondered what on earth I was laughing at. Poor old Sally didn't even realise the couple had ever been there.

I have told this story many, many times and I am sure if I had really got the devilment in me that evening I could have made it even more entertaining. I would have loved to have crept into the elderberry bushes, hidden to wait for them to see Sally and then violently shaken the bushes and let out an almighty roar like a lion. I would bet my bottom dollar that they would have cleared that five-bar gate without even touching it, despite their age and most certainly needed a change of underwear as well! I could even have caused two major heart attacks that evening!

The next signs were quite simple, identifying different buildings, rooms, areas and so forth. TOILET, well everyone knows what that is for. OFFICE, KITCHEN, CAR PARK are all quite self-explanatory, I think.

NO UNAUTHORISED CARS OR PEOPLE BEYOND THIS POINT. Why would we need this one you might ask? Well, it was because so many people just ignored the sign that read: TO CAR PARK AND OFFICE and just drove straight past it down to our house and knocked on our private front door.

Another sign was again straight forward enough. It read: NO UNAUTHORISED PERSONS TO OPEN THIS DOOR. This was fixed on the main door to the first block of kennels, but some souls just totally ignored it and walked straight into the kennels. This caused the dogs to erupt into a noise that would make a jumbo jet seem quiet! Why did people just ignore my beautiful signs? What was it with these people? Didn't they think we might have had a dog loose out of its kennel and they could have been the cause for it to escape past them? Wow, did I get frustrated or what!

This following sign caused all sorts of confusion. It was situated on the outside office wall, next to the main door of the first block of kennels. It read: PLEASE RING THE BELL FOR ATTENTION, with an arrow pointing up toward a red button just inches above. If anyone pressed the button, a bell rang in kennel block number one and of course the dogs erupted into frenzied barking. This could be as many as thirty dogs, which naturally started off a chain reaction, with the dogs following suit in the other blocks. Wow, the noise created was unbelievable!

There was also a bell that rang in the cattery at the same time. Fortunately, the cats didn't mind it ringing and as far as I know, no one has ever heard a cat bark!

The bell was necessary because the office couldn't be manned all the time, especially when dog walking. During this time we needed, 'All hands on deck', as the saying goes. It was inevitable that some dogs barked as their doggy brains weren't able to understand that they couldn't all be walked at the same time. We did our best to keep them as quiet as possible by taking the noisiest first and afterward locking them away in their sleeping quarters for the duration of the walking. If we heard a car coming up the drive one of us would almost have a hernia trying to make an effort to get to the customer before he or she rang that damn bell. The office/reception was a small room with a little window at the back; it looked into kennel block number one. We would leave the office door open to encourage customers to walk in and be able to see us working with the dogs. We were then able to acknowledge them with a wave and mouth to them, "We won't be a second."

But did they wait? Like hell they did, they just had to ring that damn bell and start the dog barking off yet again. I used to think, C*an't you please be a little patient, we are coming as quickly as we can.* Well, that was the polite version, but I really would like to have said, "Don't you realise every time you press that ***** button, the dogs bark even ***** louder? Don't you realise we know you are ***** waiting? Do you think we are all stone ***** deaf?" We could be walking back from the cattery toward a customer and even though we were in full view, they would still press that damn button.

One day I was actually talking to a customer and as I turned away, what did he do? Yes, to my utter amazement he pressed the button and rang the damn bell! I was astounded how customers reacted to the sign and would joke to the staff, "If anyone presses that button more than once I'll get it wired up to have ten thousand volts passing through them!"

We used to ask people, "Why did you press the button when you saw me coming toward you?"
They would reply, "Well, the sign says 'Please ring;' so I did."
I think once people saw the sign and it seemed to be the only one they ever read, they just had to press the button at all costs. I was sure if they were absolutely riddled with machine gun bullets they would still manage to drag themselves over to the sign and press the button and make the damn bell ring.
I think their thoughts were, *I must press that button, if it's the last thing I do!*

Wow, what stress that bell gave us and of course it gave the dogs stress too. We had to find a way to solve the problem because the bell ringing in the kennels and the dog barking that automatically followed was seriously getting right up my nose and certainly in my ears! So what could I do?

A fantastic idea came to mind, it was a flashing light that I attached to a high stanchion fixed on top of the staffroom roof so we were able to see it from everywhere on the premises— even in the woodland while we were walking the dogs. So when the dreaded button was pressed, instead of the bell ringing, the orange light flashed and instantly we knew someone needed our attention. Okay, so we had a flashing light, but people couldn't hear a bell ringing, so they just simply kept pressing and pressing and pressing the damn button, thinking it wasn't working. But we didn't mind because the dogs didn't bark and pressing the button didn't get up my nose anymore. So as far as I was concerned they could press the button as many times as they liked and I have to confess, I was highly amused with that!

Some customers used to ask, "Do you know your bell isn't working?"
We used to reply smiling, while pointing to the flashing light in the sky, "But that is!"
On returning to the office all we had to do was press another button that turned it off. Our famous flashing light was there for all to see and no dogs to hear! Tranquility had finally arrived!

Travelling a few years down the road, we had expanded big time and had four kennel blocks. So why did we need this next sign? Oh yes, would you believe this one?

One day the dogs in the second kennel block were going absolutely ballistic with their barking and for no apparent reason. I went to investigate the disturbance and to my amazement there was a man wandering around the kennels, staring at the dogs. The second block was well away from the office and no way would you think someone would have had the cheek to enter the kennels without permission. But that cheeky chappy had! As I approached him, I must have had a look of complete disbelief on my face and did an

incredible job of controlling my temper. I politely said, "I'm sorry, but you're not meant to be in here. Can I help you?"
"Oh, I'm just looking around," he calmly replied.
Trying not to blow a gasket I asked, "Didn't you see the large sign outside the kennel block?" (NO UNAUTHORISED PEOPLE BEYOND THIS POINT PLEASE)
"What sign?" he innocently asked.
I just couldn't believe the audacity of the man. I would like to have said, "You know the sign you virtually had to climb over to get to this kennel block!" But of course, I thought better of it! So what do you think? Is the customer always right?

The sign in question was fixed to a four-inch oak stake about shoulder height for an average person and you had to actually walk around it to get to the kennel block door, which was another ten yards further along. How on earth could he have missed it? It was clearly impossible, he had to be lying. I struggled to do my best to be polite and explained we didn't like customers wandering around our premises willy-nilly. He seemed to fully understand and as a bonus, he decided to book his dog into the kennels for a stay. On his illicit wanderings, he was obviously impressed with what he saw, so it does pay to bite your tongue sometimes and laugh all the way to the bank!

I think this next sign is number thirteen, but by now I could have lost count. What was number thirteen? You should be able to work this one out for yourself. Number thirteen, unlucky for some, had to be fixed to the main door of block two kennels where our gentleman friend had wandered into without permission. I initially thought about putting up a sign that read: OPEN THIS DOOR AND YOU WILL BE SHOT! Instead, I thought be sensible here Geoff lad, so it read: NO ADMITTANCE STRICTLY STAFF ONLY. That finally seemed to sink in as we never had any more strange people walking around the kennels unattended.

Down to the cattery for the next few signs and we won't worry about keeping count, the numbers just kept rapidly increasing every week. There was a simple sign that read: CATTERY. I think most people could work out what that one meant! On the outside door of the cattery there was a sign that read: PLEASE DO NOT OPEN THIS DOOR UNLESS ACCOMPANIED BY A MEMBER OF STAFF—yet another sign that was occasionally ignored.

One day we found a child wandering around the cattery. His mother had let him in because he liked stroking and playing with the nice pussycats. What a nice Mummy! How they had got down to the cattery unaccompanied in the first place, was beyond belief. Fortunately, the child couldn't get into the cat runs, we had triple spring-loaded safety doors, but he was able to stroke them through the mesh doors. If he had managed to lose any out, we could have been looking for cats for weeks after that event. His mother obviously hadn't seen the danger she had put our cats in and more importantly her son!

I politely asked, "Didn't you see the sign on the door?"

"I am sorry. My son just loves cats and I knew none could escape—especially with me standing here guarding the door," she replied.

In my usual polite manner, although I really could have throttled her at the time, I explained, "Some of these cats can be quite aggressive and could have seriously injured your son. In fact, we have one or two in here at the moment that behave more like tigers! And even I am sometimes frightened of them."

I think the little boy's mother then fully understood the danger she had put her son in and of course the lovely placid pussycats. *Placid* pussycats! I have met a few pussycats that could have ripped her little boy's arms off! If her son had let more than one cat out there could have been fighting big time and serious injuries to the cats could have occurred. And that's not counting the chaos and mix-ups that could have happened. If any cats had escaped, I hate to imagine what the cat owner's reactions would have been. Plus, who would have to tell the owners that their pussycat had escaped? It sure as hell wasn't going to be her. Was it? No, the buck always stopped with *Mr. Muggins* here. She eventually appreciated how she would have felt if we had lost her own cat while it was staying with us. The good news was she booked her cat in for a stay with us. Phew! Did we get through some traumas, or what! My next move was to put a padlock onto the outside cattery door that we kept locked when there were no members of staff there.

I even had a sign that read: HOUSE ONLY NO CATTERY AND KENNEL BUSINESS. But we still had people knocking on our front door asking, "Where do you want me to put my dog/cat?"
I certainly could have answered that question; that's for sure!

They had not only missed or even ignored the large sign that read: TO CAR PARK AND OFFICE. They had also passed the second large sign that read: NO UNAUTHORISED CARS OR PEOPLE BEYOND THIS POINT. They had driven past the car park and massive area of kennels and also ignored the large building with a sign on it reading: CATTERY. Were these people blind or what?

I think you will remember the sign that read: PLEASE KEEP OFF THE GRASS. It was from the story of 'A Chinese Take-Away'. I suppose, KEEP OFF THE GRASS, is quite common really, you see

It's Raining Cats and Dogs

it in parks and public places, but as we all know, most people just ignore them.

Another sign read: DANGER LOOK LEFT. This one was erected at the end of our drive, on the way out onto the main A41 trunk road. With it being a long straight road, cars were often overtaking and when a car leaving our premises was turning out onto the main road to turn left, the driver sometimes only looked to the right, without realising that cars could be overtaking from the opposite direction. Our sign tried to warn drivers to look left as well, I am sure this sign saved many accidents and possibly even lives, it made many people more aware of the danger.

Over the years we ran the business we only had one car accident, which happened to be caused by one of our customers pulling out of the drive. Fortunately, there were only minor injuries inflicted, but I'm afraid some serious damage to three vehicles.

There were many more signs I haven't mentioned, you must now be getting the picture that some of the signs were maybe a little bit necessary. I think most people did read what they actually stated but some totally ignored them or didn't even see them! It's a good job their lives didn't depend on our signs. Well actually, when I think about the one at the bottom of our drive, that one possibly did—not to mention other signs that could have stopped people getting ripped to bits by big dangerous doggies or little placid pussycats!

All of our signs were in large bold printing for all to see, even if people maybe needed reading glasses! I must say one thing about all our signs is we certainly had many laughs over them! I suppose I am as much to blame as anyone for not reading signs as well, its human nature, that's my excuse anyway.

Geoffrey Doody

The Sign Writer

I had contacted Adrian, the sign writer, through Yellow Pages and it turned out his business was new like ours. We quickly developed a good relationship and saw each others businesses grow quite rapidly. We became very good friends with Adrian and his wife Melanie and took skiing holidays with them. Kathy is Godmother to their daughter Hannah and we still see them, even though we now live in Spain.

All the signs I purchased most certainly helped Adrian to establish his new sign-writing business and I am sure I must have been one of his best customers. I would ring him up and he would say, 'What new sign have you come up with today Geoff?' Within a couple of days he would deliver yet another new shiny sign for me to put up where I hoped people would read it!

You could say I couldn't get enough of those signs and customers did comment I had become obsessed with my beautiful signs. Is there such a phobia called 'sign-nar-ritus'? Well, if there is, I certainly had it bad! I visited Adrian's premises quite often and was amazed at how intricate the making of a sign was. Perhaps I should have been a sign-writer myself; it could have maybe cured my so-called sign-nar-ritus phobia!

Adrian and Melanie had a little Yorkshire Terrier called *Simon*. As they liked lots of holidays, little Simon often used to board with us. Simon had a little red wellington boot he used to carry in his mouth that squeaked when he squeezed it. He also had a small football and he would play with you for ages, hitting the ball back to you with the little red boot in his mouth, using it almost like a golf club. He could even do headers! What a little character he was, as were many of the other boarders.

Back to Adrian, I thought if I gave him a good price for Simon, he would then give me a good price for the signs. You know the saying, "I'll scratch your back, if you scratch mine." I found this statement to be true in many aspects of running our business. Adrian's brother also boarded his dog with us and who recommended him, well of course, it was Adrian. So both their recommendations kept coming in with new customers using us. In return I would recommend Adrian's sign-writing to anyone I knew.

Adrian and Melanie moved house quite often. No, they weren't Gypsies; I think they were just obsessed with moving. This phobia could be called 'move-a-ritus'? Adrian loved decorating and as soon as he had refurbished their house, it was sold very quickly and they would move into their next new house and project, which was always bigger and of course more valuable.

Adrian and Melanie often spent evenings at our house coming around for dinner and they were two of the famous dog walkers involved in a future story. We in return were invited to all their new houses and didn't have to walk any dogs—not even little Simon! The four of us were working very hard in our separate businesses and all very successful, thank you very much. They liked having the best of everything, like new cars and furniture. You could say, they were quite materialistic, and why not? They earned it; they deserved it, so why not spend it! There is a famous saying, "You can't take your money with you!" And that is so true.

One day we had a phone call from Adrian and Melanie inviting us for dinner to see their latest house, or should I say *project*. We had previously seen the house a few months before, shortly after they purchased it. The interior of the house and gardens had been quite run down; it had been owned by an old lady who hadn't been able to look after it properly. The house was situated in a typical beautiful English village called Ashley in Shropshire. All the houses were very valuable in that area and we knew it was going to be the best house they had owned so far. They were really excited for us to see their finished project and we felt highly honoured, as we knew we would be their first visitors.

When we left our house to visit Adrian and Melanie, it was a cold wet windy winter's night. Normally Kathy opened and closed our five-bar gate, as she had spent ages drying her long blonde hair, she obviously didn't want it getting wet and blown about. So that is where Geoff, 'The Knight in Shining Armour', came in and offered to be her hero.

BIG, BIG MISTAKE! You will find out why later. With the umbrella, instead of sword, Kathy's hero braved the wind and rain. He got out of the vehicle, opened the gate, got back in, drove it through, got back out, closed the gate and clicked the padlock shut, back into the vehicle and finally set off down the bendy drive. Phew! What we men do for our loved ones!

We arrived at Adrian and Melanie's twenty minutes later and as we drove into their driveway, several security lights came on. I thought, *Very posh*. The front door opened to reveal the excited couple beckoning us to come in. It was still blowing a 'hooley'. The rain was lashing down more than ever and we took a desperate dive into their porch. We said our greetings at the door and Kathy asked, "Do you want us to take off our shoes?"

"No, just give them a good wipe on the doormat," Melanie replied.
After meticulously wiping our shoes we were shown into their new kitchen. Kathy exclaimed, "Wow, this is absolutely fabulous!"
I could see Kathy was envious, she looked at me and I knew exactly what she was thinking. She added, "This is fantastic, Geoff. It is a lot better than ours. It has everything I could wish for."

Hey, I told you I knew what she was thinking. We were asked what we would like to drink and shown into their lounge with its beautiful beige, almost white, plush carpet. It was so thick and deep, it just had to be expensive. After a few minutes of chatting, they left the two of us sitting on their new leather settee in front of a blazing fire. We were enjoying our drinks and taking in the ambience while they were preparing the meal in their new kitchen. The fire was so comforting on that cold winter's night and as we were absolutely shattered from our days work, it would have been very easy for both of us to have dozed off. But we made sure we stayed politely awake as we looked around the room admiring the wallpapering Adrian had done. We thought how nice the colour scheme was with all the pale shades complimenting each other. Adrian was making me feel quite guilty helping Melanie in the kitchen. I cagily said, "What a good husband Adrian is."

Kathy gave me a knowing look and replied with a sigh, "Yes, Geoff, I know your domain is outside with a chain saw or lawn mower. I accept that you do your best to help me where you can in the kitchen. It is just not your scene." I must say I felt a lot less guilty after that last calming statement of Kathy's.
We were generally chit chatting when Kathy said, "You know, they are going to need to be extra careful with this carpet. It will really show the slightest mark, especially with them having Simon."

The words had barely left Kathy's mouth when I spotted them! There were brown marks leading from the door, directly to where we were sitting, or should I say to where I was sitting. The marks were difficult to see because the lights were dimmed. I immediately thought, *She is right as always. This carpet is definitely the wrong colour. They are going to have real trouble keeping this clean and it looks to me like they have problems here already.* I studied the light brown marks intensely, they were about two inches across and there was mark, after mark, after mark, getting darker the nearer they got to where I was sitting. They certainly had a problem alright and the problem led straight to me. I knew the brown marks had nothing to do with me because I had more than meticulously wiped my feet, watched closely by Kathy. I thought, *Perhaps its Simon that has made the marks before we arrived.*

I had another sip of my drink thinking the marks didn't look that fresh anyway. What a shame somebody, or something, meaning Simon, had already spoilt their beautiful new carpet. I glanced down at Kathy's shoes; they looked spotless. I looked down at mine, they also looked spotless. Thank God, it wasn't us that had made the horrible stains on their pale carpet. They obviously hadn't been able to get the stains out and if it had been a person who was guilty, what kind of moron would do something so disrespectful to a beautiful new carpet! I thought, *I bet whoever they are, they haven't owned up to this dastardly deed.* I said to Kathy, "What on earth are they doing in the kitchen? They've been in there ages. Hey, by the way, have you noticed those marks on the carpet?"

"What marks?" Kathy asked.

"Those marks—there, coming from the door," I answered, as I pointed to them and had another refreshing sip from my drink.

"It must be us," Kathy said in a panicky tone.

"No, they're nothing to do with us and anyway, they're not even fresh," I casually replied, taking another sip from my glass of superb red wine.

Kathy took off her shoes and examined the soles underneath. "My shoes are clean! Check yours Geoff?"

"Mine are clean and the stains on the carpet are old, I told you."

Kathy repeated the order for me to take them off, I begrudgingly obeyed her as always. I took my right shoe off and knowingly retorted, "Look . . . it's clean, I told you so." I knew damn well I wasn't the cause of the stains, so I never bothered taking off my left shoe. I casually glanced down at it and moved my ankle to turn the shoe onto its side. Oh my God! My heart skipped a beat as I stared down in horror, staring right back up at me was the biggest piece of dog turd that was possible to implant directly in the middle of one's instep! The damn thing must have weighed at least a quarter of a pound. Oh hell! Why hadn't I felt it? Why hadn't I smelt it? Why hadn't it come off when I wiped my feet? Oh why, oh why, oh why?

It was artistically curled up on the right side of my shoe and looked like a horn; it could have adorned a Viking's helmet! A cobbler couldn't have made a more precise job. It was a work of art and it stared up at me triumphantly. I stared back in horror, "Arrrrrrghhhhh!"
I shrieked under my breath, as to not alert our hosts, who could have soon become our enemy!
"What's wrong?" Kathy asked in surprise.
"Shhhhh! Look at my shoe," I whispered.
She looked at my shoe and her face filled with horror and disgust, she exclaimed, "Oh, my God!"
"Perhaps they won't notice," I said defensively.
"Of course they'll notice," Kathy angrily retorted.

It's Raining Cats and Dogs

"What am I going to do?"
"You'll have to tell them," Kathy firmly said.
"I'm not telling them. You tell them.'
Kathy replied, with the tone in her voice rising, "No, it's on your shoe. You tell them. You haven't wiped your shoes properly."
"Of course I damn well did. You saw me. You even watched me. How was I to know I had a massive piece of dog turd stuck under the middle of my shoe?"
"You should have checked your shoes better," Kathy said, with an even higher panicky tone in her voice.
I retaliated, "Why didn't we smell it in the car? It's too big to belong to their Yorkshire Terrier. I must have picked it up from by our gate when I opened and closed it. You should have done the gate. You always open and close it just because you were frightened of getting your hair messed up. It's not fair. It should be on your shoe, not mine!" My temper and embarrassment was rising by the second, as I continued and snarled, "I'll kill those bloody girls at the kennels tomorrow morning. They must have walked the long-haired dogs down the drive because it was so muddy in the wood today. If I have told them once I've told them a thousand times to clear up any dog crap lying down that drive. Just wait until tomorrow. I'll give them a rollicking they won't believe."

Kathy interrupted my flow of heightening anticipation for the next mornings rollickings or even better, stranglings! She said, "Never mind what you'll do tomorrow. What the hell are you going to do tonight? What are you going to say to Adrian and Melanie?"

"Oh, I don't bloody know. Will it come off the carpet?"

"Probably..... But what are you going to say to them?" Kathy calmly said.

I thought, *It's all right for Miss. Perfect. It's not on her bloody shoe, is it? It's on my damn shoe!*

Then the inevitable happened, Melanie shouted, "Are you all right in there? We'll be with you in a second."

I thought, *Like the bloody hell we are!*

I was getting really worried about the impending embarrassment, I whispered, "Kathy, what the hell am I going to say?"

The next minute Melanie walked through the door with a nice big beaming smile on her face carrying her drink. She said to me, "Geoff, are you okay? You look a little red in the face?"

I angrily thought, *Of course I'm red in the face. I'm red in the face with embarrassment! I'm red in the face because I have probably messed up your brand new, very expensive beautiful new carpet. I'm red in the face because I've spread dog shit all over your new carpet and you haven't even damn well noticed. And I've got to own up to all this shit, haven't I!*

Eventually, I pulled myself together and politely stammered out to Melanie, "How long will Adrian be? I've got something to tell you both."

I sure as hell wasn't going to own up to the mess by telling Melanie first and then having to go through the nightmare over again with Adrian afterwards. I thought it was going to be best to tell them together and get it all over and done with in one go. I knew I had to tell them as soon as possible before I lost my nerve or blamed Simon, their little dog. I thought, *My next drink is definitely going to be a brandy. That's if I live long enough to take another drink!*

Adrian came into the lounge, also beaming from ear to ear carrying his drink. I looked up at him and thought, *I'll soon wipe that smile off your face, mate, when I tell you the good news about your new carpet!*
He said, "So what do you think of our new house then? Do you like how we have decorated it? And what about the new colour scheme?" He was so proud he could hardly wait for us to answer the previous question before he asked the next one!
"Don't you think it goes well with the carpet?"

Carpet, carpet! I couldn't believe what I was hearing. My hands had started to shake and I was almost spilling my wine, I had beads of sweat on my forehead. My immediate thoughts were, *This is a bloody nightmare. What the hell are you going to think of my new colour scheme on your* *carpet? Oh God, please help me. Beam me up, Scotty. Get me out of here right now!*

I bravely composed myself, put my hand to my mouth and gave a slight cough. It all spluttered out and I groveled, "I am so terribly, terribly sorry. There is something I need to own up to."
Their smiles slowly but surely started to evaporate, as I nervously explained the shocking news. I gave them the full story of how I must have obtained the larger than life dog turd. Surprisingly they didn't throw me out and took my devastating news exceptionally well. They could see how terribly embarrassed I was and were so understanding. They even gave me a glass of their best brandy to calm my frayed nerves. Now, that is what you call good friends!

It was the first and definitely the last time I will ever be invited to anyone's house and spend over half an hour on my hands and knees in my best clothes cleaning up dog shit from a brand-new carpet. In fact, any carpet at all. To cap it all their little Yorkshire Terrier Simon had already been banned from going into their newly carpeted lounge, I had been deviously thinking how I could have blamed him for the dastardly deed! The poor little dog would have taken at least a week of shitting to produce a turd the size of the monster that had attached itself under the instep of my shoe! Now I can guarantee you, I always take off my shoes in anyone else's house I go into!

It was a happy ending as the carpet cleaned up as good as new, with no trace of the marks to be seen at all. Hey, hang on a minute; it was new! No harm done and we enjoyed a lovely evening in the house with the proud couple and a few more clinks of glasses. I made sure I purchased another sign from Adrian within the week to make sure I was definitely back in his good books!

Shortly after I wrote this story Adrian and Melanie came to visit us in Spain and the amazing thing is they couldn't even remember my extremely embarrassing incident. Kathy and I couldn't believe they had forgotten something that we thought was so important, or to put it mildly, to us a major catastrophe! Surely, we didn't dream the same nightmare!

Geoffrey Doody

Walking Diners

As I have mentioned before, to keep costs down, it was important at the start of the business to refrain from employing staff as long as possible. In those days we had many dinner parties with our friends and found it better to be on the premises for the business. It was certainly more enjoyable to stay at home, rather than meet friends in local pubs or elsewhere.

A couple named Rick and Bet who were long-standing friends of ours came to our house for dinner quite often. Rick had been my best man at our wedding. He had sold his business a few years previously and it appeared he had become a wealthy man in the sense that he even owned his own plane!

One day Rick phoned me and suggested that he and Bet would like to come a little earlier before dinner to help us walk the dogs that evening. I thought, *What a great idea, any free help offered was never refused.* Sensibly, Bet brought a change of clothes as she knew they would be walking the dogs around the woodland. But Rick, for some unknown reason, chose to walk the dogs while he was wearing a smart jacket and tie. Obviously, this was not the correct attire for dog walking, but I have to say Rick was the best dressed dog walker of all time! We even have that particular dog walking session on video! So, some of the lucky dogs whether they appreciated it or probably not, were walked by a couple of apparent millionaires! They both had great fun helping with the dog walking and helped us quite a few times during the first summer, it was quite a novelty to them and it gave great stories to be told around the dining table.

This started a trend with many of our dinner party friends and family. In other words, if they didn't help us walk the dogs. They got no dinner! Hey, we weren't that cruel. I'm only joking!

Kathy's brother Ken and his wife Rosemarie were both from farming backgrounds. I would describe my brother-in-law as a typical farmer's son, with healthy rosy cheeks and a cheeky smile. He was well weathered, as strong as an ox and over six feet tall. He would drive a combined harvester, tirelessly wield an axe, or use a chainsaw, probably all in the same day. He wouldn't have looked out of place as a bouncer standing outside a door, wearing a bowtie and dinner jacket. He gave the impression that he wouldn't be afraid of anything or anybody that was his character and stature. What could possibly frighten big Ken? Well, just wait and see!

It was a lovely Sunday evening when Ken and Rosemarie were setting about their new task of dog walking. Boarding with us at the time was a very old black Labrador called *Bess*. She had a lovely nature and wouldn't hurt a fly. She had a habit of curling her upper lip in a greeting, while wagging her tail. I called it a happy grin; actually quite a lot of Labradors do this. Anybody not knowing anything about dogs, especially when they curl their lips back, could mistake this greeting as a vicious silent snarl. Brother Ken knew very little about dogs! Unfortunately for Bess she had arthritis and had also suffered a stroke six months previous to her stay at our kennels. This had caused her to hold her head on one side and her eyes seemed to show only the whites. I must say, she did look rather peculiar. As you can imagine poor old Bess was definitely on her last legs, albeit very happy.

I had warned her owners when they left her that she may not last her duration and explained the kennels were a different environment to her home and every day was a bonus, she could easily have expired at any moment. They accepted the risks involved and we agreed to board Bess.

I decided to put her in run number one, the one at the very end of the building, right by the exit door to the car park next to the big lawn. This enabled us to just let her out on her own, it was impossible to walk her around the wood, she was definitely not fit enough. As soon as she had walked or even stumbled ten yards, once her feet touched the grass, she would squat down and go to the toilet. She was then quite happy to stagger about having a few sniffs here and there, before slowly make her way back to her run. Bess had been doing this for almost two weeks and had got into her own routine. We trusted her and left her to do her own thing, we knew it was impossible for her to run off. (Take note, Ken knew nothing at all about Bess!)

Ken returned from the wood with two yellow Labradors on their leads and my plan was to pass Ken two more dogs for him to take for the next walk. This was the easiest and quickest way to walk the dogs when we had help. Although labelled, I knew off by heart which run each of the dogs belonged in. Ken walked along the row of kennels with his two new found friends and was about to hand them over to me, so that I could put them back into their correct run. I couldn't help noticing Ken's face as he looked beyond me. He had a look of horror in his eyes and had gone as white as a sheet! I turned around and looked behind me to see what Ken was staring at. Low and behold, there was poor old Bess, staggering mistakenly past her kennel, head lolling on one side with her curled upper-lip revealing her yellow teeth, with only the whites of her eyes showing and her tail wagging. Ken took one look at her and shouted, "Oh, shit!"

I turned to answer him, but to my amazement, Ken had fled! He had turned and left the kennels at speed, taking the two bewildered Labradors with him. He was going so fast his legs were a blur and the two bemused dogs were being dragged behind him. There was six feet of solid muscle running away from poor old Bess. Off he shot back into the wood and the two dogs were having a job to keep up with him. They must have thought it was their lucky day. After having had one nice walk, they were now going again for what could only be described as a gallop!

When I had looked into Ken's eyes I could only imagine how terrified he was of poor old black Bess. I started to laugh and I just couldn't stop. I had tears streaming down my cheeks and all the dogs were looking at me as if I had gone mad. After a few minutes I tried to pull myself together.

Kathy appeared in the kennels after walking her dogs. She gave me a puzzled look and asked, "Why is Ken running around the wood with the same dogs again?"
My laughter erupted again and so did the tears.
"What have you done to my brother this time?" She asked suspiciously.
I had often played silly tricks on Ken and Kathy knew I might have been up to something. "Honest, I haven't done anything. Your big brother is frightened to death of old Bess."

I went into fits of laughter yet again while trying to explain to Kathy how it had come to pass that her big hunk of a brother had taken flight from an old crippled dog. Kathy realised the situation and she also erupted into bursts of loud laughter. As Ann and Rosemarie arrived back in the kennels from their walks, after hearing about Ken's dilemma, they immediately joined in, which created a chorus of laughter that echoed around the kennels. The four of us were laughing hysterically and had to virtually hold each other up. The dogs in the kennels joined in the chorus with their barking and must have thought we had all gone stark staring bonkers! I would like to think the dogs had joined in with their own laughter at Kathy's little brother, big Ken!

Eventually we all calmed down when we heard Ken's stern voice shouting from the woodland, "Will somebody come and take these bloody dogs from me?"
I went out to rescue him, whilst trying hard to restrain my laughter.
"What the hell are you doing letting killer dogs roam loose in your kennels?" Ken spluttered. He could hear the three girls laughing in the kennels. "What's so funny anyway? What are you all laughing at?"
"If you come back into the kennels, I'll show you exactly what's so funny."
"You'll never get me back in those damn kennels again!" Ken snarled.

It's Raining Cats and Dogs

Ken was wrong, as eventually we did get him back into the kennels after we had explained about poor old Bess. I lead him to Bess and she was by then safely back in her run, she gave Ken that same old grin, curling her upper lip, while wagging her tail. He looked down at old Bess and as I looked into his face I still wasn't sure if he was entirely convinced that she wasn't a vicious dog. He told me later that evening that he thought Bess was the devil's dog, as she had staggered and lumbered toward him.

To Ken's credit, it never stopped him helping us in the future and we never had another dog like Bess in the kennels we needed to warn him about. Even after all these years Ken still doesn't see the funny side of this story and I am sure he thinks I set him up on purpose. Now, would I do a naughty thing like that?

Geoffrey Doody

Indian Take-Away

We have already had a Chinese take-away and now we are having an Indian!

This is a tale about two pussycats from Wolverhampton—*Fluffy* and *Teddy*. Don't worry they didn't end up in a Curry! (How about that for a bit of poetry!) Their names definitely described their appearances and characters. Fluffy was a small cat with long black fluffy fur, peeping out were her gorgeous yellow eyes and she was always purring. Teddy had short light brown fur, with two white front feet, it gave the impression he had white gloves on. He most certainly resembled a Teddy bear, hence his name. In my opinion he had some Burmese blood in him. I have always found these breeds to be quite friendly and he was certainly no exception.

When Fluffy and Teddy came to stay with us our business was two years down the road and well established. I was employing a few staff by then and I also had a manageress. We found Fridays, Saturdays, Sundays, and Mondays were always our busiest days for people delivering and collecting their pets. On Saturdays and

Sundays fortunately, there were many teenagers from school available and we were inundated with phone calls from them, asking for jobs or just volunteering to work with the animals. The teenagers absolutely loved the work and as a bonus for us, were also available throughout their school holidays. They even volunteered to work on Christmas days and Boxing days! This was a wonderful arrangement for both parties as our busiest times always revolved around the school holidays. Most of the teenagers were very good working with the cats and dogs and needed little supervision. They ranged between thirteen to sixteen years old and in fact, were more like young adults rather than children. Sorry for that important interruption.

Now get back to Fluffy and Teddy. They were delivered on a Saturday morning by their owners and as usual we went through the routine of checking vaccination certificates and any special requirements, before the cats were taken from their owner's cars. The cats would then be handed to us in their carriers and taken down to the cattery by one or two of our young staff.

Fluffy and Teddy were going to stay with us for two weeks and their owners asked if a friend could collect them, rather than themselves. I confirmed that it would all be in order as long as their friend paid when he collected. Fluffy and Teddy's owners felt it would be far simpler if they paid in advance that day, rather than complicating things later. I asked them for their friend's name and telephone number. I joked and said, "I don't want anyone turning up to steal your cats!"

Having sorted out everything with the owners, they left the two pussycats with us in their carrying containers. Cat containers came in all shapes and sizes. They could be made in plastic, basket cane, plastic-coated wire, wood, cardboard and even some strange homemade devices and contraptions. Fluffy and Teddy were in cardboard carriers, just boxes really, which I must say were very unreliable. Besides not being very safe, the cats couldn't see out of them and they would have been travelling in the dark, which is not ideal. Most cats surely would like to see where they were going. So now do you get the idea, I didn't like cardboard carriers one little bit!

The boxes that Fluffy and Teddy arrived in had most certainly seen a few years of use and it resulted in the cardboard being pliable and not very strong. This meant that if the cats were left unattended there was a possibility they would push themselves out. Also if the cardboard container was picked up by the handle, the fragile bottom could become loose and the cat could drop out. Not only might the cat injure itself as it dropped to the ground but it could have possibly escaped into a strange area it didn't know and get lost or even run over.

I instructed two girls to carry the cardboard boxes very carefully with one hand on the handle at the top and the other hand to secure the bottom. I left the two girls to go down to the cattery and returned to the office to pick up the ringing phone. I hadn't been on the phone for many seconds when I heard a loud scream, "Geoff, Geoff, come quick!"

I dropped the phone like a red hot coal into my manageress' hand for her to sort the call out. I shot outside and was mortified to see the two girls rooted to the spot. They were standing in the middle of the grass between the office and the cattery. One of the cats was slowly walking toward me, while one of the girls was left holding the empty cardboard container by the handle, with the bottom hanging down. She obviously hadn't listened to my instructions, but that was definitely not in my mind at that memorable moment. My main concern was not to panic the cat, it didn't know me and it could easily have run off into the surrounding woodland to maybe disappear forever!

This was the first time Fluffy and Teddy were visiting us and I hoped it wasn't going to be their last! I called softly to the two girls to stay still, not to panic and just leave it to me. I slowly walked up to the cat, which turned out to be Teddy and with no trouble at all, I stroked him and picked him up. Teddy was so lovable, just purring away, appearing not to be the slightest bit bothered that he was in a stranger's arms. I think he was probably just glad to be out of the dark old cardboard container! I slowly walked down to the cattery carrying Teddy in my arms and he was safely installed with no harm done. Phew . . . were we lucky, or what! I had horrible thoughts of explaining to Teddy's owners that Teddy had spent a glorious two weeks in the woodland and would they mind going to look for him. Thank goodness, that wasn't the case!

The member of staff learnt from her big mistake and her frightening experience, she turned out to be one of our best girls and lucky for us, stayed with us for many years afterwards. What the hell has all this got to do with an Indian take-away, you might well ask? Don't worry, I will eventually get there!

Fluffy and Teddy spent a happy two weeks with us and all the staff loved them, they were both so friendly. It was a Saturday when their owner's friend turned up to collect them and he just happened to be an Indian gentleman. Now we are getting to the theme. He arrived in a beautiful gleaming dark blue Jaguar saloon, looking very distinguished in his suit and tie. I thought he looked impeccable. He had the look of a doctor, lawyer, or most probably he owned a string of Indian restaurants. He didn't look to be suitably dressed for collecting and cuddling two lovely friendly pussycats, that's for sure!

I instructed the same two girls to bring Fluffy and Teddy from the cattery, because they definitely knew all about their cardboard carriers! I asked them to put the cardboard carriers directly into the car, rather than bring them into the office, which was the normal procedure. We certainly didn't want the same episode again. I feared the next time we might not have been quite so lucky! In the meantime, the Indian gentleman was explaining to me how terrified he was of cats and looking at his face I could see he had a genuine fear of them. He said in a panicky tone, "If a cat just looks at me I go into a hot sweat."

I asked myself, *Why the hell have the owners asked this guy to collect their cats?* I explained to him that he didn't have to worry, Fluffy and Teddy were in closed containers and he wouldn't even be able to see them. Even better, they wouldn't be able to see him either. I could see he was a bit more settled with my comforting words. Perhaps his ancestors had been eaten by tigers in years gone by! We will never know as I didn't dare ask him. Suddenly, his face changed to a paler shade of brown and beads of sweat had appeared on his forehead as he looked in horror at the fragile cardboard containers being carried to his car. We had even tied them up with string to make them more secure, but he still wasn't happy and he pleaded with us to put the containers into his car boot. Unfortunately for him, or should I say his peace of mind, we had to insist each cardboard container went behind the front seats, in the footwells. I explained that the containers would be more stable there and wouldn't be thrown about as they would have been in the car boot. With growing reluctance he let us put them into the inside of his car as he hesitantly accepted my explanation.

Before he got into his car he tentatively peered through the side window and could see the top of one of the containers moving up and down. We all knew it was Teddy pushing up and rubbing his head under the top of it, almost as if he was being stroked. I looked into the poor guy's face, his eyes appeared to be rolling and his face had turned from a pale brown to ashen. With my suntan I was now a darker shade than he was! I tried to explain to him they were really very friendly cats and wouldn't harm him at all. I could see I was fighting a losing battle and more importantly so was the cardboard container holding Teddy!
I said, "It won't take you long to get back to Wolverhampton."
"You bet it won't," he determinedly replied.

With that, he leapt into his car, started the powerful engine of the Jaguar and was gone in a flash with screeching tyres smoking, leaving the smell of burning rubber and exhaust fumes. He made a

Grand Prix driver look like a tortoise on the starting grid! I knew if I drove fast to Wolverhampton I could get there in twenty minutes. I was sure this guy was going to do it in ten! The two girls burst into laughter as the Jaguar sped down the drive, I just couldn't help myself and joined in with their laughter and said, "If those two cats get out of their containers, I wouldn't like to be his wife washing his underwear!"
One of the girls jokingly added, "I'm sure I could smell something, even before he got into his car!" We certainly had a good laugh about it and knew it would have been a miracle if the two cardboard containers held all the way to Wolverhampton and if they had, he would have ended up being one very lucky man!

I must say, we did feel a little guilty toward him but we were only doing what was best for our friends, Fluffy and Teddy. We really hoped they wouldn't get out as they could have caused an accident. I had asked him to phone me at his journey's end, I really was concerned for him and the cats. Fortunately, he did ring me twenty minutes later to tell me the three of them had all arrived safely. Thank goodness!

Fluffy and Teddy became regular guests of ours so this is how we know the ending of the story.

When the Indian gentleman got back he immediately vacated his lovely Jaguar, I am sure

It's Raining Cats and Dogs

at speed and left Fluffy and Teddy to it. He was frightened to go anywhere near them, let alone touch them. Unfortunately, Fluffy and Teddy's owners were delayed by five hours and within that time Fluffy and Teddy escaped out of their boxes into the luxurious car, making themselves well at home, but unavoidably leaving cat hairs everywhere. When the owners eventually arrived to greet Fluffy and Teddy, they found the Jaguar abandoned with no sign of the fleeing driver. To cap it all or should it read 'cat it all', the two cats were blissfully cuddled up together fast asleep in sheer luxury on the driver's leather seat. The two harmless pussycats hadn't felt any trauma at all over the last two weeks, unlike their Indian friend, who very nearly had a nervous breakdown!

The lovely Jaguar was sold within weeks of Fluffy and Teddy's luxury sleep. I am sure someone must have had a bargain! And surprise, surprise, the Indian gentleman never collected them again! At least he did remain a good friend with the owners, but he could never overcome his fear of their friendly pussycats.

In conclusion, I can't understand why someone should ask a friend to pick up two cats when he was obviously terrified of them. He must have been an extremely good friend of theirs and possibly hadn't told them of his tremendous fear of cats or maybe he owed them a favour! If that was the case, it must have been a big one—that's all I can say!

At least we knew there was one cat he liked, the Jaguar and that was the one he had driven at breakneck speed to Wolverhampton. The tyre marks remained on the car park for the best part of a year, reminding us of "A very fast, rubber-burning, Indian take-away." So now you know, folks!

Geoffrey Doody

The Love of My Life and the Lustful Lab

When you go to dinner parties the hosts and their guests inevitably talk about their pets, which usually mean cats and dogs. That's one reason why I wrote this book! I've never heard anyone talking about their pet goldfish yet! I mean, what can goldfish do besides open and close their mouths while swimming in circles around their bowl. I suppose somebody one day will bore us to tears around the dinner table with the incredible adventures of Goldy, their beloved goldfish.

Yes, everybody talks about their own pets, because to them they are unique. Some of the stories are interesting, but some are unbelievably boring. It's just like looking at other people's holiday photographs; they can also be incredibly boring. Especially if you are not in them! I call them visitor repellents. It's a good way of getting rid of your dinner guests when it's late and you're tired, they soon make a move to leave when your holiday snaps come out!

This story is mainly about *Sally* my Springer Spaniel, she was the liver and white variety and no different to anyone else's dog. In fact, she was pretty similar in appearance, possessing a head, a body, four legs and a docked tail. But Sally was very special to me, quite unique in many ways and became an important member of our family.

I was a gamekeeper when I acquired Sally and had virtually bought her before even seeing her. I heard through the grapevine, via another gamekeeper, of a litter of five pure pedigree Springer Spaniel pups—one bitch and four dogs, from champion parents. I immediately made the phone call and to cut a long conversation short said, "Please save the bitch for me." The last thing I wanted was another randy male dog, like the one in the next few paragraphs.

My first gundog before Sally was a black Labrador. I bought him when he was eight weeks old and named him *Ricky*. If I had known how his character was going to turn out I should have named him Randy! If a dog moved or even breathed, it didn't make any difference to him, dog or bitch, he would try to have his wicked way. As a lustful lab he succeeded on many occasions and in one instance made his victim pregnant, having climbed over a six-foot fence to get into her kennel run. When the owner of the black Labrador bitch, a gamekeeper friend of mine called Ken found them, they were both locked together in love, standing back to back as mating dogs do. And that is probably where the phrase, 'Get knotted', comes from. Ricky looked shattered, the black Labrador bitch looked embarrassed and Ken looked absolutely furious. Ken snarled at me, "That's twice in three days your randy dog has had my bitch. I've taken her to the vets once to prevent a pregnancy and I can't take her again. He wants seeing too!" I think he meant Ricky not the vet!

What could I say, I felt really guilty. Ricky had climbed over and done the dirty deed. What could I do? Hey it was my dog not me! I grovelled and apologised profusely, it should have been Ricky apologising—not me! I should have trained the randy devil to talk! After a few minutes of ranting and raving Ken eventually calmed down.

With a female dog, if she has been mated, it is possible for her to have an injection administered by a vet to stop her conceiving. If she was mated again virtually straight away, the second injection could be fatal, so the pregnancy just has to take its course. If the bitch was lucky, she would not be pregnant with the second unwanted mating!

But Ken's bitch was not so lucky. As time eventually proved, Ricky, the Lustful Lab, sired five beautiful pedigree black Labrador puppies. Ken wasn't too unhappy then, Ricky had a good pedigree and so had his bitch. The five puppies were eventually sold for a good price and Ken was smiling happily with money in his back pocket, he wasn't exactly forthcoming in offering me the pick of the litter, which is the normal procedure for the owner of the male dog to have. So Ricky the proud father and I just kept stum. I was fortunate enough not to lose Ken as a friend, we had known each other for many years, that was a happy ending to one of Randy Ricky's dastardly, dirty deeds!

Ricky also embarrassed me many times with people, by cocking his leg up them and peeing on their legs. It got even worse when he wrapped his front legs around them and started to gyrate! Gender didn't seem to matter to him, but it was terribly embarrassing for me, especially when it happened to be a lady!

Shortly after the saga with Ken's bitch, I spoke to the vet about Ricky's over sexual nature and he suggested castration. I didn't like the sound of that and I'm sure neither did Ricky! The other option was to insert two caponising tablets into the back of his neck, which I went for or should I say for Ricky, not for me! The tablets gave Ricky female hormones for eighteen months. The poor lad couldn't understand why he was attracting so much lovable attention from the male gender of his species! Mind you he had grown quite large teats! Well, all the gamekeepers certainly had a laugh about that one, especially Ken!

It's Raining Cats and Dogs

Good old Ricky managed to attain the age of twelve, which wasn't a bad age for a Labrador, but as you can imagine, having been a gundog and a sex maniac as well, he had led quite an active life! In the winter of his life Randy Ricky had suffered many minor heart attacks, it is quite normal for dogs. Unlike humans, most dogs bounce back, almost as if nothing had happened and some dogs can go on for years . . . it is quite amazing. Poor Ricky didn't last too long after his first major coronary. Only three days before Randy Ricky died, he still had designs on Sally, who at that time was only eighteen months old. That's what you call stamina from Ricky the Lustful Lab, who always seemed to have a smile on his face, even the day he died. I can think of far worse ways of going!

Let's get back to Sally. It was a cold February day in a light snow storm when I collected her. She was only nine weeks old, perfectly marked in liver and white, with a thin white blaze running centrally down her face. She could only be described as cute, not that looks had ever mattered to Randy Ricky! I knew I would have to guard my little Sally very carefully against the amorous advances from the lustful devil! As it turned out Sally could always handle herself and she always let him know in no uncertain terms that she was a real lady and wasn't available under any circumstances. Every time he tried to get his wicked way, there was a snap and a flash of white teeth from her and a cowardly yelp omitted from the optimistic offender. It was the only aggression Sally ever showed.

Sally's temperament was outstanding. She was incredibly intelligent, which was fortunate for me because it enabled me to train her very easily as a gundog. She soon obeyed all commands from my whistle, even at long distance. She was fearless of the thorniest thickets and would go through them as if she had the skin of a rhinoceros. When shot game birds couldn't be found by other dogs, Sally would be sent for and would come to the rescue. With her nose down to pick up the scent, she quickly made the retrieve. She certainly showed the other gundogs how superior her nose was and her ability to track the wounded birds. Even when retrieving she still had a gentle mouth, while taking a severe battering from the flapping wings of a wounded cock pheasant.

Sally's memory was amazing too. She even knew when to protect pheasants, rather than catch them. In summer time when the pheasant chicks were tiny, they were just like bumble bees on two legs and each evening had to be driven into a heated brooder shed from a thirty by thirty foot wire mesh pen. Every year as soon as she saw the freshly erected rearing sheds and pens containing the pheasant chicks, she would be springing up and down in anticipation outside the gate waiting to be let in, hence the name, Springer Spaniel.

Pheasant chicks are very well camouflaged so they could be missed easily as they hid in the long grass in the pen. If left outside they would have died from the cold. In the shed there was a gas heater, it gave off heat just like a brooding hen pheasant would in the wild. Sally's job was to seek out the chicks I had missed, pointing them out with her nose, while raising her front paw. This is known as the *pointing stance*, it is a term used in the gundog world. She would gently pick them up in her mouth, totally unharmed and pass them to me so I could put them into the shed for the night. Pheasants needed to be shut away every night, right up to the age of four weeks and by this time they were called *poults*. Sally and I did this job for nine consecutive summers.

One weekend in late spring, we had friends Pete and Sue visit us, who happened to play golf and they tried to teach us how to hit golf balls. At that time, Kathy and I had no idea about golf and didn't know one end of a golf club from the other. I now play golf and my friend's joke that I still don't! Well, I hope they are joking! To show us how to hit a golf ball Pete hit twelve balls down a twenty-acre grass field, it was situated right behind our cottage. I was quite impressed with how far Pete was hitting them, although I had never seen anyone hit a golf ball before. As usual Sally was close by and I must say looking rather bored with the proceedings. I am sure she must have been thinking, *I don't like this new kind of gun.* After a while she trotted off to her favourite mat outside our back door and I am sure went to sleep to dream of better things, such as pheasants and partridges—not stupid golf balls. The four of us trailed down the field to look for the golf balls and after searching for at least half an hour, we could only find one. It sure looked like an expensive sport to me! Pete seemed to have hit the balls in more or less the same area, but we didn't seem to stand 'a cat in hells chance' of finding any of them. The grass was only about three inches high, but the base was thick with clover. I said, "I have an idea. I know how we can find these balls. Sally will be able to find them."

I blew my dog whistle, it was always hung around my neck and on hearing the sound, just like the Lone Ranger's horse, Silver, Sally sped flat out toward me. She pulled up at my feet with her docked tail and backside furiously wagging. In anticipation, she looked up at me with her eager brown eyes, as if to say, "What can I do for you Master?"

I asked Pete to give me the one ball we had managed to find so Sally could take in the new scent. She sniffed it, and then I extended my arm, pointed my finger in the direction of the missing balls and commanded, "Get on. Good dog."

Sally rocketed off with her nose to the ground and her rump excitedly wagging from side to side. Within thirty seconds, she had retrieved her very first golf ball and delicately placed it in my hand, just as if it was an egg or a tiny pheasant chick. Pete stared in absolute amazement and exclaimed, "I don't believe it!"

I sent her to retrieve one after the other and she was really enjoying showing off her skills. Pete and Sue had never seen a gundog work before and really enjoyed the demonstration. Pete said, "Wait until I tell my friends at the golf club they will offer Sally a job, we lose loads of balls there."

Sally retrieved the remaining balls in less than ten minutes and we knew we weren't going to lose anymore with her around, many more were hit down the field. She was in her element and by then she was really interested in this new type of gun—the golf club!

When it was Kathy's and my turn, the golf balls were hit all over the place, not unlike when I play golf today! Military golf they call it—left right, left right. Perhaps I'm being hard on myself, I do actually manage to hit them straight occasionally!

Sally turned out to be a legend in her own time and my shooting associates kept pestering me with the words, "If ever you breed from Sally please let me buy one of her pups."

I decided when Sally was six years old we would breed some little Sallys. She was mated with a Springer Spaniel with a long pedigree named *Rufus*. My plan was to keep two of the puppies, but only if they were bitches. No more Randy Ricky's for me, thank you very much! Any puppies that were left would have been sold many times over with all the requests I had.

Sally eventually looked well pregnant and we couldn't wait to meet her puppies, damn and blast she fooled us all, it was a phantom pregnancy. We had to wait until she came back into season again, which was six months later before she could be ready for another amorous meeting, with the handsome lucky boy Rufus.

After the second renaissance Sally produced five beautiful liver and white puppies, four bitches and one dog. Kathy had checked on her before leaving for work early one morning. She could tell Sally was acting differently and by the time Kathy had called me from the house, Sally had already given birth to one of her puppies. We watched the rest being born and found it absolutely amazing how she knew exactly what to do. She bit off each umbilical cord and then licked the puppy clean. In between each birth she even found time to look up at us while proudly wagging her tail. We kept two of the bitches which we named *Jemma* and *Jess*. The male puppy went to the owner of Rufus, sadly we could only sell the two remaining bitches to the top of the long list of friends.

Sally was nine years old when I started building the cattery and kennels and she became semi-retired from the shooting world. Although we still went pheasant and partridge shooting at least once a week during the season, she was now getting past her prime. She had started to put on weight and had got a little bit naughty where food was concerned. Her main hobby became eating. She would go to great lengths to get any food she could and I had to keep a watchful eye on her because being overweight wasn't good for an ageing Springer Spaniel, or in fact any other breed.

I warned all the workmen to keep their sandwiches in a safe place, as she had been known to steal them in the past. She would go to them at their breaks and look pleadingly at the sandwiches with her hypnotic brown eyes. Unfortunately, they just couldn't resist her bewitching pleas. I married a lady like that! Hey, I could be creeping here! Most times Sally triumphantly walked away from them with her rump wagging and a sandwich in her mouth. (No, my wife definitely doesn't do that trick!) This was always against my wishes but I'm sure they must have thought the way she begged I was starving her to death.

One day the workmen had left their sandwiches in their van as usual, they had carelessly left a side window half open. All Sally had to do was follow her keen nose to the tempting aroma and it wasn't long before she found where they were hidden. She dived straight through the open window; it was no problem at all for a gundog like Sally that had been used to jumping fences much higher over the years. She wolfed down the lot, the fat little pig really gorged herself that day and to put it mildly, the workmen weren't exactly over the moon about it either. I said, "She's not as daft as you think. I did warn you."
Unfortunately, the workmen had learnt the hard way.

When the cattery and kennels eventually opened, Sally was always there with me to greet all the new customers. They usually booked their pets in after Sally had rolled over on her back and they had patted and stroked her. I am sure she must have been the best public relations officer you could ever wish to meet!

Geoffrey Doody

When Arthur Met Sally

One day a customer arrived delivering his large pampered dog, a Great Dane named *Arthur*. He was as big a Great Dane as you will ever see, he was absolutely enormous and his colouring was light brown. He was nearly as big as a donkey and he had a brain to match, that's for sure. We christened him King Arthur because he was so big and aristocratic. He always arrived in a brand new Range Rover, like royalty sometimes do. I could never understand why people wanted dogs that big and six years is a good age for a Great Dane. Well I suppose everyone to their own.

We had another owner who boarded two of the giant dogs with us and because of their black and white patchwork colouring they were a very special type of Great Dane, known as *Harlequins*. I have to admit, those two dogs were gorgeous and because of their colouring and size it looked like we had a pair of Frisian cows on leads! Have you ever tried walking one Great Dane on a lead, let alone two! It was an absolute nightmare I can assure you of that! Having experienced hanging onto Arthur at my peril after he had spotted a rabbit in the woodland, I thought I was being dragged by a four-wheel drive tractor—not a dog!

Unfortunately for me I always walked him, as I was the strongest person there and probably the most foolhardy.

Due to Arthur's size and weight, his owner always brought him a large bean bag to sleep on, it was necessary to stop him getting bed sores as he spent a lot of time lying down, like all heavy Great Danes do. The bean bag had been dumped unceremoniously by his owner on the concrete path outside the office right next to where Sally was lying down, minding her own business. Arthur had met Sally many times before, but on this particular day, he seemed to be in a bad mood. Perhaps it was because Sally was sitting too close to his bean bag I had no idea what the cause was, but as he jumped out of the vehicle, fortunately still on his lead with me grimly hanging on the other end, he made an aggressive lunge toward my Sally. I could barely hang on to the massive brute, he was far bigger and heavier than me! He dragged me along toward Sally and she submissively rolled over on her back whimpering, showing absolutely no aggression at all. The big bully tried to rough her up and I only just managed to drag him off her as she screamed blue murder, thankfully that put him off his attack. His owner shouted at Arthur for being a naughty boy. Luckily there was no damage done, except maybe to Sally's pride. It was lucky for Arthur that he hadn't hurt my precious Sally, because if he had done, I would have felt like shooting the big bullying brute. I didn't shoot him I just dragged him around the corner of the kennel buildings, to take him into the wood for his walk. At least the one good thing was I had a safe walk as the big boy didn't see any rabbits. Thank God. That would have been the last straw!

I installed King Arthur into his kennel and went into the office to have a word with Kathy, who had witnessed the fracas, while doing some paperwork. I asked, "Where's Sally?"
"Oh don't worry; she's okay, she's just gone down to the house. But have I got news for you!"
"What do you mean?"
"Well, Arthur's owner was very apologetic for Arthur's boisterous behaviour."
"Boisterous! Boisterous! I have seen tanks in war films put to shame in comparison to that brute!"
"Calm down Geoff. Listen to what I have to tell you. You are going to really laugh."
"Okay, okay, carry on."
I looked through the window and Sally was licking her coat as if she was wounded. Suddenly, she got up and shook herself, had a sniff at Arthur's bean bag. And what do you think she did next?"
I rudely butted in, "Well, come on tell me."
"She squatted with one of her back legs raised high in the air and did a small pee right in the centre of Arthur's bean bag! She looked just like a male dog marking his territory. She then calmly sauntered off down to the house with her nose held high in the air."

On hearing this I was astonished, Sally had never ever cocked her leg in the air when she had a pee. I am sure she had done the amusing deed as if to say to Arthur, "That'll teach you for attacking me. You big bully!"

I examined the bean bag where Sally had made her mark and there was no more than a teaspoonful. I thought, *Good girl Sal, that'll teach that great big lummox.* So why did Sally do it? It was obviously the only way she could pay Arthur back and I'm sure she must have thought every time the big brute lay on his bed, he would smell her urine. Sally, the little dog that never did him or any other dog any harm would remind Arthur of his bad behaviour to 'Sally Queen of the Kennels'. So the little Queen ended up being the ruler over the giant King.

I don't know if King Arthur had thought that it was me who had put Sally up to peeing on his bean bag, but pay back time very nearly came to me. After three weeks of walking Arthur twice a day, the big boy had really grown on me, even though he had upset my Sally. We appeared to be very good mates and when it came to the day for Arthur to leave, I must admit, I was quite sad as I led him out of the kennels, to the waiting Range Rover. The tail door was open and the giant dog jumped in, I let go of his lead and reached out to stroke his head which I had done many times before. Suddenly, with no warning at all, my previously best mate Arthur lunged at me with teeth flashing and very nearly ripped my hand off! If it hadn't been for my quick reflexes, I would definitely have been a hospital case. The big ungrateful brute had missed me by only a hair's breath. Arthur's unconcerned owner, who had obviously seen the performance before said, "Oh, he gets a bit possessive now and again, especially when he is in his own vehicle."

My immediate thoughts were, *A bit possessive, a bit possessive, the bloody big brute nearly took my hand off right up to my armpit!* Well, they do say you live and learn something everyday and I can assure you it was the very last time I tried to stroke a dog in its owners car.

Arthur met Sally many more times after the bean bag event and King Arthur always showed Queen Sally the utmost respect the great lady deserved and to me, she was definitely the Queen of all dogs.

Geoffrey Doody

Temperament!

From the beginning of our business we used the same booking form throughout and it was a form you could say we invented. We checked out other forms belonging to our opposition that we had collected on our initial visits at our investigation stage, (remember when we were doing our '008' spying bit). We didn't want anything similar to our competitors, we wanted to be completely different. Basically our booking form was a questionnaire, giving details of the pets that would be staying with us. We had a form for cats and a similar one for dogs. It was obvious they couldn't be exactly the same, because they are as different as cats and dogs, excuse the pun. You wouldn't ask a cat owner, "Is your cat likely to be in season during its stay with us?"

Equally we wouldn't ask a dog owner, "Has your dog been neutered?" The doggy word for doctored, is *castrated*; the pussycat word for doctored is *neutered*. Now those words definitely bring tears to my eyes.

On the cat-booking form there was a very important statement. It read quite boldly, "No male cats are allowed in the cattery unless they are neutered." Somehow, I don't think the owners of a top pedigree dog would go for that one!

I must clarify those few points, as it may seem rather strange to some of you why our rules and regulations had to be stipulated. If a bitch was in season or likely to come into season, it was always better to be aware of it, we wouldn't want to put a bitch next door to a male dog that would obviously be teased with her close proximity. For sure, many male dogs would howl their heads off, hoping to get to the bitch to have their wicked way. No way, did we want to hear lots of howling or accidentally become a breeding kennels, as well as a boarding kennels! So it was always wise to keep bitches in season next door to each other and well away from the noses of the amorous macho dogs! And yes, it did seem unfair that we would accept the macho dogs and not the macho cats.

Tomcats that haven't been neutered spray everywhere when they have a pee and *wow* does it smell, or should I say it absolutely stinks! Another point for male cats that aren't neutered is they are usually pedigree cats, which are kept solely for breeding. They are usually owned by people who are running a breeding cattery. If female cats were ready for mating, it made no difference to us, as we had no male cats with testicles in the cattery, unless they were kittens. But more often than not people tended to have their female cats neutered anyway; they didn't want to have their cat pregnant when it roamed outside its own house. As we all know, not all cats are pets and there are many cats roaming around our neighbourhoods—especially toms, they are semi wild and not cared for. When tomcats are having their wicked way, they yowl their heads off, while biting the neck of a female cat . . . just like bloodsucking vampires. So when you hear a yowling sound outside in the middle of the night, I can assure you it is a cat and not a vampire! Anyway, sure as hell I hope so! Tomcats are a lot harder to control because it is difficult to keep them indoors, unlike macho dogs that can trot around with their owners while on their leads, hopefully while being restrained from doing the dirty deed.

Let's go back to the booking form and the title of this chapter, 'Temperament?' What would your answer be if I asked, "What sort of temperament has your dog got?" Would your pet be the most placid animal to ever walk this planet? Is that what you would say? Would you tell the truth? Is there a slight chance that your little *Fido* might give us a little nibble on the back of our hand in gratitude for a lovely walk in our beautiful surrounding woodland? Or, is there a remote possibility that big *Bruno* might want to rip us up into tiny bloody shreds if we dared set a foot in his kennel?
No, of course not. Joe Public wouldn't tell the truth and put down on a questionnaire that the

love of their life could be lethal! Because if they told us the truth, they knew damn well their dog wouldn't stand 'a dog in hell's chance', of being accepted into our kennels for one minute, let alone two or three weeks!

Ninety percent of all forms that came back accompanied with their deposit were completed in full and by the word *temperament*, it read words like, "Friendly, loved to be cuddled, playful and boisterous," or something similar. All these descriptions we had no problem with—especially "Loved to be cuddled." It was the ten percent that gave us the problems—the ones that were left blank by the word *temperament*, or said, "Nervous... *nervous... nervous!*"
What the hell is that bloody word, supposed to mean?
I had a look in a dictionary and found out the true meaning of the word *nervous. Nervous* is a very ambiguous word and it was often used by owners for their dog's temperament. So what did the dictionary say? I will now give you my interpretation of the word, *nervous*.

The first meaning of nervous was to do with the nerves. Does this mean "Nervous Breakdown?" I read, "Loss of emotional and mental stability." Does this mean *mad dog*? Or has the dog lost its marbles? I definitely don't like the sound of that! The word also relates to the nervous system in the body, whether it means sinewy or muscular.

Well, I have no problem with that explanation, it obviously doesn't apply to vicious dogs.

The second meaning of nervous uses words like *vigorous* or *terse*. *Vigorous, terse*, sounds a bit dodgy to me! I said *dodgy* not *doggy*.

The third meaning of *nervous* is described as having disordered or delicate nerves. *I don't like the sound of that one either!* Anyway, after meeting a few of these so called nervous characters my nerves have certainly been in total disorder and quite delicate as well. I can well assure you of that!

Here are a few more words relating to the word *nervous*.

Excitable	Hey up!
Highly strung	Jesus! Here we go!
Easily agitated	Is that a temperament similar to a rhinoceros? Well figure that one out for yourselves!
Timid	Now I don't mind timid doggies. They are right up my street, unless they looked timid and then change their minds and decide they want to rip me apart!

Does that clarify the word *nervous* for a dog's temperament? You tell me!

I also decided to check the word *ambiguous*. So here goes. Ambiguous can mean, "Double meaning, doubtful classification, uncertain issue or even obscure." Could this mean a schizophrenic dog? I don't like the sound of that one either!
Are you now starting to get the picture? So when I read the word *nervous* on the booking form, it certainly made me more than nervous.

Let's go back to the first real meaning—simply good old *mad dog*, which could also conjure up the word *psychopath*. Now, this word can play tricks with your imagination. Like the devil's dog, an Alfred Hitchcock movie, a long, sharp, pointed knife, shower curtain and blood.
Blood? Who's blood? The dog's blood? My blood?
Yes, I'm afraid it usually meant my precious blood! That's if I wasn't as careful with a nervous dog as a 'White Hunter' would have to be, to track down a wounded lion in ten feet of long grass. By the way, the hunter at least would be armed with a rifle. What it really means is somebody is going to die, mate! I will also guarantee it wouldn't be the dog! I am certain that my blood would have been everywhere, caused by the so called nervous dog, if I wasn't as careful as the 'White Hunter'! Of course, it would always be my blood because no other silly fool would dare go anywhere near any of those nervous nutters.

When we had a nervous dog in for a stay, the staff would say, "Oh my God! It's a nervous dog, it could be dangerous. Get Geoff quick."
The staff wouldn't even let me bring my little gun to defend myself; at least the great White Hunter had his big rifle! So, who was the bravest, me or the White Hunter?

Now let me try and remember some of my epic moments with some of my cuddly canine friends that happened to cross the step into my domain. Usually on their booking form for temperament it would be left blank or say '*nervous*'!

The first dog's owner didn't even try to lie to us or even bend the truth, he came to see me to have a talk about his schizophrenic Golden Retriever bitch called *Lucy.* Yes, this was a real explanation of a nervous dog that had actually been diagnosed as *schizophrenic*! The poor man was at his wits end, not knowing what to do with his dog. I could have told him exactly what to do with it, but I thought better of it.

Over the years in the business and even today I would say the same if asked, "What breed of dog would I consider to be the most placid family dog?" My reply would always be a Labrador or a Golden Retriever. It is a good job we never saw any other schizophrenic Golden Retrievers because I would have definitely crossed Golden Retrievers off my placid family dog list.

Lucy was something else! Unfortunately, she should have been shot on sight! The owner explained to me that he had owned her from being a puppy and how her personality had drastically changed. When I met her she was three years old and I might add very lucky to attain that age without being put down. Lucy was definitely in the category, of *highly bloody dangerous!* Her owner even showed me the white scars on both his arms and on the back of his hands where she had bitten him previously. He told me he had heard I was a good dog trainer and he wanted to know if we would board her, knowing she was a schizophrenic. He also asked if I could train her or do anything to help solve her problem. I am sure he didn't mean shoot her . . . or did he? I pointed out to him that I had no scars on my body and I intended to keep it that way. Well, being the good soul that I was and obviously thinking about the boarding and training fees, I agreed to board Lucy for five days and then give him my opinion afterwards, that's if I was still in one piece, or God willing, still alive!

Lucy was delivered two days later and I immediately walked her around the wood. She was okay on the lead but had a disconcerting habit of rolling her eye nearest to me backwards, while looking up into my eyes with her head still pointing forwards. I've seen Great White Sharks do similar on television, but never a dog! This definitely set my alarm bells ringing and also made the hairs stand up on the back of my neck. I thought, *Be careful Geoff. Be damn well careful!*

After the walk I was thankfully still in one piece and entered the kennels with Lucy. The gate to her run had been left open on my instructions because I must admit, I was a little cautious of there being a problem with her when I got her back.

Cautious, cautious! I was even more than bloody cautious. Now there's an understatement if ever I made one! I ran her into the run before she knew what was going on, released the lead from her collar and quickly stepped out, shutting and bolting the mesh gate behind me. The moment I was out of her run, she spun around and gave me a blood chilling look that I will never forget. Her name should have been '*Medusa*'. I felt I was going to turn to stone. She certainly sent a chill down my spine for sure. I clipped a notice on the front of her run and it read in big blood red letters, DANGEROUS DOG TO BE HANDLED BY GEOFF ONLY.

During Lucy's five-day stay, *HANDLED* proved to be the wrong choice of word. She would never let me get anywhere near her again—not even to walk her. She used to give me that 'Medusa look' as if to say, "Over my dead body! Come in here mate and you won't be going out in one piece!"

I think she actually meant my dead body—not her own. I thought cleaning Lucy's run out would be an absolute nightmare but luckily she didn't like the noise of the power hose or the water near her. So when I switched it on she just quietly slinked away into her sleeping quarters. Thank God for that small mercy. It enabled me to close the door to her sleeping quarters while I hosed her run out. At least she didn't fret being with us was and always ate all her food.

Lucy's owner came to collect her after the five days and I gave him the sad news, "In my opinion she should be put down, especially as you have a five-year-old daughter."
Although he had previously told me Lucy had been okay where his daughter was concerned, with her schizophrenic condition she could turn at any time and God knows what would have happened.

Unfortunately, Lucy's owner didn't heed my warning straight away, as a few weeks later she bit him quite badly yet again, so he had her put down. I found all this out because a few months later he brought a lovely yellow Labrador puppy to board with us for many years afterwards. That was very good news for him and his family and of course for me it was double-sided, not only did we get the boarding fees, but we also had a lovely dog with a lovely temperament to look after. More importantly, after my encounter with

It's Raining Cats and Dogs

Lucy the schizophrenic Golden Retriever, I was still in one piece with no loss of blood, my skin wasn't even slightly punctured after those five nerve-racking days!

Does the name *Linus* conjure up thoughts for a dog's name? Well, to me it sounds more suitable for a lion!

We had a large Tibetan Mastiff board with us with just that very name and on his booking form for 'Temperament', it read, 'Prefers ladies'. Well, who doesn't? I sure hoped it didn't mean to eat them! But that left a bit of a grey area concerning gentleman, which I am 100 percent included in that gender. Because of my self-preservation tendencies I must add, I definitely don't like the sight of my own blood. I thought it would be very wise to clear up the 'grey area', before it turned to 'red', excuse the pun.

When Linus arrived I decided to make myself available to sort out the paperwork with his owner, coincidentally he happened to be called Mr. Savage, (very appropriate name for his dog, *Linus Savage*). With Mr. Savage sitting in front of me I quickly looked over the details on the booking form, almost ignoring everything else on it and asked, "On Linus's booking form I see against his temperament you have put prefers ladies. Can you be a little bit more specific, please?"

During the conversation I was looking at the size of Linus in the back of Mr. Savage's car and I hoped it didn't mean he really did prefer ladies, to eat!

Mr. Savage replied, "Well, Linus did used to like men as well, (to eat?) until a man accidentally dropped an iron bar on his front feet."

I said, "Wow that sounds painful."

Mr. Savage continued, "Linus was only five months old when we had builders working in our house and that was when the accident happened. I took him to the vets to see if anything was broken and the vet concluded that Linus's feet were badly bruised. Unfortunately, the vet who was also a male hurt him while examining him. Since that day Linus has held a grudge against all men. When I take him to the vets I have to make sure that it is now a lady vet who will be attending him. So apart from me, he just doesn't like men at all."

"Oh, I see," I replied thoughtfully. But, I thought differently because I seem to have an affinity with most animals—especially dogs. I was confident I would win Linus over and make friends with him during his two week's stay. But boy, I couldn't have been more *wrong!*

My manageress went to get Linus out of the car to take him for his introductory walk. I had never seen such a beautiful dog before and he could only be described as being magnificent. His dark brown coat glistened in the sun, making his fur look a bit like mink. His coat was about three inches long and even thicker around his neck, just like a mane. As he walked, his whole coat swayed with each step. So apart from his colour, he could have easily been mistaken for a male lion from a distance. Considering he was only twelve months old, he looked absolutely enormous and very powerful. I stood outside the office and I thought, *What an awesome looking animal.* Linus walked within two yards of me and totally ignored me, which I must say I didn't mind one little bit.

The first day I stayed well away from Linus to let him settle in and he took to the girls with no problem at all. The second morning of his stay, he happened to brush past me as one of the girls was walking him back to his kennel and there was no acknowledgement at all to my gender. I watched the girl take him off his lead, stroke him and fuss him before she left his kennel. He appeared to be very placid, so that afternoon I decided I would take him for his walk around the wood and make friends with him, to prove there really were some nice men on his planet. Is Geoff an idiot or what? Linus didn't want to know. He looked at me holding his lead in my hand, turned his back on me, after giving me a sullen look and walked back into his sleeping quarters. I gave his lead to the manageress and she called his name, to my utter amazement he bounded straight out to her, just as if nothing had happened. I might as well have been invisible! She put him on his lead and off they went for a walk. I did take note that he gave me a strange look as he passed by me, which made the hairs on the back of my neck stand up. I thought, *Why bother him, he likes the girls. Why risk my neck or even the hairs on it*!

The following day one of the girls phoned in sick. With animals, it is not possible to leave things until the next day. There is a routine that must be followed and all jobs have to be done, even if we were one person down. So whenever we were a member of staff short, I would offer to help with the manual work. My manageress usually put me on the task of power hosing.

When we first started the business, I used to do the hosing everyday and I must say there was no one quicker than myself. I set the power hose up and quickly got back into my old routine. Everybody seemed to enjoy power hosing and I was no exception. The power hose could easily remove anything that had stuck to the concrete floor of the dog runs, including the most stubborn dog crap, or whatever you would like to call it! I must point out that only a small percentage of our doggy guests couldn't wait to go to the toilet until they had their 'walkies' in the wood, so not all runs needed to be power hosed everyday. We always shovelled up the doggy dirt first and then hosed the run down to remove any debris.

I had completed half the block when I came to Linus's run. The card on the outside of the run, which had been put there by my manageress read in large red writing (coincidentally the colour of blood), DOES NOT LIKE MEN. ESPECIALLY YOU GEOFF - KEEP THE HELL OUT. Linus was nowhere to be seen. I thought, *Maybe he's asleep in his kennel. Do I get one of the girls or do I risk it?* I only had a few strides to go across his run to enable me to close the door to his sleeping quarters and then I could safely hose him out. I thought, *He who dares wins.* I tentatively slid the bolt on the gate of his run and cautiously made my way in. Just as I edged forward and reached out to close the door, I heard an ear-splitting growl, Linus charged through the doorway entrance. I instantly thought, *Oh my God, I'm going to die.*

Luckily, I still had the power hose gun in my hand. I instinctively pointed it straight at Linus's face and squeezed the trigger. I am sorry, but it was the only defence I had. Fortunately, it stopped him in his tracks for just a brief moment, which gave me a split second to get the hell out of there. I bolted out, slammed the gate, jamming the power hose gun in it, which stopped me from closing it properly. Lucky for me, Linus immediately switched his aggression to the end of the power hose nozzle and grabbed it in his mouth. It was still jetting water out, at a pressure of 1,800 pounds per square inch and in his temper he didn't take a blind bit of notice of the power. I thought, *Hell that could have been my arm—or even worse a much more sensitive part of my lower body!* I released the power hose trigger and as soon as the jet of water stopped, he immediately transferred his aggression toward me. He stood on his hind legs and looked more like a grizzly bear than a dog! His eyes had unbelievingly changed from brown to a glowing red colour and his mouth was wide open with barred teeth. He was so close to my face I could feel his hot breath. I thought, *God, I hope this mesh is strong enough to hold him.* Thank God, his weight was keeping the gate shut as it closed toward me. He was going absolutely ballistic as he snarled and chewed at the strong mesh, blood even started to come from his gums as he was frantically trying to get part of me in his mouth. The only good news was that the blood wasn't mine! I still hadn't managed to bolt the gate to his run because I couldn't get the jammed power hose gun out. I was desperately holding on, hoping he wouldn't seize my fingers through the mesh. If he had, it was most definitely, goodbye fingers! With all the commotion going on, fortunately for me, help soon arrived in the form of my manageress. She looked at me in disappointment, turned away and simply said in a stern voice, "Get down Linus. You naughty, naughty boy."

To my utter amazement, his temper was completely extinguished and he sullenly walked back into his sleeping quarters. It was just like turning off a switch. One moment Linus was a

frenzied beast trying to tear me apart and the next he was as meek and mild as a lamb.
The manageress sternly said to me, "Have you got a bloody death wish or what?"
She went into his run and closed the door behind her. I decided to get the hell out of there while the going was good and watched what was happening from the safety of my office window. I just couldn't believe what I was seeing, there was Linus and his lady friend cuddling in his run. It just didn't seem possible to be the same dog as he had been a few minutes before. Talk about Jekyll and Hyde! Well, as you can imagine, I stayed well clear of him for the rest of his stay and decided he was definitely one animal I wasn't going to get to like me.

On a couple of occasions during his first week, I happened to be near the gate of Linus's run, he would growl at me while staring right back into my eyes with an evil, evil look. His eyes seemed to turn from deep brown to red and they glowed like red hot coals from within the dark brown fur on his face. I had seen this happen in horror films, but I couldn't believe it was happening here to me in real life. It was just like seeing the devil's dog. I called to the manageress to come and witness this unbelievable phenomenon. She arrived in less than a minute and by then his eyes had gone back to the normal colour of brown. She really thought I was pulling her leg when I told her his eyes were changing to red when

he saw me. We both stood there and 'Sod's law', his eyes stayed the same normal colour as he looked at the manageress, completely ignoring me. I said, "It's because you're standing there. Go and hide in another kennel where he can't see you and make sure you can see his eyes."
"Are you joking or what?" The manageress replied.
"No, no, I am deadly serious. His eyes did change colour. I definitely saw them and I'll prove it to you."
I distracted Linus while she hid and I stared into his eyes, he immediately started to growl. It was incredible, unbelievably his eyes instantly turned red and he had that evil look on his face.
"I don't believe it," the manageress shouted from her hiding place.

I later discussed the strange occurrence with my vet and even other vets that used us for boarding their own animals. None of them had ever heard anything like it before except in fictional horror movies. I swore it was true and I even had a witness to prove it. Did my manageress and I both witness this phenomenon, or did we imagine it? Linus remained silent, it was his dark red secret.

I ended up having the greatest of respect for Linus and felt sorry that the accident he had when he was a puppy had totally made him mistrust men, probably until his dying day. The only male person he ever accepted was his owner and I bet my bottom dollar, Linus's owner was thankful for that one!

The next guest was described on the booking form to have a nervous temperament. Here we go again, with that ambiguous word *nervous*. He was a large German Shepherd dog called *Kaiser*. Jet black in colour and he was a very handsome dog indeed. His owner was a lady who was dressed exceptionally smart and I must say as handsome as the dog was (sorry I mean handsome in her own way). She excelled in her attractiveness.
I thought, *Um.. you're in good nick for your age.* I politely asked her, "On Kaiser's booking form you have written down nervous for temperament. Can you be a little bit more specific please?"
"Well, he is nervous," she replied.
"Does that mean he might bite us?"
"Well, he hasn't bitten anyone yet."
I immediately thought, *What the hell is that supposed to mean?* Anyway, I bit my tongue and kept my thoughts to myself I didn't want to upset her and said, "If you put him on his lead I'll get one of the girls to take him for a walk around the wood."
She immediately replied, "Oh, I don't think that's a very good idea. Kaiser was never walked at the boarding kennels where I used to leave him before."
I thought, *Is she trying to tell me something, or what*

She continued, "I would prefer to put him in the kennel myself, like I used to at the other boarding kennels."
"As you wish," I replied.

We never liked the owners putting their dogs straight into the kennels, we preferred taking them for a walk first ourselves, so that they got used to us and it helped them to settle down quickly. Anyway, she had her way, we put Kaiser's bed in his sleeping quarters and left a clean bowl of drinking water for him. Kaiser's owner put him on his lead and he walked placidly to where he would be staying for his two-week duration.
You could tell the way he looked at her, that he thought the world of her. I asked her, "I presume he will be okay with us when we walk him?"
"I would prefer that if he isn't interested, just leave him alone," she replied.
As she drove down the drive, I looked through the office window and Kaiser was pacing silently up and down his run. I gave Kaiser half an hour before I went to check him out, to make sure he was okay and that he had hopefully settled in. He was in his sleeping quarters, I quietly called his name and with absolutely no warning at all, he launched himself in a flying fury of black fur and white teeth smashed into the gate of his run—just inches from my throat. I jumped back in horror.
I thought, *Thank God, I'm not in the run with you!*

It's Raining Cats and Dogs

The handsome black German Shepherd had turned into probably the most vicious brute I ever had the misfortune to clap my eyes on. Kaiser made my friend, Linus, look like a puppy dog! He was attacking the mesh gate with intense fury and aggression as he tried to rip it off its hinges, biting the steel mesh so hard that his gums were damaged and bleeding, pink froth mixed with his saliva was coming from his mouth. The frenzied animal stood on his hind legs for at least twenty minutes non-stop, trying to bite his way out of his new home. No mean feat, for a breed that has a profound weakness in its back legs! Every time one of the girls went into the kennel block, Kaiser would start again and get into an even worse frenzy.

I thought, *If this is what he's going to be like, there is no way I am going to keep this animal in here for two hours, let alone two weeks.*

I had no alternative but to ring Kaiser's owner up and ask her to collect him from our premises immediately. As far as I was concerned, he was the most dangerous thing, I had ever met on four legs! The frenzied German Shepherd had virtually turned into a Werewolf! At least Linus could be calmed down by a friendly female, but anything human was fair game for Kaiser, no matter what sex it was!

Kaiser's owner arrived in a real panic and said, "I'm catching a plane in five hours time. What am I going to do?"

"Why don't you take him to where you boarded him before?" I asked.

"Oh, they're full," she instantly replied.

I sarcastically thought, *I bet they are. They're just saying that because they don't want your raving lunatic of a dog back again.*

With an irritable tone in her voice she said, "Oh, I suppose my husband will have to look after him."

I inquisitively asked, "Why isn't he looking after him anyway?"

"Oh, sometimes he has trouble handling him and he is away from the house for such long hours. I'm the only one who can do anything with him. He's as quiet as a lamb for me."

I gave her one of those Benny Hill looks of amazement and thought, *Oh yes. The truth is really coming out now, isn't it? That's why you put nervous on the booking form!*

I could hear Kaiser still going absolutely berserk in his run. Amazingly, as soon as she went into the kennels, the dog completely changed. It was just like waving a magic wand. He was yet another Jekyll and Hyde!

Kaiser's owner put him in the car without saying another word and angrily drove off with tyres squealing. How irresponsible can some people be? That animal was seriously dangerous and that's a gross understatement if ever I heard one! I had young girls working for me walking dogs and what chance would a young person, or even an adult, stand against a frenzied attack like the one he had just made! For sure, no chance at all!

His owner had said, "He hasn't bitten anyone yet!"

She never said whether he had devoured anyone though!

In hindsight, I should have refused Kaiser from the very start when my alarm bells had first started ringing. Of course, I wanted the boarding fees but not at any cost and most certainly not to endanger my staff. Kaiser didn't want to just bite us, he wanted to shred us and eat the little pieces as well. I wondered what would have happened if a new customer had come along to view the kennels and as they passed Kaiser's kennel, the nutter had launched at them. I am sure it would have almost frightened them to death! And they wouldn't have made their booking.

On rare occasions, we accepted a few nervous dogs that could have become dangerous, like our friend *Zara*. She was quite small for a German Shepherd, but still had the usual set of big teeth. Zara's owner used to take her to her run and she would quietly follow him with no hesitation at all, but whenever we went near her run to change her water, give her food, or clean her out, she would just slink away to her sleeping quarters. She never wanted to be walked or touched. As long as we left her alone, she left us alone, she just wanted her own privacy. She always ate well, as long as we weren't watching her and was always quiet. In fact, she never caused us any problems at all.

Zara came to us for many years right up to the day she died with always the same routine. And no, she didn't die in our kennels, she just died of old age at home. Sadly, she could never quite overcome her fear of us and just became less agitated as the years went by. We all became quite fond of her and felt she really wanted to be our friend. When we found out she had died we were all quite upset. But sometimes from bad news comes good news and we were delighted when her owners bought a new puppy to stay with us and yes it was a German Shepherd, with an excellent friendly temperament.

Over the years we found out which breeds could generally be classified as the most dangerous and quite a few German Shepherd dogs certainly came into that category. Jack Russells were on an equal par, but their size helped the situation. If the 'Little Jacks' were as large as German Shepherds, they would very likely have been shot on sight. The size of a Jack Russell definitely takes the loss-of-life factor out of the equation. We found Dobermans and Rottweiler puppy dogs, in comparison to Little Jacks. Personally, I think German Shepherd dogs are one of the most intelligent of all the breeds, they are a fantastic family dog and are so loyal. I know, I grew up with a German Shepherd named *Jassey*, I had first-hand experience from an early age, of how faithful they are to a family. Taken out of their environment, they can become frightened and start to protect their new territory, which in our case was their kennel and run. Some boarding kennels wouldn't even take German Shepherds at all—well, well, what a surprise.

Now from big dogs to little dogs, to one named Heidi, that thought she was a Doberman. Perhaps she had looked in the mirror and imagined she looked like a ferocious Doberman, well at least she was a similar colour. Miniature Dachshunds do look a little bit like Dobermans, although their legs are somewhat shorter! Now what a lovely feminine name Heidi is. Doesn't it conjure up a pretty little girl with pigtails swishing as she runs through the spring flowers and green grass on a mountain in the sunshine. Anyway, don't be fooled by that lovely name of Heidi. She was a little dog that could pack a punch—and a sly punch at that!

Not many dogs came more miniature than Heidi and she was a crafty little devil to boot. On Heidi's booking form under temperament, it read: "Friendly, but will bite if she can get away with it."

That sounded more like a Jack Russell to me! Her greatest ambition in life was to bite any fingers that came near her. I humorously wondered if her owners fed her fingers at home, as a little treat now and again—hopefully chocolate ones. She most definitely had a taste for pink meaty ones! Well, I can assure you, we did our damnedest to make sure she didn't get any of ours!

On Heidi's first visit her owner said quite proudly, "She bit the postman last week, so be careful with her. For some reason, she seems to thinks she's a Doberman. Not a Dachshund." I thought, *Careful, careful, be careful with her! Was he kidding, or what?*

Heidi visited us many times over the years and was quite a little character. We got used to handling her with the respect she most certainly deserved. She loved to be walked in the woods, although at times it was fun, if you can call it that, trying to put her lead on and then after her walk trying to take the damn thing off! On every gate of each dog's run, there was a card printed with the dog's name and any comments necessary. On Heidi's card in large red writing it read: DANGEROUS LITTLE DEVIL WILL TRY TO NIP YOU IF SHE CAN!

During dog walking, every time we went into Heidi's run, with the intention of putting her lead on she would come running to us, looking very

It's Raining Cats and Dogs

friendly, with her thin short tail raised in the air wagging furiously. Now, believe me, if we didn't watch what we were doing big, big time, she would have preferred our fingers, instead of her walk! We had to treat her a bit like a dangerous ferret by quickly grabbing her collar at the back of her neck and then gently lifting her up. This suspended her onto her back legs, giving her less manoeuvrability. We were then able to quickly clip the lead onto her collar, while keeping our fingers well and truly out of her way, but the crafty little devil still attempted to twist around to try and bite us.

On her return from the walk, she thanked us by trying to nip us as we took her lead off. At least taking her off was a little easier because we had her lead to suspend her onto her back legs and our fingers were well out of the way, which enabled us to safely unclip the lead from her collar. But it was virtually guaranteed that the moment her front feet touched the floor, we would hear her little teeth click, as her jaws snapped together searching for our fingers. Wow, just missed again! I can't recall if she ever managed to a get hold of any of us, but I can assure you, it wasn't through her lack of trying!

Heidi generally never seemed to be too interested in biting any other parts of our body during dog walking. All I can say is, thank God for that! But occasionally when we were cleaning her out she did go for our ankles—that was if she could manage to sneak up from behind. She also developed a habit of running at us yapping like mad, if we stamped our feet at her and shouted no, she would about turn and run back twice as quickly. I don't know the things we had to do to save our vulnerable body parts from getting punctured.

One day little Heidi really frightened a new member of staff and cornered her in the run. The poor girl was absolutely terrified, luckily help was near at hand from the manageress, with a broom in her hand to push the little sod away and no harm was done. Over the years we got to know Heidi's little moods and tantrums but always found it quite an exciting challenge. No one ever dared to attempt to pick her up to give her a loving cuddle, like her owner did. We all preferred to retain our fingers instead!

Another dog that had *nervous* printed on the booking form definitely came in the category of dangerous. It was a Chihuahua—yes, a dangerous Chihuahua, can you believe? Do you realise how tiny a Chihuahua is? The Chihuahua's name was *Tanya* and I asked her owner, "I see on the booking form you have written *nervous* under temperament. What do you mean by nervous? He replied, "Well, Tanya is likely to bite, it shouldn't be a problem because of her size."

I thought, *No problem! Who for, the dog or for us?* We found out later that if Tanya had been big enough, she would have ripped us to bits!

We soon got to realise why the so-called nervous dogs came to stay with us. It's because you can't really ask your next-door neighbour to look after *Fido*, when it's more than likely that Fido would put him or her into hospital. Why do people keep dogs like these? Yes, maybe the dogs love their owners, but what about the rest of us?

If we had known about Tanya's unusual nature, I can guarantee we would never have let her set paws in our establishment. We had great difficulty looking after her because of her tendency to be rather violent toward us. If we went into her territory we had to be armed with a large bass broom to protect us from being savaged. And this is only a Chihuahua I am describing! The broom head was larger than her, so we were able to gently push her back into her sleeping quarters with it and then lock her in while we cleaned her run out. We felt a little bit like a lion tamer with whip and chair, but we were missing the whip and the broom sufficed as the chair!

With a diminutive Chihuahua, you might think taking a broom to her was perhaps a little bit over the top, but with Tanya being so quick, we had to walk out backwards with the broom at the ready, because her favourite form of attack was from behind! Mind you, I suppose you couldn't blame her for her sneaky attack from the back, considering the size of a Chihuahua to a human being! I certainly wouldn't entertain attacking any creature that is more than twenty times bigger than me, even if I was armed with an elephant gun. To have only your teeth to attack with, doesn't even bare thinking about, so at least Tanya was definitely a brave little Chihuahua.

Sadly, Tanya was one of the few dogs that actually died while staying with us, it was inevitable an occasional death happened when dealing with so many cats and dogs. First thing one morning one of the girls found Tanya lying in a pool of blood, which appeared to have come from her ears. It was a tremendous shock for the girl to find the little dog in that condition. According to our vet, Tanya's death was caused by a terminal brain tumour, which apparently had been there for some considerable time. Thank God, it was no fault of ours. No wonder the poor little thing was so violent. A suffering dog can't even tell you it has a headache, let alone the extreme pain it may have when it has a brain tumour! That was obviously why Tanya had a nervous temperament, or should I say, in her case, an extremely violent one!

We had never dealt with the situation of a pet dying before and I was unsure what the procedure should be. I decided to keep Tanya's body at the vets, just in case the owners wanted to take her body for burial or wanted a second opinion. I was dreading telling the owners, who were quite elderly, that their beloved Tanya had died. But as usual, the 'buck' always stopped with me. I didn't want to phone them while they were away, there was no point in spoiling their holiday and there was nothing they could do anyway. All I could do was wait for the dreaded day when they were due to collect Tanya and then phone them at home to break the sad news. I thought it would give them time to come to terms with her sad loss and I didn't want them turning up in a happy mood, only to be presented with a dead dog. Not only would it have been devastating for them, but it wouldn't have been a very good advert for our business, especially if we had other customers in the office listening to the fact that a dog had just died with us. I could just have imagined the scene. Tanya's owners would be crying and other customers would be thinking, *Jesus, they let dogs die in here. It could be a bit dodgy using this establishment.* Of course, the customers wouldn't be listening to the full story of how Tanya had died, just to the fact that she was dead and I mean well and truly dead. Bad rumours soon spread rapidly and it wouldn't have been too long before our premises became taboo, when it was certainly no fault of our own.

On the day that Tanya was meant to be collected, I definitely wasn't looking forward to the phone call one little bit. I decided to make the phone call from the house rather than the office because I didn't want any customers overhearing me and getting the wrong impression. In other words, they might think dogs died at our premises on a regular basis. I rang the owner's house many times and eventually made contact just before they left to come and collect her. They were obviously heart-broken and in no way held us responsible for Tanya's unhappy end. On their arrival to get the full details of her death, they actually insisted on paying for her full stay with us, even though I suggested we didn't want paying at all. They were absolutely adamant on paying for the full fifteen days. Good news followed as the next year they booked Tanya's successor in with us, which was a puppy named *Tara* and yes she was a Chihuahua as well. Her temperament said *friendly* and that was exactly how she was. In fact, she liked to be picked up and cuddled. Now that's the type of doggies we really liked!

It might sound a bit like running a boarding kennels is a form of business where you risk your life almost every day. Well, it's not quite as bad as it sounds because dangerous dogs, thank God, were few and far between. I would say there were less than one percent of dogs that came to us over the years that were in that category. And I can assure you we went through thousands. We just made absolutely sure we thoroughly checked out those ambiguous words that were put on the booking form for describing that word *TEMPERAMENT*!

As the business progressed over the years every new dog that came to board with us, if the temperament said something that wasn't similar to friendly, either my manageress or I would carefully vet them. If there was any doubt that the owner could not be specific about the temperament we would refuse to take their dog. It just wasn't worth the risk, but over the years, it was only a small percentage that we refused. We certainly did, 'live and learn' as the saying goes. And hey, I do like that word *live* and hey, I am still here with no scars to prove it!

Geoffrey Doody

Are Rotties Aggressive?

Well, of course, some Rottweilers are aggressive, but they generally are a much maligned breed, probably because they are portrayed in lots of films as being aggressive guard dogs. I must admit, I hadn't had much experience with Rottweilers before I had the business; actually my knowledge of this breed was virtually zero. All I knew was they could be potentially dangerous.

The very first booking I took for a Rottweiler wasn't for one but for two of the fearsome looking monsters. With a little bit of trepidation I took the booking (actually a lot of trepidation). When they arrived on the due day, I looked into the car containing the two extremely large new guests. The car was swaying from side to side and the suspension was heaving up and down, caused by the power of the two giant heavyweights excitedly jumping about in their keenness to get out for a walk. Looking at the size of them, I sincerely hoped it was for a walk and not to get at me to rip me into tiny shreds or even eat me!

The Rotties were absolutely massive and their owner proudly informed me their combined weight was seventeen stone. Can you believe seventeen bloody stone? Well, I certainly believed it, as I looked directly at the huge hounds and to my mounting concern they looked directly back at poor little me and there was only eleven stone of me! I thought I would need help, there would be no way I could manage the two giants on my own. If my manageress helped me, a consoling thought was, at least I wouldn't be dying alone. Their owner insisted I would be able to manage them on my own and said, "My wife always walks them by herself." I sadly thought, *I'm going to die on my own after all.*

The Rottie's owner struggled to hook their leads onto their collars as they bounded and pounded about in the back of his car. Their collars were of the strong wide variety with dull silver studs on, which made the two brutish-looking dogs appear even more fearsome than ever. At that moment in time, I would have given a million pounds to change them into miniature Poodles. Stuff what my macho gamekeeper friends would have thought of me walking tiny dogs, because I can assure you, miniature Pugs or Poodles were by then rapidly growing on me by the second!

The two giant Rottweilers were lumps of powerful solid muscle and teeth. After being put onto their leads, they were barking louder than loud, spitting saliva all over themselves in their excitement to go for a walk, hopefully not a meal (meaning yours truly)! I prepared to meet my maker as the

two leads were handed to me. Was I nervous or what! But I had no choice, so off we jolly well went as I left their owner standing on the car park. I wondered, *Is this going to be the last time I would ever be seen again?*
Well, it was all right for him to say his wife walked them, they knew her and they most certainly had never met me before. I just hoped he couldn't see that I was a little dubious of his two fearsome-looking brutes. *A little dubious* is a serious understatement if ever I made one! I certainly hoped the enormous Rottie's didn't sense my fear and at that stage of the proceedings, I also hoped my underwear was still clean and was going to remain so!

I hadn't been walking the two monsters for long when it suddenly dawned on me that I was still alive and in one piece. They didn't pull on their leads one little bit, in fact, they were quite gentle, which believe me, was to my utmost relief. As far as the black and tan giants were concerned, I might as well have been invisible, they didn't even take the slightest bit of notice of me. Phew, I didn't get ambushed in the woods and torn into little shreds after all, it finally dawned on me I was actually enjoying myself with the fearsome looking monsters. When I miraculously returned without the slightest scratch on me, I had made friends with two lovely natured Rottweiler gentlemen and their names were *Taz* and *Fritz.* I could tell they really liked me and I thought they were great, in fact, they were absolutely fantastic. My two new friends didn't act anything like the ferocious breed they had apparently portrayed, they acted more like pussycats or even lambs and they were so gentle.

There was only one problem we had with the two gentle giants and that was when potential customers came to inspect the kennels before they hopefully booked in their loved ones. When in their run, Taz and Fritz were normally like quiet little lambs but on spotting strangers walking around they would change into roaring lions. Up they would get onto their hind legs, which raised them to a height in excess of six feet, spitting slobber and fiercely barking their heads off. We all knew they weren't really dangerous and only wanted to protect their territory, but the potential customers didn't realise that one little bit! They almost frightened the crap out of some of them, to say the least. Causing them to nearly have a coronary would probably be a more appropriate description! Who could blame them into thinking that Taz and Fritz wanted to rip their heads off from their shoulders. Taz and Fritz never made a murmur when any of the staff or I entered the kennels, it was just when they saw someone strange.

We soon figured out how to get over Taz and Fritz's fearsome excitement when someone was viewing, well we most certainly had to, didn't we! The customers would have thought if they boarded their miniature pooches with us that Taz and Fritz acting in that ferocious way could have frightened their little doggies to death. There was no way I wanted to get sued for a customer dropping dead from fright on our premises, thank you very much! The problem was solved by shutting Taz and Fritz away into their sleeping quarters, where thank God, the two giants were as quite as church mice. The prospective customers took their time walking around and inspecting the kennels, little did they realise what muscle, teeth and power was lurking behind that closed steel door.

Taz and Fritz stayed with us dozens of times over the years and it was to our utmost pleasure that we had met two gentle German giants. On reflection, we wouldn't have missed that wonderful experience for the world.

Geoffrey Doody

Are Cats More Dangerous Than Dogs?

It may come as a surprise to you, but in my opinion, of course they are. It is quite logical really because cats have two sets of weapons, their teeth and claws. Dogs only have the one weapon, their teeth. Believe me, I have met some dogs that can make the great white shark in the film *Jaws* look a bit tame. Unlike sharks, with most dogs at least you normally get a warning. You certainly don't get any warning with most pussycats, take my word for it.

One thing all cats love to do is sharpen those lethal claws, whether it is on a tree, scratching post, or even your own expensive furniture. Have you ever been into someone's house where their cat has clawed the furniture? What a mess they make! I don't know the things we allow our furry friends to get away with!

The other major weapon in a cat's armoury is a very nasty set of teeth that are as sharp as needles and lurk in a small, powerful jaw. We had many cats coming to us that were recovering from abscesses that had been caused from another cat's bite, with whom they had been fighting. Cat's teeth are far more dangerous than a dog's because they will penetrate skin very easily, especially if it is of the delicate human variety like mine. Cats also carry a lot of bacteria in their teeth, due to their varied diet of live animals! So if anyone or anything is bitten by a cat, the risk of infection is very high. You could say that a cat's bite is a little like a venomous snakes, with the added danger of four sets of very sharp claws that move like lightening. I can honestly say I love cats, but I am much more frightened, or should I say, wary of a cat, especially when it is in full attack mode.

After many years of running the cattery and kennels I became aware that the percentage of cats being dangerous was probably 25 percent higher than dogs! And that was far too high for my liking!

On a cats departure, the problem we had with some of the aggressive little blighters was we needed to pick them up to put them in their carrying containers. I often thought, *Why should we get our arteries ripped out? Why not send the cat's owner down to the cattery to put their loved ones back into their carriers? Let them get ripped to bits instead of us*! Now that was a really good idea. Don't you think? Do you know some owners wouldn't even pick their own cat up! No way would they go down to the cattery and help.

Sometimes I would like to have said, "If you won't or can't pick up your own cat, then how are we expected to do it?"

I am sure their reply would have been, "Well you are the experts."

Are we? Because sometimes for sure, we wished we weren't! We had no choice in the matter. Although we were supposedly experts, we didn't always quite know how to deal with the occasional little lion or tiger in our cattery!

When we had trouble with a cat that wouldn't go into its carrier, who do you think had to do the dirty work? Yes, you guessed it, good old Geoff—Mr. Muggins here. Off I would charge, down to the cattery like a knight in shining armour, but unfortunately, without the armour! Believe you me at times I needed the armour. I did wear a strong pair of gloves with long cuffs, which I had purchased from our vets. Can you imagine what trouble vets must have with some of our pussycat friends! At least they could sedate them. For sure, some cats are definitely lions and tigers in drag!

The most efficient way of picking up a cat is by the scruff of its neck where there is plenty of loose skin. This method doesn't hurt them in anyway at all and was used by their mother to carry them around when they were kittens. Grabbing the scruff of a cat's neck is sometimes a problem because it is protected by deadly needle-like teeth at the front end, not forgetting the four sets of claws. So that was when I needed to be much craftier than the far-from-placid pussycat, which was awaiting my attention. I would slowly manoeuvre my pussycat friend into a corner of its run, trying hard not to frighten it and by slowly waving a towel in my left hand, I would hopefully distract it. Then with my right gloved hand, I would grab puss puss by the scruff of its neck. The towel was quickly dropped, making the left hand free, enabling me to grab the base of the pussycat's tail. Then I would quickly lift my pussycat friend up, which brought two more weapons into play, meaning the back sets of claws. So I had to be ultra careful of its teeth and four sets of razor sharp claws as well, which would by then be thrashing and slashing about in all directions and could hook deeply into delicate human skin! My skin, I hoped not!

Yes, it adds up to five dangerous weapons, you should now be getting the picture. If it did manage to make contact with anything human, meaning me or one of my staff or if it was able to hook its claws around something else, no way would it let go. We just had to do our utmost best to prise our little pussycat friend off and believe me, it wasn't easy. The moment I slightly suspended my feline friend, the spitting and growling would really start and it would scream absolute blue murder. If a diminutive pussycat can make that amount of noise and be so dangerous, it doesn't bear thinking what a lion or tiger is like! This is where I needed help from another member of staff with the cat carrier at hand and it took quite some skill and bravery from the two of us to get the little bundle of spitting fury gently lowered, with precision, into its carrier. From start to finish the process had to be done in seconds because if it wasn't, it meant you had failed and lost the battle, other methods then had to be used. Fortunately, in most cases my gloved-hand approach usually worked and with all the practice we became quite skilful at it.

The girls where always aware which cats there would be problems with, they would have got to know their little habits during their stay. Like trying to rip us to bits! Thankfully, a good percentage of the cats walked into their carrier, others just needed a little bit of friendly persuasion!

In my time I've had more than a few small cats frighten the hell out of me! They say the worst big cats in the world for their bad temper are leopards. I can tell you I have met a few little leopards in my time! And for sure, one of my main ambitions in life is not to meet a big one!
Owners wanted their little leopards at home as quickly as possible and I can assure you, so did we! The day before yesterday wouldn't have been soon enough! I am only talking about dangerous cats here. Some only turned that way because they hated their carriers. One moment a cat

could be friendly and lovable, but once it saw its carrier, it probably thought something unpleasant was about to happen. It would probably have connections in the cat's memory of being used for a trip down to the vets for an injection or even something nastier. So, we couldn't blame our feline friends for associating the cat carrier with unpleasant experiences—usually meaning pain! It's a pity cats can't read. I could have worn a t-shirt for protection that read: I'm definitely not a bloody vet!

If all else failed getting the spitting, growling bundle of fur into its carrier, then more extreme emergency measures were necessary. That is when we used one of Geoff's new toys, the dreaded 'cat tongues' and I must say, they were only used in extreme cases. This was an implement or even defensive weapon I had purchased from our local vets. In the instructions it read: Only use in extreme emergencies. One emergency was one too many for my liking!

Cat tongues are a little bit like the tongues you use for putting coal onto a fire or to rearrange the hot coals therein. Yes, we could be dealing with a red hot cat, rather than red hot coals. *Was there a difference*? I ask myself. The tongues were about two feet long and were designed to clamp around the cats neck, which enabled us to safely pin the cat down. Then we could grab it by the scruff of its neck. I know it sounds a bit barbaric, but in some cases we just had no choice.

One day a cat called *Tiddles* was leaving the cattery and on that day he was definitely no Tiddles but a little leopard had taken his place! I had successfully grabbed him by the scruff of his neck with my gloved hand, but his legs had shot out sideways, rigidly attaching himself with his four sets of claws to either side of his carrier. There I was holding him, while he was growling and spitting with the manageress and another member of staff who were trying their utmost best to gently bend his stiffened legs into his carrier. There was absolutely no way the little demon was ever going in that carrier! And no way was he going to give in! A lump hammer came to mind!

After our unsuccessful struggle with Tiddles, we suggested to his owners, they should try to get him in. They agreed to have a go, which I thought was very sporting of them because they were well aware of his hatred of the carrier. His owners tried various ways to bag him up, so to speak. I watched them doing battle with him, while keeping well out of the way of the furious contest that was taking place. Tiddles was having none of it! The more they tried, the more ferocious he got. His fur was completely puffed out, his ears were flattened to his head and his yellow teeth were barred. He was a tabby cat but he looked

more like a Scottish wild cat by the second, and I can assure you, you don't mess with them!
The lady owner said, "I have never seen him act like this before. I know he doesn't like his carrier, but this is absolutely ridiculous. What on earth are we going to do?"

I had no alternative but to introduce my brand new toy, the dreaded cat tongues. I looked at Tiddles with his sharp yellow teeth protruding out of his bright red gums. He was huddled in the corner of his run, looking absolutely exhausted and terrified after his traumatic struggling session. I must admit I was beginning to feel sorry for him, but that soon changed because as soon as he saw Geoff's magic tongues, the little sod had another lease of life. His adrenaline started to flow and he became even more aggressive than ever. The yowling noise Tiddles made was incredible. It was obvious this cat had seen cat tongues before—probably at the vets.

So the magic tongues weren't so magic after all, he went absolutely berserk. All hell was let loose. He was going ballistic and it was poor little me locked in the run with the little maniac leopard! He started to ricochet off the walls, uncomfortably close to my face and even worse my eyes, he was screaming blue murder.

Quite a large audience, meaning most of the staff, as well as the intrepid owners had gathered to watch the entertainment and I'm sure they were really waiting to see whose blood was going to get spilt first. Tiddles or mine! Guess what, everyone including me, thought it was going to be mine!

During the epic struggle, another member of staff came running down to the cattery to inform us that two new customers had turned up to view the cattery. I thought, *That's the last bloody thing we need at the moment.*
The manageress was mesmerized, watching my big battle with little Tiddles as I said to her, "Quick, go back to the office and whatever you do, don't let them come near here until we come back to the office. God knows, what they will think. With all this noise going on we could be killing cats not looking after them. Show them some nice dogs or something. Do anything. Just keep them well away from here! Go, go, go."
In my garbled message to my manageress I felt like swearing, which was not my normal practice and certainly not in front of owners, but I think whatever I uttered, Tiddles' owners would have totally understood.

It was raining quite hard at the time, so keeping the prospective new customers talking in the office wasn't too much of a problem for the manageress. I was getting more and more frustrated with Tiddles and I am sure in his temper he wanted to kill me! I was doing my utmost best to keep as calm as possible and it didn't help the situation, especially with his owners watching everything that was going on.

Eventually, Tiddles succumbed to the cat tongues and was safely installed in his carrier. His owners thought I was very brave. They sympathised with me and apologised profusely over their little pussycat's behaviour. Brave I was for sure, because there was blood on the floor tiles and it was all mine, not one drop from our little leopard impressionist!

During one of his spectacular flights, which would have put Concorde to shame, Tiddles had nicked my right ear lobe as he flew past me. And I had always insisted I would never get my ears pierced! After that little episode, I was certainly not into body piercing, especially after I had found out just how painful it could be. When I finally nailed the ill-tempered little sod and closed the lid on his carrier I privately thought, *It should be nailed down for bloody good!*

When we were walking back to the office with the back-to-normal placid little Tiddles, the lady owner asked sheepishly, "Would you have Tiddles in your cattery again?"
I thought, *That's the question of the year!*
But I politely answered, "Of course we will, but the next time, please bring some tranquilisers

with you. We will give them to him a couple of hours before you come to collect him."

At that moment, I wasn't sure who needed the tranquilisers, that damn cat or me!

"Oh thank you. You are very brave," she said.

We occasionally used tranquilisers for cats that didn't like their carriers, but the owners had to supply them, having obtained them from their own vet.

My mother's cat *Ben*, was definitely high up in the dangerous pussy category list
(CAT- EGORY). Do you like that? He was possibly even our number one contender! He was yet another Jekyll and Hyde character and there were a lot of them about, especially where cats were concerned.

Ben used to stay with us quite often, especially in the wintertime when we had our holidays, which was the low season in our trade. Good job we loved skiing! Mother used to stay in our house to take care of things and answer the phone when the girls were busy. As I mentioned previously, we had an answer machine, but I hated using the infernal thing. On hearing it a lot of customers would immediately hang up, others would leave messages that sounded more like they spoke Swahili or even some kind of cryptic code. Trying to decipher them was a real headache. Hence Ben used to stay in the cattery free of charge. You can't charge your own Mother. Can you?

Especially when she's doing you one hell of a big favour! But the conniving Ben should have been charged double! There was no need to fill in the cat-booking form to find out Ben's temperament, because for sure, we all knew what he was like. In fact, on the cat-booking form, we didn't have, "What is your cat's temperament?" Generally it was never necessary to know, although perhaps in some cases, it would have been a good idea.

On Ben's many visits to the cattery he turned out to be a real con artist. All the girls were told of his nature and warned not to be fooled by him. But I think he got all of them at least once because you couldn't resist his initial charms. The amount of rubber gloves he ruined with his swipes doesn't bear thinking about. He didn't look like a wild cat at all, as his colouring was predominantly grey on top with white running down under his chin, chest and stomach. In fact, he looked quite cute and cuddly and as innocent as a teddy bear. It can most certainly be quite deceptive how looks can fool you.

Kathy had got Ben as a six-week-old kitten from a friend who had a farm in Cheshire. Mother was ill in bed at the time with a bout of flu and Kathy thought it would cheer her up to have a tiny playful kitten with her. Ben certainly worked wonders as he initially spent most of his time on her bed and when she was well again, on her knee, where he loved to stretch out and be stroked.

When visiting Mother's house you could be sitting quite comfortably on the sofa minding your own business. Ben would come up to you purring away loudly, with his tail swishing high in the air, obviously wanting a fuss made of him. He would rub his head up and down your legs, just the same as all the pussycat tribe do. Well, let's face it, that's why we keep the little devils as pets, isn't it! So, he was no exception to the rule, but the difference with Ben was that it was just one of his many ploys and he would for sure lead you into a false sense of security. You could be holding your cup of tea in one hand, while scratching and stroking him with the other, still purring away, he appeared to really enjoy the loving attention. To prove his acceptance of all your fussing, he would press his body even harder against your hand, therefore asking for more attention. Or was he? Suddenly, without any warning at all, he would hiss and spit, while taking a swipe at your hand or anything else that was in range of his razor-sharp claws. Ben never missed, he always drew blood! He would then walk off triumphantly, striding away with the fur standing up along the ridge of his back. You would have spilt your piping hot cup of tea all over you and the carpet, be left in a distressed condition, examining the wounds he had inflicted and maybe thinking he had ripped open a main artery! I must admit, Ben got me quite a few times before I eventually became wise to his charming, conniving ways. I learnt the best way was to totally ignore him, which was a good idea. I kept my own blood where it belonged!

Another trick of Ben's was to sit halfway up Mother's stairs that became his watching post. The bad news was the toilet was upstairs, so you had no alternative but to pass him. As you went by him you would hear him purring. So what do you naturally do? Yes, of course, you would bend down and stroke the little sod. Who can resist stroking a purring pussycat! As you went by him believing you were safe to do so, he again would have led you into a false sense of security. Then what would the little devil do? He would pounce at you and wrap himself round one of your legs, with his back legs kicking and digging in with all his claws fully out. Now if you were lucky enough to be wearing jeans, they would help to protect you a little bit, but if you had bare legs or stockings like most ladies do—wow, he could inflict some damage and give you some serious pain. I think he just about caught out everyone with that little ploy. It was a habit he never grew out of and he for sure, had a long list of victims in his time. There was only one way to get up the stairs in one piece and that was to call Mother to remove him before you even set one foot on the stairway. Fortunately, Mother moved to a bungalow and everyone knows bungalows don't have stairs, so that was one little trick he was never able to play there!

As Ben grew older he turned into a real killer. He loved to catch birds and mice, always bringing his trophies back to Mother as a gift. Like most cat owners, she didn't like him killing the birds that came into her garden, so she got him a collar with a bell on it. That initially seemed to do the trick and the bird population seemed to thrive in her garden. One day, Mother was watching Ben trying to ambush a sparrow, she could hardly believe her eyes because the crafty little sod was creeping with his chin low, pressing the bell down on his chest, therefore stopping it from ringing. Now that is what you call a pussycat with brains!

Another funny story Mother told me about Ben was most certainly what you would call a cat with innovative skills. One day he came home to present Mother with a dead mouse. It was dead alright, but would you believe the mouse came with a mousetrap attached to it as well! Why should Ben go to all the effort and trouble chasing a mouse when something else had done the job for him!

In conclusion, I think you could have stroked Ben for about ten seconds and know you would get away with it. Anytime longer, for sure, you were really, really pushing your luck! The point that should be coming over from Ben's story is that he had claws, four sets of them, as all cats do and you never knew when he would use them!

Mother loved Ben dearly and fussed over him all the time, but even she wasn't safe from the little horror, occasionally he drew blood from her as well. Even so, she would have nothing said against him. Her excuse was that he had come from a farm and he still had the wildness in him. Some excuse that was!

In my younger days we had a cat, his name was *Randy.* No, he wasn't named Randy because he was a randy devil; he was named after Randolph Turpin, a famous boxer. His colouring was tabby on top and white underneath. When he walked his stomach swayed from side to side, sometimes touching the floor. This rubbed away most of his white fur to expose his skin, which gave his stomach a pink glow. Can you believe it, he was well in excess of two stone! No wonder he got so fat, the crafty devil was getting food elsewhere. We found out he was also being fed at three of our neighbour's houses!

Randy would often sit in the sun on the footpath outside our house licking himself. Sometimes a dog would spot him and come hurtling toward him expecting him to run, but to the dog's surprise, Randy just stood his ground. He would puff his fur out, arch his back with his tail in the air, which made him look twice as big. The horrified dog would hit the breaks big time, skidding to a halt with only inches to spare from the big cat. Suddenly, Randy would swipe his paw across the dog's nose which drew blood, making the dog yelp and turn tail in the opposite direction, while loudly whimpering. Randy, totally unconcerned continued cleaning himself, just as if nothing had ever happened.

It sure wasn't long before the canine race in our neighbourhood learned to respect that giant cat. But I must say it wasn't just the canine race that respected Randy, it was also the feline varieties, as they would learn from their fist meeting or even fight with him, never to approach him again. I would often see both dogs and cats giving Randy a very wide berth.

Would a cat take on a German Shepherd dog? Now that's a very good question. I grew up with a German Shepherd called *Jassey* and she would more than enthusiastically chase cats. She was perfectly marked with black and tan colouring and a lovely black diamond on the middle of her forehead. I suppose she should have been beautiful and handsomely marked because she had a pedigree as long as your arm and had cost my parents a small fortune.

Jassey never bothered about Randy, not because he was a great big pussycat, but she actually liked him. They could often be seen lying together in the sun and in wintertime by the fire. However, with Jassey, where other cats were concerned, that was most certainly another story!

One day Jassey unfortunately chased and caught a cat then killed it! The unlucky cat belonged to one of our neighbours and that created some sort of a stir, I can tell you. After that sad day, we always made sure we kept a close watch on her. She was quite obedient and if we spotted a cat before her, we made her know in no uncertain terms, that the pussycat was taboo.

Jassey was my constant companion and one day when I was walking with her to the local grocers shop, she spotted a cat before I did. By the way, there was no such thing as a supermarket in those days. I hope I'm not giving my age away here! She instantly launched herself like a rocket into the attack and the small cat, which was completely black, ran like the wind, not in the opposite direction as I expected, but to my utter amazement straight at Jassey. This was braver than David taking on Goliath! It certainly looked like the little black cat was surely going to die in style and there wasn't a thing I could do about it. I visualised that small cat disappearing right down Jassey's throat without even touching the sides. I wondered who was going to be in the most trouble, me or the dog! The brave little hissing, spitting, pussy sprang with all four feet in the air, straight at the face of Jassey. I had seen Jassey take on dogs of all shapes and sizes and she always won quite easily. She had also killed hundreds of rats, some almost the same size as the little black cat in this story! But even Jassey was no match for the little black bundle of spitting fury of teeth and claws. Jassey just turned tail and fled for her life. I just stood and stared rooted to the spot as I watched in total disbelief. The brave little cat gave chase with her hackles and tail high in the air for at least fifty yards, while Jassey ran yelping with her tail between her legs! I started laughing until I could hardly stand up, it was just like watching a Tom and Jerry cartoon. I couldn't believe the little black cat had been so brave and it wasn't long before I found out why. When I walked into the shop, I told the shopkeeper what had happened and how I couldn't believe what I had witnessed. The shopkeeper told me the little black cat that belonged to him was a she cat and she had given birth to six kittens two weeks previously. Is that what you call a protective mother, or what? The maternal instincts were certainly running high that day! That's for sure!

Over the years cats have drawn blood from me on quite a few occasions and thank God, it was with their claws and not their teeth! Dogs have never been much of a problem, even though some of them could have been twenty times bigger than my little pussycat friend Tiddles! If you take a Jack Russell and a similar sized cat, which one would you fancy your chances against if it came at you in full attack mode? If you took a Rottweiler, a similar sized cat would be a leopard, so my case rests here. So what do all my cat stories tell you? Are cats more dangerous than dogs? I don't know about you, but cats certainly have my utmost respect.

Geoffrey Doody

Tiger, Tiger, Shining Not So Bright

One day, I was called down to the cattery because the staff couldn't find a so-called 'dangerous' cat hidden in the shrubbery. Guess what, it had to be a well-camouflaged tabby, didn't it! On the tabby cats label by its name, which by the way was *Tiger*, very appropriate, it read in large writing: STRIKES OUT WITHOUT ANY WARNING. Apparently he had ruined many a pair of rubber gloves as he had swiped out with his claws, just like Ben, while the girls worked in his run. It was fortunate that they were wearing the gloves for cleaning or it could have been their hands. But I must say, a rubber glove doesn't give much protection to a cat's razor sharp claws!

The girls had been looking for Tiger for over thirty minutes but I am sure they were maybe a little bit more cautious due to his violent nature. I asked the girls, "Are you sure he hasn't escaped out through the main door?"
"No. Other than coming for you, we haven't been out of the cattery," one of them replied in a worried tone.

I thought, *Oh God, please let him still be in the shrubbery. Just please don't do this to me.*

I imagined myself saying the dreaded words to the distraught owners, "Sorry, we have lost your cat. It's now roaming around the woodland."

I sarcastically thought, *What a good advert for us, bring your well-loved pussycats to us. We can let them loose in 100 acres of woodland, where they can have the time of their little lives.*

If I walked and crawled up and down that shrubbery once, I did it a hundred times, being an ex-gamekeeper, my eyes missed nothing, I was absolutely certain Tiger wasn't in the shrubbery. I thought, *Oh my God he's gone.* I had been looking for him for well over an hour and considering the shrubbery was only thirty feet long and six feet wide, there was no way he could possibly still have been hidden there. By then, I knew every leaf on every shrub in that bit of a garden.

I thought, *This shrubbery is going as soon as I can get round to it. I'm not having this every time a cat goes past one of the girls.*

I searched and searched, but still no cat! What on earth was I going to do? I decided to check out Tiger's run from where he had gone missing and yes, the door was slightly ajar. Maybe, just maybe he had gone back on his own. I could only hope for a miracle, bearing in mind there was fifteen runs on each side and the door in question was number seven, which just happened to be my lucky number and still is. I crossed my fingers, of course not being the slightest bit superstitious, I walk under ladders on purpose and have never been hurt yet! Mind you I did fall off one once! I looked into his run, but there was no sign of you know who. I went in and closed the door behind me, just in case Tiger was hiding in his bed. Well you never know your luck, do you? He could have been sleeping. I gently lifted the lid to where his bed was and yes, would you believe it. There he was curled up fast asleep. His feet were twitching, he was obviously dreaming about playing hide and seek in the shrubbery with my staff. I just couldn't believe my eyes. I could have kissed the little devil, even if he could have swiped out at me, the dangerous cat bit had gone clean out of my head and so had the time I had wasted. Thank you my lucky number seven. I'm not sure what finding the cat had to do with me walking under ladders, but seven was definitely my lucky number that day.

What I believe happened, was while the girls were away from the cattery giving me the bad news, Tiger had slipped back into his bed. Why on earth, didn't I look in the obvious place in the first instance? So this episode was definitely the last straw and that is why the shrubbery had to go. You wouldn't think tranquil things like shrubs could give you so much stress!

The shrubbery ran down the middle of the cattery and caused us many problems over the first two years, although it looked very nice. It made the cattery look very tranquil, which was a very good selling point, especially when prospective new customers came down to have a look at where their loved ones could be staying.

Cattery and kennels are built like prisons and I am afraid that is the way they have to be. It is not a good idea to have any chance of an escape route the ambitious escapee might find. With all the steel and mesh everywhere, the shrubbery softened the cattery, making it look less stark.

The shrubs had grown very large and had bushed out much more than I had anticipated. I purchased them from a local garden centre, supposedly as dwarf shrubs. No way were they dwarf shrubs. They had grown into what could only be described as, a mini jungle. They overflowed into the walkways and the decorative gravel accumulated a lot of cat hairs, which were very difficult to pick up. The worst problem we had with our unwanted jungle, was when mischievous pussycats, dodged around members of staff when they were cleaning them out. This wasn't a cause for major concern because there was no escape route, as there was a mesh roof over the shrubbery. The hardest task we had was finding the mischievous pussycat that had hidden in the jungle—sorry I mean shrubbery. Locating a white pussycat was no problem but trying to find a well-camouflaged tabby like Tiger amongst that lot was an absolute nightmare. Having eventually located our pussycat friend, we had to try and catch it and then put it back into its run. Maybe the staff hadn't had any fun playing hide and seek, but I am sure our pussycat friends had. It was as time consuming as trying to find a needle in a haystack! I didn't need to be a rocket scientist to realise that it wasted time and time was costing me money! Therefore, the shrubbery had to go!

I have never been one to hang about once I have made a decision. The shrubs had been growing for over two years and had done exceptionally well. This made the job of digging them up even harder and I really didn't want to waste them. My idea was to replant the shrubs in our own grounds in between the cattery and the kennels. Yes, the work was hard, but I managed to dig all the shrubs up and replant them. I must say, they did look rather nice dotted about on the grass lawn. Once the shrubs were planted, I used to whip around them on my tractor, like they were slalom gate posts on a ski run. This kept me wide awake, therefore getting rid of those occasional kinks!

Removing the shrubs left a big space in the middle of the cattery, so out came the lovely knee pads, down on his lovely knees went Geoff, to have some more lovely days laying those lovely cream tiles! All my alterations turned out to be a great success, it made the cattery look a lot larger, cleaner, and tidier and it certainly made a lot more space for the girls to work.

When the weather was fine, the girls even wore carpet slippers, this kept the tiles always looking spotlessly clean. To soften the spacious area and steelwork we put up more hanging baskets and we never found one pussycat in any of them! So now try and play hide and seek you fun-loving pussycats! Ah, well, there is nothing like learning the hard way!

Once I had re-straightened my back after laying those lovely tiles, I decided to put another door on the outside of the cattery, this made triple security. I designed a cage that was ten feet by ten feet and bolted it onto the exterior cattery wall, it was virtually impossible for any cat to slip out of my cattery. No cat was ever going to escape out of our cattery. Would those be my famous last words? Mind you, with our previous double security, we had never lost a cat, but you can never be too careful. My motto always was, "Never be over cautious." You never know what is around the corner, especially when dealing with other people's animals!

Geoffrey Doody

The Escape Artist

Kathy didn't want me to write this story, as it could possibly be detrimental to our past reputation, but this is yet another true story. It is a very sad story about a cat that escaped and was never found. After all my security this was definitely, 'A Cat on the Run'.

This particular day was as good as it gets for mowing grass. As we all know in the UK, fitting grass mowing in between the showers in the normal wet summers we have too endure, can be a nightmare. Mowing the grass turned out to be one of my biggest tasks. I always used to try and cut it all on the same day, which included the large lawn in between the cattery and kennels and the lawns in my own garden. This task used to take me just under four hours—that was if I had no interruptions. Fortunately, I really enjoyed sitting on my little red tractor and I was more than satisfied with the finished result.

I had been on my lovely red tractor for about an hour (sounds like a sentence from a Noddy and Big Ears story) reflecting how good life was, as I watched my friends the swallows whizzing past. I was totally my own boss, or should I say when Kathy wasn't around! Although I did get more than enough stick from my manageress at times! The business was booming and I am quite proud to say we had become one of the most famous cattery and kennels in the Midlands for our service to our customers and of course to our furry friends. To cap it all, we were making money as well! Yes, life was really, really good, but as usual it doesn't last for long. Does it?

The times I heard one of the members of staff shouting, "Geoff, Geoff," at the top of their voices, to get my attention, just doesn't bear thinking about. Little did I know that day was going to be no exception. I was cutting the grass by the car park and turned the red tractor to make my way back down toward the cattery. I was about halfway when I saw Ann, looking more than a little bit impatient. In fact, she was jumping up and down and at the same time gesticulating for me to hurry up. I could faintly hear that well used name, "Geoff," being screamed out, even though I was wearing my ear defenders. I was driving the tractor in second gear because the grass was too thick and long for me to put it into third gear and I knew I would be there in less than twenty seconds anyway.

I thought, *I've seen it all before. You'll just have to wait until I get down there. It can't be that important!* But the closer I was getting to Ann, the more impatient she appeared to be getting. I wondered, *What on earth is the matter with her?*

It dawned on me, my fantastic day, was soon going to be fantastically screwed up, to say the least. I felt like turning the red machine around and disappear over the green horizon, but I did the decent thing and carried on toward Ann. When I got to her, I immediately switched the engine off and removed my ear defenders.
I asked, "Whatever is the matter with you?"
"We've lost a cat," Ann distressfully replied.
"What do you mean? We've lost a cat?"
"I tell you; we have lost a cat."
"How can we lose a cat with all the security we've got?" I retorted.
Ann was getting quite tearful and I knew she could be a joker at times, but I was beginning to feel that this wasn't a practical joke.
She said, "I'm telling you, we've lost a cat. It's gone."
I was trying to keep calm, as I could see Ann was almost hysterical. "Tell me what happened?"
"He's gone. There's just no sign of him anywhere. The other cat that was with him is still there. But he's gone!" she said even more tearfully.
"What do you mean he's gone . . . gone where? How's he got out and why is the other one still there, if he's gone?"
"For God's sake Geoff! Stop asking me stupid questions and come and have a look for yourself," Ann replied in desperation.
I followed her into the cattery and walked down to where he, the missing cat, should have been.

As usual, Ann was right. It seems to run in Kathy's family, they're always right!

Sure enough there was only one cat there and definitely no sign of the other.

Ann said, "He was here when I fed them this morning and when I came to check his bedding, there was just no sign of him. He has just disappeared."

"Have you checked the other cat runs? He could possibly have got into one of the empty ones," I hopefully enquired.

"I'm not stupid. I have checked absolutely everywhere and that cat is not in this cattery," she said in even more desperation.

"Oh hell!" I exclaimed. "When is he due to be collected by the owners?' Now that was when the really bad news came out.

"This afternoon!" Ann exclaimed.

"This afternoon! Oh, my God!" I shouted.

"How are we going to find him before they arrive to collect him?" Ann asked.

That was a question, to which I had no answer.

The missing cat's name was Thomas and all we could do was search for him, but where would we start? How long had he been gone? How far could he have got? How long is a piece of string? Ann had seen him less than two hours ago but that meant nothing now. We searched high and low for him for over three hours and searching in 100 acres of woodland was like looking for a needle in the proverbial haystack. Unfortunately for us and of course Thomas, there was no sign of him. I was the one who was going to have to face the music. So much for the perks of running a first-class boarding cattery and kennels establishment!

When Thomas's owners arrived, I tried to explain in the most calming way we had lost their lovely pussycat. As you can imagine, they were far from happy. The only consolation I could offer them was, at least we still had the other cat. Thomas's 'dad' had gone as white as a sheet and was shaking with temper. His wife was crying, their two children were crying, Ann was crying in the background, and I wanted to cry too. But where the hell was that going to get me! Big boys don't cry, do they? I certainly didn't feel very big at that moment in time. Mind you, I am only five feet seven inches tall!

If only Thomas's owners had collected him the day before, we would have had their two cats waiting for them—or even first thing that morning. Thomas had been there when Ann had fed them both. Thomas's 'dad' looked at me savagely, almost as if I had lost his cat on purpose! I could tell he wanted to break my neck. And who could blame him? With every word I uttered, I just made things worse and seemed to be digging a hole for me that was getting deeper and deeper by the second. I felt as if I was in a bottomless pit. At that moment, I wished

I could have disappeared into that bottomless pit. Thomas's 'dad' who had risen into a seething temper said, "I told you he was an escape artist and he hates being touched."
"I am really sorry. We just don't know how he's got out."
"But he damn well has, hasn't he?"
"Yes, I am afraid he has," I quietly replied.
"Well what are you going to do about it?'
"Everything we can."
"Well, what does that mean?" he retorted with the tone in his voice rising even more.
I was dumbfounded and replied, "I don't know."
"Well, you had better bloody well find out!"

Thomas's owner had totally lost it by then and I could see he was shaking with even more anger. I couldn't do or say anymore at that time that could have helped the ugly situation. I decided to take the distressed family down to the cattery to show them where their 'Houdini' had lived for two weeks. Even they reluctantly agreed Thomas had done the impossible. He had escaped but none of us could fathom how. Even if he had escaped out of his run, he would then have had to get out through two more spring-loaded doors.
"I told you this place is like 'Fort Knox,' " I said.
He looked at me very aggressively as if to say, "If you don't shut up, I will bloody shut you up!"
I decided if I wanted to see tomorrow in one piece, I was best to keep as quiet as possible.

The whole family spent the next two hours with me, walking around the 100-acre woodland, searching and calling Thomas's name, sadly to no avail.

Unfortunately, there was no happy ending to this sad story of this particular 'Houdini'. Thomas had made a great escape to freedom and there was just no sign of him, he was never to be seen or heard of again. But how had he escaped? I just had to find out. It was obviously a real worry. If one cat could get out, then other cats could follow. That doesn't take much working out. Does it? I trusted all my staff implicitly and I knew if they had seen him escape, when they were cleaning, they would definitely have told me. There had to be an escape route from Houdini's run. And I was absolutely determined to find out where. I went back into his run and I just couldn't see anyway out, he had done the impossible! How could I advertise our cattery as being the most secure cattery in the Midlands if there was a secret way out, even I didn't know of! If one cat could find its way out of the secret escape route, then an army of cats would have been able to do the same. But why hadn't Houdini's pussycat friend followed him out that morning? Where would it all end? We could have lost dozens of cats, if I hadn't been able to solve the mystery. I knew there just had to be a solution and I was determined to solve the riddle, but the more I searched, the more puzzled I became. I had looked from all sorts of angles from within the cattery and I wasn't able to see any way a cat could have possibly escaped. I presume by now, you have noticed I am calling Thomas *Houdini.* The reason is because of the feat Thomas had achieved. I think Houdini is a more appropriate name and rolls off the tongue better!

I later decided to get the ladder and climb onto the cattery roof to check it out. The roof was made of corrugated fibreglass and I knew if I walked on the areas which were bolted to the wooden joists, I would be able to walk quite safely without damaging it, or God forbid, me falling through. I made my way very carefully along toward Houdini's run, checking along the line of bolts above each run, which I had meticulously bolted down myself. I had made sure that there was a bolt fixed in each raised contour of the corrugation. Every other one would have been sufficient, but I had taken no chance at all and secured every last one. A cat wouldn't have 'a cat in hell's chance' of escaping through the roof. All the bolts were intact and none were missing. So how had Houdini done it? I was totally baffled. I knelt down and closely inspected each bolt by feeling them and making sure they were all tightly fitted. To my complete disbelief, in the end row of bolts which was attached to the wall plate, one moved, the damn bolt was loose.
I thought, *Absolutely impossible. How can it be loose?* There were three inch brass bolts screwed

deeply into wooden joists and it would have been impossible for a man to loosen one of those bolts, let alone a cat. But the one above Houdini's run was definitely loose! I pulled at the fibreglass corrugated sheet and it lifted slightly. It had to be his escape route. I shot back down the ladder in my excitement of maybe solving the distressing riddle and ran around the back of the cattery to what was previously Houdini's run. I pushed the corrugated sheet upward, which took quite some effort and managed to create a gap that was no more than three inches wide by one and a half inches high. Using my past gamekeeping skills in this case like a detective, I inspected the gap closely to see if there was any cat hair attached to the ends of the corrugated sheet, and yes, there was, just a couple of hairs clinging to the ends of the corrugation and they were the same colour as Houdini's. Riddle solved, but that was no consolation for me having lost a valuable family cat. I pledged no other cat was ever going to escape from our cattery again! I went back up onto the roof again, checked and double checked every last bolt and thankfully, no more bolts were the slightest bit loose. The bolt above Houdini's run was the only one that had been loose, and he had damn well found it. But why? I was totally puzzled. Why was this the one and only bolt, out of hundreds, that was loose? Why did it have to be coincidentally the bolt above his run? The jammy little devil in his attempts to get out had been pushing his head hard and I mean hard up against the corrugated roofing. Obviously, he had loosened the bolt by his continued pushing with his head. I could see it was in an area of wooden joist, which had a knot in it, the knot had dried out and cracked slightly. Houdini must have been very determined to escape by working so hard and pushing himself up against the weakened area. We were just so unlucky he had managed to achieve his aim and squeeze through the tiny gap he had created and on the morning he was due to leave. If you could have seen the minute gap that he had managed to squeeze through, you would never have believed it and he was a full-grown cat as well, not a kitten. Houdini would most probably have been, the only cat to have found that way out. 'Sods Law', I suppose!

After that awful disaster I decided to lift every bolt on the roof and fix a galvanised metal strap across all the corrugated sheets. I painstakingly completed the task in record time, which then made the cattery roof escape-proof and as a bonus, totally windproof. No other cat ever managed to escape from our cattery after that, thank goodness.

I believe that Houdini was a cat in a million. Only he could have achieved the amazing feat and to this very day, I still feel very sorry toward his owners. I also think I was very lucky that I wasn't set upon by Houdini's dad that day, who I am absolutely sure wanted to kill me at the time and I don't blame him either. I would have felt exactly the same if the roles had been reversed and Houdini had been my cat. It was a pure miracle their cat had managed to do a runner and no one was really to blame, but the escape artist Houdini! The other strange thing was we knew he had been happy with us, as he had been playing pussycat games with his partner, while the girls had watched them. He had eaten well, which meant that he hadn't been under any stress and the girls had even been able to pick him up and cuddle him—unlike the advice given by the owners, that Houdini didn't like being picked up.

I only hope that Houdini cat did find what he was looking for, out in the wild woodland. I can assure you of one thing, he wouldn't have starved, as there would have been plenty of wildlife about. If any cat is hungry, it soon turns wild and becomes a very good hunter. All cats have a natural instinct to hunt.

Hopefully by telling this story, I will have proven it shouldn't be detrimental to our past reputation, which by the way, we are still very proud of. Even with new proprietors running the business, the cattery even to this day should still be, 'Houdini proof'! After all, it was me who built it! At the end of the day, all can say is this was one hell of an experience I didn't want repeated.

Geoffrey Doody

Not the Sweetest of Smells

I am sure all you knowledgeable readers know, but just in case you don't, the word *Tom* is used for a male cat. Normally, people always say crap smells and it does, but what do you think about pee? On the whole, crap easily outranks pee in the smell league. Dog pee is quite a common smell that's quite pungent anyway. We get used to the smell of dog pee because male dogs are always cocking their legs here, there and everywhere. Have you ever cleaned your car, left it sparkling in the sun, only to come out a little later to find some dirty dog has cocked his leg and peed all over your lovely alloy wheels? Lampposts are a favourite peeing venue as well, but thankfully we don't have to clean them! Have you ever heard of the saying, "As happy as a dog with twelve lampposts?"

Fox pee has a very strong scent and they use it to mark their territories like a lot of other animals do. Horse pee smells strongly of ammonia, but you can put up with that as long as you don't take a deep breath. My personal view on pee odours is, our pussycat friends are pretty high up near the top of the most pungent smell list. Most of us have smelt cat pee in our time, but this is usually from a neutered Tom that has peed, without your permission in your beautiful flower bed. Cats also like cat mint and that's why the little chappies use it as a toilet.

Well, people think the smell of cat pee is pretty bad, but not that many people have smelt the pee of an unneutered Tom. This pure unspoilt smell of pee is strongly advisable to be avoided at all costs. The smell from the cat that has kept his testicles is probably ten times stronger than a poor Tom that has lost his. Most owners of male cats have them neutered when they are six months old. This is mainly to stop the country being overrun with masses of cats, but it also stops cats from spraying when they mark their territories.

The vile smell of an unneutered Tom was the reason we put on the cat booking form, IS YOUR CAT NEUTERED? If they answer no, our alarm bells would start ringing. If a Tom was in the region of six months old, we would insist on it being neutered before it stayed with us. Any Tom over that age would get an instant ban or the chop, not performed by me of course, but the local vet. I will now explain why.

In the early days we had one or two Toms that managed to slip through our net, so to speak. Having experienced first-hand what it is like to look after an unneutered Tom for a week, I can sure tell you it's a real bad experience, which I don't want to ever repeat in my whole lifetime, or hopefully the next! It's not just the smell, that's bad enough on its own, it's where the pee could end up that was our major concern. For instance, dripping off the ceiling, would you believe! How does it get there? You might well ask, because they spray it there. That's how!

When Toms did occasionally manage to penetrate our defences, they have covered every inch of their six-foot high by six-foot long and three-foot wide accommodation with the obnoxious, foul stinking pee. They usually performed the dirty deed in the night, totally ignoring their litter tray which we had provided for them. Cats generally being clean creatures rarely urinated in their sleeping quarters, thank God!

When a Tom with his dangly bits had slipped through our net, we always knew we had made a mistake because as we were about to enter the cattery, even before we ever set foot in the place, the foul smell would bombard our nostrils. I can assure you our nostrils got even more sensitive after our first experience. If the stinking stuff managed to get on our hands, it would take days to rid our skin of the dreadful pungent smell. During that period of time I made doubly sure I avoided eating any food that required using my hands, like sandwiches for instance. Eating sandwiches, while wearing rubber gloves, didn't do too much for my appetite either!

When I worked alone, I had the unavoidable responsibility of looking after one of those, thankfully rare, cats with testicles. The vile problems it caused made me lie awake all night wondering, *What sight or what smell will be waiting for me in the morning?*

Once we had made the mistake and accepted a Tom, there was no way of getting rid of him until his owner collected him. I must admit, I was more than tempted to throw it out into the wood, where it would have been able to pee to its hearts content. Having an unneutered Tom in the family, probably wouldn't matter to its owners, because of course, their Tom would pee outside and mark its territory out there, not in their house or garden, but probably on some other poor soul's property!

I am sure you can now see the reason for that very important question on the cat booking form: IS YOUR CAT NUETERED? I suppose it could have been much worse. We could have been unfortunate enough to have been looking after lions! Have you ever seen lions on the television marking their territories? I don't mean peeing on the actual television, I mean on a television wildlife programme! Wow, do they release some amount of pee and what about the power when it squirts out! It is a bit like having a power hose, but with one of the most obnoxious smells in the world jetting out! Not in our cattery, thank you very much!

After reading this story, I think you must now get the picture that Tom pee is most certainly 'not the sweetest of smells'!

Geoffrey Doody

Percy Police Dog

Percy was a West Highland Terrier, we called them Westies for short and he was a little character that I will most certainly never forget. What has this got to do with being a police dog, you might well ask. Well, his owner was a humorous happy character and just happened to be a member of the police force. The first time I met Percy's 'dad', he turned up in a 'Jam Butty Patrol Car', (a white car with a thick red stripe running along the middle).

I was down at the house when Kathy shouted, "Geoff, there's a Police car on the car park. I think you should go down and see what he wants."
I looked out of the window thinking Kathy was joking. Sure enough she wasn't, there as large as life, walking from the patrol car toward the office was a very large policeman. It flashed through my mind, *Oh hell, I've been recorded for speeding and he's come to deliver the fine.* It wouldn't have been a surprise to me because I was always rushing about in some sort of an emergency, which could have been a journey to the vets or getting supplies of some sort or other. It would have been my first speeding offence, so I supposed I had done pretty well to get away

with it for so long. Surely the speeding offence wouldn't be for Miss. Goody Two Shoes (Kathy), mind you. She had been caught once already.

I just can't resist in quickly deviating to tell this short story. A few days before a Christmas break, Kathy had been driving along in her new Toyota Celica with Margaret, a friend from work. They had been collecting the Christmas raffle prizes for their work's draw. Margaret had been telling Kathy about all the latest office gossip and Kathy had been totally oblivious, to the fact that a police patrol car had been following her for well over a mile in a built-up area, virtually on her back bumper. She had been speeding at twenty miles per hour over the speed limit! As pretty as she was and still is, (I have to put that in, don't I,) she couldn't persuade the police officer to wavier the booking. She came home most disgruntled and said, "He even had the gall to wish me a Happy Christmas!"

Back to maybe my own speeding problem. I obviously wasn't as good looking as Kathy, so I stood little chance of getting away with it. I decided it would be better to go and face the music and get it over and done with. As I approached the kennel buildings I could hear laughter coming from the office. The policeman was talking to the manageress, I thought it couldn't be anything too seriously—especially if there was humour in the air. What a nice surprise I had. This very pleasant policeman had been recommended to us and he wanted to book his dog *Percy* in for a two-week stay. Little did I know that Percy was going to become one of our most memorable and regular guests.

One day, Percy's 'dad' turned up on a police patrol motor bike to book Percy a holiday with us. As he was leaving he said, "Okay, I suppose I will have to see if I can make somebody's day!"
Does that remind you of a famous movie starring Clint Eastwood? After those famous words, off he roared on his patrol bike laughing all over his round humorous face. I often wondered what would have happened if the laughing policeman had caught me speeding, especially after I had become such a good friend of Percy. Would he have let me go with a friendly caution?

Percy loved coming to us and we loved having him. He never looked back toward his owner when he was dropped off, which was often in a police vehicle! Whoops, perhaps I shouldn't have mentioned that! Percy was so keen to get into the wood, where all those wonderful smells were waiting to titillate his shiny black doggy nose. But for anybody new walking him he had a little surprise waiting for them, hiding up his sleeve you might say.

Yes, Percy could most certainly make your day, a day to remember alright because he had a very unusual habit. In fact, we never ever saw another dog in all the years of running our boarding kennels come even close to the amazing trick of Percy's. I don't know if I was fortunate, or unfortunate to be the first one to find out about it. I just happened to be the first person to walk him on his very first day with us. I thought walking Percy would impress his dad, the big laughing policeman, especially if Geoff, the boss of the best boarding kennels in Great Britain actually walked the dogs as well. I also thought he might recommend his police pals to use our facilities and sure enough he did!

On Percy's first walk I set off around the wood with him and he was thoroughly enjoying himself, strutting away so importantly. Did he think he was a police dog? Suddenly, with no warning whatsoever he did a handstand. I thought that was a good trick for a circus but his trick got even better. While his two back legs were waving at the sky and the other more handsome end, his face I mean, was contemplating living in Australia, a powerful jet of dog pee shot straight out like a bullet from the secret pistol that lived between Percy's legs! Not in any way expecting this unlikely stunt, a jet of soothingly warm dog pee hit me full blast in my left ear! To say I was shocked was a gross understatement! I was absolutely dumbfounded and wasn't too amused either! The last thing I needed was to have my left ear syringed out by dog pee! What is more I had only had my ears syringed by my doctor the day before! I looked down at Percy in amazement as I groped in my pocket for a handkerchief. Thank God, I had one with me. He looked up at me while wagging his little tail, (I don't mean the one that had just squirted me in my ear-hole!) as if to say, "Come on Geoff, stop dawdling, let's get on with my walk."

Percy wasn't malicious in any way and I am sure he had no idea what he had done. I thought, *I bet that laughing policeman knows all about Percy's little trick! And he is laughing all the way down our drive.* As far as I knew, the laughing policeman hadn't told anyone else about Percy's little trick, so why should I? What a naughty thought, the last thing I wanted was my staff laughing at me because Percy had peed in my ear. To say they would take the pee would have been another understatement! No, I decided not to tell a soul. I thought, *let nature take its natural course*, or was it, *let Percy take his aim*!

It was mid-morning when I had taken Percy on that more than memorable first walk, so when he was due to be taken out for the late afternoon walk, I would make sure to wangle it would be my manageress who would walk him in the afternoon. She had played a few tricks on me in the past, this was going to be payback time, and big time! I completed Percy's first walk while drying my ear and walked him to his kennel, stroked him on his head and whispered in his ear, "May your aim be true little chap."

I went into the office to see the Manageress and said, "Make sure you walk Percy this afternoon and give him your very best attention, especially with his owner being a policeman. Anyway, it's perks of the job being able to walk a nice little dog like that. You don't want to be dragged around the wood with the usual lunatics pulling away at you. Do you?"
She smiled at me and I knew I had sold her the job of walking Percy.

In later years I didn't always help with dog walking, especially in the afternoons, but I most certainly put myself in a position to make sure I was available to help that particular day. Dog walking began at the usual time of four o'clock and my good lady friend, the manageress, put Percy on his lead. I took the dog next door to Percy so I could follow or should I say tail my manageress and watch the little chap in action. I was eagerly following her from about fifteen yards, to my disappointment Percy stopped, cocked his leg, just like any normal dog and then had a little pee. There was no handstand to be seen anywhere! I thought, *What's going on? What's gone wrong? Is Percy taking the pee or what? Have I imagined it? No, I don't think so. I would remember his warm dog pee penetrating my inner ear for the rest of my life!*

Ignoring my disappointment I carried on following from a discreet fifteen yards and suddenly, with no warning for Percy's intended victim, up he went on his front legs into a perfect handstand, a gymnast would be proud of.
I excitedly thought, *Good old Percy.*
A jet of pee shot out from Percy's secret pistol and hit the unsuspecting victim full on the side of her neck. My evil thoughts were, *Now Percy, it would have been much better in the ear-hole!*
I suppose beggars can't be choosers. I nearly keeled over with laughter.
My manageress turned to me and gave me the filthiest look possible, she obviously hadn't seen the funny side of Percy's stunt!
She yelled at me, "You swine. I thought it was unusual that you were helping with the dog walking. You knew damn well he was going to do that. Didn't you?" (Not the way to talk to your boss, but perhaps I deserved it.)
"Who me? Now what makes you think I would do a thing like that?" I replied trying to keep a straight face.
I could see my manageress wasn't particularly amused with the prank, as she tried to wipe Percy's cooling pee from her neck. I was sure I could see a hint of a smile on her face as she said, "Don't you worry Geoff. You won't get away with this one. I'll remember and I'll get you back one of these days. You just wait and see."
True to her word my manageress did get me back, take note and watch out for a later story

about *MY FRIEND BEN* in my second book. How about that for an advert!

Percy's fame spread rapidly to all the staff and they made sure they were very vigilant and not in the firing line when he did his handstands to fire his pistol. I told all the staff he had just missed me when I first walked him. I kept Percy's and my little secret for a long time. After all, it could have been much more than my life was worth if my manageress had found out!

Percy always came to us spotlessly white, which never lasted long because after he had been around the wood a few times he began to turn a yellowy brown colour. This was caused by his frequent handstands which made his pee trickle onto his upturned tummy. The pee made it damp and when the dry ground was flicked up by his paws it stuck to his hair growing on his undercarriage. Each day he lost some of his whiteness and turned more and more yellowy brown. The day before he was collected he had a bath and was once again transformed into a bright, fluffy little white dog.

Geoffrey Doody

Bath Time

It didn't take us long to realise when dogs stayed with us there was a good chance that they could smell when they were collected. *Could smell* is the operative word, because they could absolutely stink, or even honk, would be a more appropriate description. The smell some dogs acquired was no fault of yours truly, because we kept the kennels spotlessly clean, but we couldn't keep them clean twenty-four hours a day. That would have been impossible. So, why did some dogs stink or honk, if our kennels were so clean? They smelt because they were peeing and crapping throughout the night and then sitting in it, before we were able to clean the mess up the following morning. Most dogs didn't sit in their crap too much, but they definitely sat in their own pee—and I mean big time! The dogs were usually male by the way, bitches were usually much cleaner and would patiently wait for their walkies in the morning. The male dogs used to pee in their runs and then sit in it, lie in it, or even roll in it! The concrete floor of each run had a slight fall sloping down from the sleeping quarters to the mesh gate, so the water or any other liquid like pee would trickle down to the open gulley, which was just the other side of the gate.

I designed special steel-and-carbon fibre benches to fit where the dogs liked to sit or lie, up against the gate. But did they use them? No, of course they damn well didn't. My idea was to raise the dogs up off the floor, so as well as being more comfortable, any pee they had peed higher up the run, could flow or seep underneath and their doggy coats wouldn't get soiled.
Lots of dogs would just simply ignore my benches and lie in their own pee. And boy, oh boy, they didn't half-whiff after they had been with us for a few days. Nobody in their right mind would have wanted to cuddle those smelly characters, especially when they had a couple of weeks staying with us, that's for sure. Can you imagine what those canines would smell like in a confined space, such as a car on their way home? Not only would you smell the stench, you would probably be able to see it as well! I would hate to think what it would be like riding along with the smell getting worse and worse by the second. I can assure you it would become disgustingly unbearable! The owners more than likely would have blamed us for the state of their little doggies' obnoxious aroma that was wafting from its coat. But we all knew whose damn fault it really was!

We had to sort out the big smelly problem once and for all because I knew if it was not sorted, we were going to get a very bad or even smelly name for our business. Bath the doggies! Yes, that was the answer. That's exactly what we did!

Even a clean dog that had been with us for more than four days was automatically bathed because they would have developed a natural doggy odour. They sweat just like humans and like humans, unfortunately some smell much stronger than others! Well, the dogs were not quite automatically bathed because we didn't have a machine which could have been likened to a dishwasher, called a dog washer! Perhaps I should have invented one! No, the girls did the bathing and they really enjoyed it too. That's the girls, not the dogs! Having said that, a lot of the dogs really did enjoy it too. There was only a minority that weren't too keen to get wet.

Some of our regular guests enjoyed being bathed so much, I'm sure they got dirty on purpose, just to get another bath before they went home. Occasionally some dogs had been known to roll in the mud while being walked, shortly after their nice warm bath. Hey ho, more work for the girls! Bath the little blighters again! Once this had happened a few times we got wise to them and in wet weather we stopped walking those clean hounds in the wood and took them down our tarmac drive instead. (Hey remember, that's the place where I put my foot right in it, on the way out to Adrian and Melanie's new home!) So that was yet another major problem solved. I'm sure some of the dogs left our premises cleaner than when they came in!

One customer had a white Samoyed, you would never guess his name was *Sam*. How about that for originality? The first time Sam's owners collected him they thought we had brought out the wrong dog because he was so white and fluffy. Not only had the girls bathed him but they had given him a good grooming as well.

An English Mastiff boarded with us called *Tiny*. Now that's a great name isn't it, because an English Mastiff is an incredibly large breed of dog. He was almost full-grown being fifteen months old, but already he was a giant of a dog. He was quite easily the biggest dog I had ever seen. He could have been compared to a donkey or even a young giraffe with a short neck. It took three girls to bath him and he was so big he couldn't even fit in the bath, which was actually designed for human use perhaps that puts his size into perspective. The only way the girls could shampoo him was outside on the grass. The four of them, that is the three girls and Tiny, made a lovely picture on a warm summer's day. One of the girls stood on a chair showering him with a hose pipe, while another tended to his every need and the third girl held on to his lead. He just stood there with a daft expression on his face and I must say he did appear to enjoy himself.

One customer who was collecting her own dog actually took a photograph of the memorable event.

When we bathed the dogs (or should I say the girls did), they used shampoo meant for humans. What a rip off dog shampoo was. It was extortionate price for only a small container. I used to travel twenty miles to a wholesaler who provided a service for the hairdressers in the area. I would go into the large warehouse and purchase twenty five to thirty one-gallon containers of shampoo and it came in all sorts of exotic perfumes too. It was never possible to get all the shampoo in the same perfume because we always needed so much. I always telephoned first to make sure they had enough stock in. The lemon scent was my personal favourite but it also came in peach, pear, strawberry, almond and even coconut to name a few.

The owner of the warehouse thought I had a chain of hairdressing shops because I was there on such a regular basis. It was a big surprise for him when I told him the shampoo was for dogs. He looked at me in disbelief and eventually realised I wasn't taking the 'Mickey' after all! He in actual fact found it quite amusing that I was using the human shampoo on dogs! I should imagine Tiny's fur coat would have added up to the equivalent of at least 100 human heads of hair! We used at least half a gallon of shampoo on his coat and that was no exaggeration, when a tablespoon would have been more than enough for humans.

I could never understand why the girls always moaned about washing my new Toyota Land Cruiser, which I was very proud of, because they also needed a chair to stand on. The girls never seemed to moan when they bathed Tiny, which used to take them at least three times longer and in the process they got themselves extremely wet! At least the Land Cruiser didn't shake its coat all over them like Tiny did, soaking them even more and creating sounds of girlie squeals and laughter. Well, I suppose the answer was bathing Tiny was much more fun, than the boss's boring Land Cruiser!

When the girls had finished a good bathing session I sometimes wondered if the dogs had bathed the girls, they appeared to be wetter than the dogs!

After having happily collected their recently shampooed sweet-smelling perfumed pooches, dog owners would ring up and congratulate us on how lovely their pooches looked and smelt. As far as I was concerned *smelt* was the key word. They would ask, "Is that lovely smell from the disinfectant you use?"
"No, we shampooed your dog."
"Really, that's incredible he never lets us shampoo him!"

The free shampooing service we provided definitely increased our trade and we never told the majority of owners we had bathed their little doggies because sometimes they might have wanted to know the reason why. They could have asked, "But why did you bath him?"

"Oh, because he likes lying in his crap and pee," should have been my answer.

I'm sure they would like to have known that, wouldn't they? Of course, I knew exactly what the blighters did. How the hell could I tell the owners that their little Fido was a filthy little sod!

Some dogs had to be bathed because they had a slobber problem. What I mean is they would have saliva drooling, or even worse, at times it was wrapped around their jaws like slimy, clingfilm! They were usually dogs that had big jowls like Bulldogs, Great Danes, and especially Boxers. We always used to have to watch dogs like that, not because they were dangerous, but because if they shook their heads the slobber hanging six inches from their jaws could easily fly through the air when the dog shook its head. The slimy slobber could hit you on the side of your face, attaching itself in a cold, wet, horrible slimy string, or if you were really unlucky. Oh my God, your mouth! Now that was one good reason to keep your mouth closed! Not a very pleasant feeling, believe me. So those slobbery characters needed a good clean-up as well. Good luck girls—rather you than me!

The afternoon before a busy collection day the girls could bath as many as thirty dogs. It was just like a conveyer belt of dogs going past the office. A dirty doggy bounding all over the place would go past the office door not knowing what was in store for him. He probably thought he was going for a walk, albeit it in a different direction. Straight into the bathing room they went.

Most dogs enjoyed the ruff and tumble with the girls and there were only a few that found it wasn't quite to their liking. After the bathing session the wet bedraggled doggies would be passed over to the drying team who stood on the lawn with towels at the ready, waiting in anticipation to find how boisterous the next doggy was going to be.

Fortunately, it was usually the summer when the very busy bathing days took place, so a good towelling down would usually suffice. In the winter a nice warm hairdryer was used. With lots of rubs from the towel and many violent shakes from the dog. No wonder the girls got soaked. When a dog shakes water from its coat, watched in slow motion, it resembles a spin drier in action. It wasn't long before the dog would look like it was about to be shown at Crufts! The dogs would be clean, fluffy and more importantly smelling sweetly from the perfumed shampoo, whichever the bathing girls had fancied using on the day.

It's Raining Cats and Dogs

I often used to watch all this action with a big grin on my face. The girls were happy, the dogs were happy, the owners were happy and of course Geoff's big nose, with his super sense of smell was happy.

Geoffrey Doody

Spots before Your Eyes

We have just had two doggy stories, now let us have one about our pussycat friends in the cattery.

When you start your own business from scratch, by the way the word *scratch* is very appropriate to this story, you have to learn things the hard way. There is nobody there to give you any advice and like in life, we learned new things at the cattery and kennels almost every day. This particular story is based on learning from a new experience in the cattery.

In the early days when I was still on my own, I occasionally found tiny spots on the cream floor tiles when I was cleaning out some of the cats in the cattery. The spots were reddy brown in colour and looked a little bit like fly dirt, I thought no more about it. As the business grew we had more cats and the reddy brown spots seemed to get more frequent. We also noticed there were tiny brown specks that looked like large dust particles, or even fine particles of soil. The look-a-like specks were no bigger than a pin head. In some instances they were all over the floor—especially if there were two cats living in the same run. Of course, two or even three cats living together in the same run were from the same household. We were certainly not stupid enough to mix cats together, like some Catteries did! If we had, God knows what we would have found after a night of cat fighting.

We naively thought that all the dirt was from the cat's fur. I imagined they had been rolling about in a flower bed at their home before they had come to us. Who knows what the pussycats might have been up to!

On one particular day I was asked to go to the cattery and inspect the tiled floor in one of the runs, where two new cats had arrived the day before. The staff wanted me to see the state of the floor before they cleaned it. I stared at the cream tiles, well they were a cream colour the day before but what greeted my eyes was absolutely disgusting. The floor was covered in reddy brown spots and they were bigger than any I had ever seen before. Some of them were the size of, let's say the top of a pencil and they were more like splashes. The horrible part of this was, even to the untrained eye, they looked more like blood than anything else. In fact, *UGH,* it was blood! I thought, *Oh my God, these cats are bleeding to death!*

I gently picked each cat up and carefully examined them. Both cats seemed to be okay and I couldn't see any wounds or blood coming from either of them. The cats looked really healthy and had eaten all the food from their morning meal. They were brother and sister and there appeared to be no antagonism between them. They had definitely not been fighting and were totally unmarked. Perhaps a mouse had wandered in and they had been lucky enough to have had some live food as a tasty extra on their menu! There seemed to be nothing to worry about, so I gave the okay for the girls to go ahead with the cleaning.

The next morning the girls were greeted with the same *bloody* (to coin a phrase), problem again. Low and behold the cream tiles had been tarnished with the same bloody mess. That was the only and best way of describing it—a bloody mess—that's for sure! Something was definitely taking the blood from the two cats and I wanted to know exactly what it was.

I was thinking along the lines of vampire bats! I knew they didn't reside in our country, I think they actually come from South America. Perhaps some stupid idiot has been keeping the vampire bats as pets and they have escaped, or even worse, let loose on purpose! Well, your imagination can run amok. Can't it? I thought, *Maybe the vet can throw some light on this.*

I immediately phoned him and said in an urgent tone, "I think something is taking blood from two cats that came in a couple of days ago. There are spots of blood all over the floor tiles."

The vet spontaneously replied, "Oh, that's a simple problem. They've only got fleas."

On hearing that statement I was absolutely devastated. "Fleas!" I blurted out.

I privately panicked and thought, *They've only got fleas! Fleas! How the hell can having fleas in my cattery be a simple problem? What is this simple problem going to do to our bloody reputation? If this simple problem got out we'll be dead in the water!*

All these problems were going through my mind and I tried to think calmly. I suppose it could have been worse. Fleas were far better than a vampire bat problem! But why did I have to get the problem just when the business was building up steadily? My mind eventually stopped racing and I calmly asked the vet, "How do we eradicate these fleas?"

I sure hoped it would be a lot simpler solution than vampire bats!

The vet replied, "All you need is a special chemical. It comes in an aerosol can. You simply spray the infected cats all over. But be very careful not to get it in their eyes."

"Do you sell it?" I asked eagerly.

"Yes, we do have some in stock," he replied.

"I'll be right down." I banged down the receiver, raced to the vehicle and drove down to the vet's like a madman. I was back in record time with three cans of spray.

It's Raining Cats and Dogs

The vet had advised we would need two people to perform the operation, a simple task he made it sound. Perhaps he hadn't met as many little 'tigers' as I had!

One person was to pick the cat up by the scruff of its neck and while the cat was suspended, put their other hand over the cat's eyes to shield them from the spray. The other person would spray the cat all over, being very careful not to get the spray in the cat's or even human eyes—especially Geoff's! Yes, it sounded simple, but time would tell. Guess who was going to be holding that bundle of fur that concealed all those teeth and claws. Well surprise, surprise. Yes it would be good old Geoff as usual. To be fair, it was my cattery! While performing the potentially dangerous operation I just hoped there wasn't going to be more blood on the floor that belonged to me, to join the previously deposited splats from the cat-biting fleas. Is anybody itching yet? Because I am!

So this was the start of my first exciting exercise of spraying a cat and hopefully eradicating its nasty parasites. I armed one of the girls with the aerosol can and made it abundantly clear it was the cat that had the fleas. Not me! I politely said to her, "Just please make sure you watch where you're pointing that damn thing!"

I had no idea how the first cat was going to react when I picked it up by the scruff of its neck and more importantly, what its reaction would be when we started spraying it. I imagined a full-scale war could erupt. I thought, *Well here goes. No guts no glory.* I gently slid my hand around the back of the cats head and stroked our furry guest or should I say the first guinea pig, to let him know I was friendly and wasn't going to hurt him. I confidently located the loose skin on the scruff of his neck and smoothly picked him up. I was pleasantly surprised how he reacted. My pussycat friend went completely placid and tucked his back legs up, as if I was going to carry him off to somewhere new, just like his mummy had done when he was a kitten a few years previously. The aerosol can then made an appearance from behind the girl's back. We had previously decided to hide it because we didn't want to frighten the poor chap before we even got started. It could have possibly made him go a tiny bit berserk! And berserk cats can be an absolute nightmare! To our amazement the cat never even batted an eyelid! He remained perfectly calm and allowed us to spray him all over. I said, "Well, that was a piece of cake. Okay, next pussycat please."

Knowing animals like I did, I could have virtually guaranteed that the next cat wouldn't be so easy. Of course as usual, thank God, I was absolutely wrong. You thought I was going to say right then, didn't you? Amazingly, the second cat did an exact repeat performance as the first cat. Then it hit me, not the cat, the idea. They had obviously been sprayed many times before by their owners and probably from when they were kittens. Anyway, no major cat war had occurred and as a bonus none of my blood had been splattered all over the cream tiles! And more importantly, I hadn't been sprayed either!

First thing the following morning I couldn't wait to get into the cattery to check out the two flea-bitten pussycat's floor. To my relief it was spotless, not a disgusting blood splat anywhere. So it became routine, if the cream tiles were splattered with blood spots the day after a cat had arrived, it was zapped immediately with the magic spray. Cats only needed just the one zapping and they would be flee from fleas. Oh I'm sorry, I mean free from fleas. (Bit of a tongue-twister that one!) But that was only until the cats were let out into the outside fleas.

We decided from the very first case of fleas we would never tell the owners and I am absolutely sure it had been the right decision. We knew it was impossible for cats to get fleas in our cattery. I had built it with no nooks and crannies for fleas to hide in. As soon as any cat finished its stay, its area was totally disinfected and fleas could not exist without a warm body, full of lovely warm blood to feed on!

Take note you cat lovers! At least 50 percent of cats that came to our cattery were infested with fleas but because of our vigilance and our cream tiles, there was no way any cat would ever leave our premises with the horrible blood-sucking little parasites living in their fur. By the way, have you had an itch and a scratch while you have been reading this?

Cats obtain their little passengers from the small mammals they kill. Wild rabbits are absolutely crawling with fleas and even moles that live their lives 99 percent underground carry the horrible parasites. So the fleas riding in on their host into a warm house, where there are usually fitted carpets, arrive in paradise. I know of quite a few people who have had to have their houses fumigated by professionals.

To me the most alarming thing about fleas is they often carry a tapeworm larva in their blood. When the flea bites a cat, the horrible larva transfers itself into the cat's bloodstream and that is why you have to worm cats on a regular basis. Even worse, humans can be bitten by the horrible blood sucking parasites and humans have been known to have tapeworms well in excess of twelve feet long in their intestines! Whether humans obtain tapeworms from fleas, I don't know, but it doesn't even bear thinking about. Does it? I started to itch when I was writing this story and I am sure as hell itching now. How about you?

It's Raining Cats and Dogs

Unfortunately, especially for me, not all cats had previously been sprayed before they came to stay with us, hence, it wasn't always so easy to pick those cats up. If it looked like we were going to become worse off from the occasional spitting, hissing furry bundle of fighting fury, we sprayed those cats without handling them. We did this by cornering them and giving them a squirt from the magic can. Often they wouldn't stand still, especially when somebody was spraying a strange-smelling chemical liquid at them. Well, would you? I soon got quite adapt at hitting a moving target, spraying an airborne cat as it flashed past me in its run, was some sort of experience, I can tell you. I was always very careful to avoid the cat's eyes and of course my own. I knew the spray really stung, I had been hit several times by the girls, when I had been holding a cat! I have to say, the girls were definitely not as good a shot as me!

It wasn't so easy to tell if a dog had fleas, but I can assure you, if a cat came in with fleas and the owners also had a dog staying with us, the dog would also be zapped with the good old faithful spray. Our reasoning was if the cat had fleas, then the dog living in the same house would most certainly have them too. I can definitely verify that because if I go back to the very first cats I sprayed there, was also a dog from the same family boarding with us. I decided to check her out and yes, she was also covered in the nasty parasites. And oh my God, her bedding had tiny specks of blood on it!

My very first experience of spraying a dog with the magic zapper was yet another exercise that I wasn't sure how the dog would react. Would it bite me or the girl? Would it go berserk? The member of staff and me discussed it in great detail beforehand and I decided I would hold the dog by the collar, as I was the strongest. The girl would do the zapping. I said to her, "Just remember the dog has fleas not me!" Well to our utmost pleasure it was a piece of cake. This dog had been sprayed before!

After all our zapping the good news was we never had a complaint about a cat or even a dog leaving our premises with fleas.

I know to this day if a cat or dog had gone home with the nasty blood sucking parasites infested in its coat, *Joe Public* would have most certainly had a field day and blamed us for it. Joe Public would never have believed it was impossible for their pets to catch fleas from our premises! So be warned, if your cats or dogs are scratching a lot, they could have fleas. Oh, I've just scratched my head yet again . . . oh, now my chest. Are you itching now? Well you should be!

I will now explain how fleas manufacture and produce spots of blood, whether they landed on our cream tiles in the cattery or the carpets in your clean house!

The fleas carried by your cat or dog are all the time sucking and feeding on your pet's blood. Every now and again your cat or dog might shake or scratch its body quite furiously. It is quite normal for cats and dogs to do this, whether they have got fleas or not, just like a person having a good old scratch. So when a flea-infested cat or dog shakes or scratches, some of the flea crap, which is the end product from the blood, is shaken off.

In the cattery we were lucky because the flea crap, (posh word for shit) in the form of red spots, were splattered onto our lovely cream tiles, which we could easily see. Now your carpet is 'a different kettle of fish', to coin a phrase, because more likely than not you won't be able to see it!

Here is a warning to all you cat and dog owners. If your pet goes outside and has anything to do with all the little mammals out there, then you must spray them on a regular basis because those blood splats could be going all over your lovely carpets or even worse, maybe your bed!

Don't take my word on this, speak with your own vets and I am sure they will tell you the same thing. It doesn't bear thinking about. Does it? Surely you are scratching now and what about the thought of the good old tapeworms! Now that's food for thought! Isn't it! YUK!

Geoffrey Doody

Filipino Take-Away

I bet you think this book sounds more like stories from a restaurant business with all these take-away titles!

I had never heard of a Filipino take-away until I met a certain Scottish gentleman. The person concerned was very much a Scot in his appearance and also his lingo. Basically I couldn't understand a word he was talking about, due to his very broad accent, unless I asked him to slow down.

From his appearance you would think he had arrived from two or three centuries past. If you had given him a kilt, claymore and shield, he would definitely have got a part in the film *Braveheart*. He had a long straggly ginger beard and wore a tartan beret. He looked like he was wearing a false beard and cap with the red hair that sticks out at the sides, which are often worn by folks portraying comical Scotsmen you see on television. Also some spectators wear them at football and rugby matches. But this guy was definitely for real. He wore glasses and I mean glasses. The lenses were so thick that describing them as the bottom of bottles would have been a gross understatement. They made his eyes look enormous. I could just imagine a young child looking into his eyes and bursting into tears. I am sorry to sound so cruel but I am describing exactly what I saw.

My Scottish friend was dressed in tweedy-type clothes and wore large brown boots; they shone so much I was almost able to see my face in the broad toe caps. He gave the appearance of being a man from the mountains, undoubtedly a Scottish Highlander. I must say, he was a very pleasant man. It was just his appearance that was a little unusual, to say the least. I was intrigued to know what sort of work he did but I was never able to hold a very long conversation because of his strong accent. I nicknamed him *Braveheart* and he used our facilities two or three times a year over a number of years.

Every time he came he was dressed similar and I still never got any better at understanding his Highland twang. Can you believe he had five Border Collies named after the apostles, Matthew, Mark, Luke, John, and Peter, obviously a religious man. Perhaps he needed all the Collies because he was a sheep farmer. But whatever his appearance or profession, he became a very good customer and what did it matter anyway, I was just interested. Or was it nosey? Sometimes I am not sure what the difference is. But let's face it, not many people have five Border Collies. Do they?

Braveheart had been using us for about three years and on this particular day his five apostles were dropped off as usual in tip top condition. They were as happy as Larry. He wasn't an apostle by the way! They looked so sleek with their shiny coats, which were almost as shiny as their dad's toe caps on his brown boots! When he dropped them off, he informed me he was off to the Philippines. Normally he never said where he was going, that's if I managed to understand him. It was always simpler to wish him a good holiday, rather than get into a conversation and keep asking him to repeat what he had said. But I became interested when I actually understood what he had said, I replied, "I believe the Philippines are a nice place to go for a holiday?"
"Och, I'm not going for a holiday. I'm collecting a wife," he replied in his broad Highland twang.
I looked at him in amazement and stuttered, "Oh, how nice." I was totally dumbfounded and stuck for words. (Yes even me, it's never been known before.)

I didn't blame him because I thought he would never pull a dolly bird with his looks, even though he was a nice guy. I was sure he would have undoubtedly frightened off any females before he would even have a chance to talk to them in his Highland twang, because if I had trouble understanding him, how on earth would a foreigner cope? I thought, *Good for you mate. Perhaps you'll come back with a Filipino girl that will make many a man envious!*

Buying Filipino girls for a wife in those days was common news. I was never sure whether to believe it or not, but it looked very likely we were actually going to witness it happening on our very doorstep!

Braveheart was away for two weeks, perhaps in with the price he was throwing in a honeymoon as well! Not a bad place to spend a honeymoon either. If they made each other happy, I personally couldn't see anything wrong in it.

I mentioned to Kathy that evening what he was up to and I jokingly said, "If he comes back with a real cracker, you had better watch your step." I looked at her face and without saying a word she gave me one of those looks, only your wife can give you. I inwardly shuddered and thought, *Time to shut up, Geoff lad!*

Braveheart returned after his two weeks away and he looked very triumphant with his spoils. I took one look at his bride and thought, *I hope they haven't charged you too much money for that one!* She most certainly wasn't the dolly bird I had envisaged. Does it really matter what other people think? No, of course it doesn't. They both looked very happy together and I bet he thought he had got a bargain as well. Perhaps there had been a sale on in the Philippines!

Before he left, he booked his dogs in for yet another stay.

Braveheart and his wife arrived four months later and he was dressed in his usual attire, but strangely they had two dogs less. I wondered what could have happened to them. I didn't dare ask because I knew he thought the world of them all and also I couldn't spare the hour that would be needed to understand him. The reason could have been something simple or even sad like a road accident. But I did happen to notice when he and his new wife dropped off the three remaining dogs, they had put on considerable weight—I mean the newly weds, not the dogs! I suppose his Filipino wife could have been pregnant, even though it had only been four months since I had last seen them! But what about Braveheart? Why had he also put on weight? No, no, no, Geoff, don't even think about it! Don't go there!

I knew his wife was Filipino and what certain type of foods were eaten as a delicacy in some Asian countries. But I had no intention of going down that road, that's for sure. For some of you readers that may not be aware, unfortunately dog meat is farmed and eaten big time in some of these countries!

They returned from their holiday looking very happy and relaxed together and collected the remaining three apostles. Yet again they booked for another stay six weeks later.

Braveheart and his wife arrived on the given day, but—wait for it—minus yet another Collie! What on earth was bloody happening to his dogs and where were the loving couple going every few weeks? How long would it have taken them to eat a Border Collie? It's none of my business, stop thinking about it, Geoff lad. My God, I didn't really fancy hearing the answer!

After Braveheart and his Filipino wife collected the last two surviving apostles, we never heard anymore from them again. Were the two remaining Collies eaten? We will never know.

I have always known dogs are a delicacy in parts of Asia and after all they had both put on weight! I just hoped beyond hope that I hadn't really witnessed a Filipino take-away of the
Border Collie variety!

Geoffrey Doody

Mother

My Mothers name is *Irene*, but while telling these stories, I will refer to her as *Mother*.

At the time of writing this book she had two cats, which were named *Ben* (who I made famous in an earlier chapter) and *Jimmy*, also a dog that was a small Border Collie cross, named *Zoe*. My sister Gail has also had many animals ranging from cats, dogs, horses and even goats, let alone the small animals she collected over the years. Gail was well on the way to having a small zoo! In the initial years, Mother and Gail helped in the cattery and kennels, but this story is all about the adventures of Mother.

Mother has always loved animals; it obviously runs in my family. When we opened the cattery and kennels she couldn't wait to help us. In fact, she was chomping at the bit! She was in her early sixties, well sixty-two actually, but certainly didn't look it and her energy levels were like someone twenty years younger. All her family were long-lived, her mother was still alive at that time—my grandmother, being twenty three years Mother's senior. I will let you readers do the mathematics on that one.

Mother was only just over five feet tall, which made her look a lot younger. She was very fit for her age and keen to help us in any way possible. Not only did she love being with the animals, she knew as a bonus, it would have kept her even fitter and younger. She loved to help with the dog walking and went onto the payroll, just like any other member of staff. Hey, and you can't get anyone more reliable than your mum. Can you?

Well, Mother certainly was very reliable in turning up for the dog walking, she was always there on time and raring to go. But how reliable was she at walking dogs? She certainly turned out to be very reliable indeed at making us laugh with her many adventures whilst dog walking.

We used to give Mother the dogs that were easiest to walk and unlikely to pull her over. Could you imagine giving my five-feet nothing Mother, two German Shepherds to walk? No, never! I always told her, "Whatever happens, never let go of the lead!" I knew if we had given Mother two German Shepherds to walk, she would have ended up face down on her stomach, whilst still hanging onto their leads being dragged at ten miles per hour. Mother would certainly have been round that wood in record time! No, we just gave her little dogs that she could manage, like Yorkshire Terriers, Jack Russells, and Westies, but certainly not Percy, because she may not have been quick enough to duck away from his deadly aim! You can't play that sort of trick on your own Mother. Can you?

After a few weeks as a successful dog walker, Mother had ambitions—ambitions in the form of two very nice yellow Labrador bitches called *Jess* and *Emma*, probably because she had always wanted a Labrador of her own. And at that time it looked like she was hoping for a chance of two! The biggest dogs Mother had walked together previously were two Westies. I don't know how, but she managed to persuade me to let her walk the two yellow Labradors. Sales talk obviously runs in the family! At least I knew they didn't pull on their leads.

Off Mother proudly went, full of her new self-importance along with Jess and Emma. As she left the kennels, I hoped the warning I had brainwashed her with, was still ringing in her ears, "Whatever happens, don't let go of their leads!"
I also asked all the staff who were walking the other dogs to keep a watchful eye on Mother.

Jess and Emma were actually well-trained gundogs and I knew they were very obedient. There shouldn't have been any problems at all, or so I thought. The first time she walked them there was nothing for me to worry about because she came back with a big grin on her face, after successfully completing the circuit in the wood.

So I was right that time, makes a pleasant change doesn't it! Mother came back eager to take two more big dogs out for walkies but I decided not to push our luck too far. With great disappointment for her she went back to walking smaller dogs.

The dog walking was keeping Mother really fit and she had no problem doing the circuit at least ten times a day. She enjoyed herself so much with Jess and Emma that everyday while they were with us, she insisted on taking them. But inevitably disaster struck, as it usually does.

One day, Jess and Emma ran back into the kennels dragging their leads and surprise, surprise, no Mother in tow. Jess and Emma were okay, but more importantly where was Mother? I ran like the wind into the wood, trying hard not to imagine what might have befallen her. I had only got twenty yards into the wood when an apparition appeared before me. The only way it resembled Mother was in height. Other than that, it looked like the 'thing' from the bog! She looked like some sort of mud monster. Only this monster wasn't very frightening at all because it was sobbing.
I said to her in a very concerned tone, "Are you okay mum?"
"Yes." she sobbed back, "But I let go of their leads."
"Don't worry about Jess and Emma. They're all right. They're back in the kennels."

I could see Mother's face brighten up with the good news.

Mother looked a rare sight and her white hair had turned almost black with the wet mud clinging to it. I could tell she had been dragged a fair way, as her clothes were covered in wet mud and one of her wellington boots was missing. Thankfully, she wasn't hurt, but just a little shaken up and I won't talk about her pride. I am sorry but I just couldn't help myself. I started to laugh out aloud and it wasn't long before she started to laugh with me. We laughed until we nearly cried. Thank God, Mother could see the funny side to her misadventure. I wiped the tears from my eyes and said, "I've just got to take a photograph of you." And we both laughed even more.

It turned out a cock pheasant had run out in front of the two Labradors and of course being gundogs, they couldn't resist their natural instinct. Jess and Emma had bolted after the pheasant, yanking Mother clean off her feet. She had hung on desperately, leaving one Wellington boot behind in the mud. But true to her promise, she had gamely hung on to the leads for as long as possible. She had remembered what my explicit instructions were and had been very brave hanging on for at least ten yards. We could see her drag marks in the mud to prove it! Ten yards is an awful long way to be dragged, by two Labradors in their prime, while lying face down in mud! To this day, Mother still holds the record of a ten-yard drag, a record I am sure will never be broken. Who knows, it could be an Olympic sport one day! I am sure you must have heard of drag racing! Maybe Mother's new sport should be called drog racing!!!

Another dog that Mother walked many times, which became one of her favourites, was a little black mongrel called *Bill*. One day Mother came wandering back to the kennels with Bill's lead and collar trailing behind her—but no Bill! Either Bill had turned invisible, or he had disappeared over the horizon. I rapidly assessed it had to be the latter, at least she had hung onto Bill's lead, as instructed. But where the hell was Bill?
To this day, I don't think she even knew that Bill wasn't behind her on the end of his collar and lead.

As Mother proudly walked into the kennels "Bill-less", I asked, "Where's Bill?"
She looked at me in amazement and then turned round to where little Bill should have been. I didn't have time to wait for an answer, I just dashed straight past her to make the 150-yard sprint to the five-bar gate, to try to seal Bill's escape. I thought, *Déjà vu.* Before I got back to the kennels, good old prodigal Bill had returned under his own steam. He didn't need Mother, or anyone else for that matter, to show him his way back. As the years passed by, we have had many

a laugh over Mother taking a collar and lead for a walk!

Another of Mother's walks was with an aged Bulldog called *Fred*. A lot of people don't realise that Bulldogs haven't a very long shelf life and every new day over six years is a bonus. Fred was six and a half years old at that time and definitely had one foot in the grave.

Fred was most definitely on borrowed time, but like any other dog, he really enjoyed his walks. As he was so old and slow, Mother was the prime candidate to take him for walkies. She had loads of patience with him because it took poor old Fred three times as long to cover the same distance, as a younger fitter dog.

One day Mother was out with Fred for a lot longer than normal, so I decided to investigate. As I entered the wood poor Mother was walking toward me crying.
"What on earth is wrong, mum?" I enquired with some concern.
"Fred's dead," she sobbed.
"Oh no! Are you sure?"
"Yes, I'm positive. He just dropped like a stone. I tried to revive him but there was just no response," she sobbed even more.
I thought, *Oh no, I hope she hasn't attempted to give him the kiss of life!* I certainly didn't fancy a go, as Fred wasn't particularly that good-looking

and if you know what a Bulldog looks like, neither would you! Bulldogs have a big fat mouth with protruding lips and usually a load of slobber coming from within! Yuk!

Mother pointed to where she had left Fred and we walked rapidly over to his dead body. Dead body! What dead body? Fred was nowhere to be seen.
"Are you sure this is the right place, mum?"
"Well, I think so," she replied as she looked all around totally bewildered.
We walked on a little further, but still no Fred.
"Are you absolutely certain he was dead?' I asked Mother in a very puzzled tone.
"I'm positive. He wasn't breathing. Perhaps we are in the wrong place."
We walked on even further, but still no dead Fred. I quietly said, "Surely, he hasn't gone to heaven already!"
Mother turned around to me and to my amazement said, "Really! Do you think he could have?"
I did hope she was joking. Surely she was joking!
"Gone to heaven, gone to heaven, like the hell he has! He's over there, look!" I exclaimed.
Mother looked over to where I was pointing and sure enough there was Fred, who was most definitely not dead. In fact, he was very much alive, mooching along at his own tortoise-like speed with not a care in the world. We were both

extremely relieved to see him, as I am sure Fred was relieved to know he wasn't dead!

"Okay Mum, no false alarms next time you walk him. My heart can't stand anymore frights like that, let alone yours . . . and we won't mention Fred's!"

"Don't worry. I'm not walking him again," Mother snapped back bitterly.

"Of course you will. He's a lovely dog and anyway lightening doesn't strike twice. Perhaps he just toppled over and felt like he needed a little rest."

Mother was persuaded to walk good old Fred, only because nobody else wanted to do it with him being so slow. Everything went well over the next two days, until Mother arrived five minutes after the morning walks had finished, Fredless. "He's definitely dead now." Mother blurted out. I had a sneaky feeling she could have been right this time.

Fred's owners had told us when they delivered him, he had been suffering with mild heart attacks and as long as he appeared to be okay and recovered from them quite quickly, there would be no need to call the vet. They had been hanging on all year trying to get a holiday, not wanting to leave poor old Fred with anyone, but in the end they just felt they had to take a much-needed break.

We were quite used to taking in old pets and caring for them as long as the owners were prepared for what could be the worst. Fortunately, we lost very few old pets and I can assure you, we didn't lose any young ones either! But when it did occasionally happen, with old ones that is, it was always very sad for us and of course the owners.

Anyway, back to Fred lying, dying, or dead in the wood. I walked with Mother to where she had left him and said, "Let's go and check the old man out."
This time we found Fred keeled over on his side. 'As dead as a door nail'. There was definitely no sign of life and there was most certainly no 'kiss of life' forthcoming from me, and I sure wasn't even going to ask Mother. Knowing her, she might very well have attempted it!

Fred was lying on his back with his feet and nose pointing to heaven and was about one hundred and twenty yards away from the kennels. I knew Fred was going to be really heavy to carry. Do you realise how heavy a Bulldog can be? There was no way I was going to attempt to carry poor old Fred such a long distance, he would have been a solid 'dead weight'. I am sure there is a joke there somewhere. So I thought it would be a good idea to fetch a wheelbarrow and a hessian sack to cover him up.

I led Mother back to the kennels as she was sobbing a little, it was always quite a shock to see a dead animal and especially when you had got attached to them. Mother had indeed got quite fond of poor old Fred. As we walked back I tried to console her and said, "You must remember he's had a good life. What could be a better way to die, than when you are having a lovely walk with a lovely lady, in beautiful woodland and just keel over peacefully? Not a bad way to go is it?" Mother seemed to perk up a little with those few kind words.

I continued, "The best thing you can do is go and help with the rest of the dog walking. I'm sure that'll take your mind of it. Don't worry. I'll sort poor old Fred out."

I left Mother and went to get my trusty wheelbarrow, a hessian sack and more importantly a strong girl. It would definitely need two of us to lift Fred gently into the wheelbarrow. My idea was to roll Fred onto the hessian sack and then lift him in. We both rounded the corner to where I had left dead Fred lying. Now, you are not going to believe this and nor could I! But dead Fred was nowhere to be seen! Fred had disappeared yet again! Does this remind you of a story from the Bible? Had Fred been resurrected?

The kennel maid gave me a knowing look, as if I was playing a practical joke on her. I said, "Honestly this is definitely the place I left him.

How many lives has that bloody Bulldog got?" I was looking around totally bewildered and thought, *No wonder most of these Bulldogs get called Churchill or Winston. They are bloody indestructible!*

Well, I must say, it was a fantastic relief to see good old Fred, just around the next corner, wandering about with not a care in the world, just sniffing around as if nothing unusual had ever happened. When I told Mother the good news she started smiling again. Her tranquil world had returned back to normal.

Fred's owners turned up a few days later to collect him, dead or alive. They were absolutely thrilled to see him alive and looking so well. I told them all about Fred's two great escapes from the 'Grim Reaper' and how my mother who loved him to bits, was so relieved he had come back to life.
Fred's owner casually said, "Oh, he does that quite often. He's been doing it for a couple of years now and is often out cold for ages."
I thought, *Oh great. Thanks for letting us know now you are collecting him!* They could have warned us when they delivered him—not just give us the heart pills and say, he should be okay.

Of course, most owners are too afraid to say too much, because we might have refused to take their dying doggies. I must add it was very rare we refused to take any dog, whatever the medical condition was. Anyway, Mother could at least sleep at night, not having the stress of dead Fred on her mind. In fact, he actually made it to the good old age of eight, a great age for a Bulldog and I am sure he must have died with a smile on his face. I just hope they didn't bury the poor old lad alive!

I have another little story about a dog Mother used to walk, which she became very fond of too. This dog was an old black Labrador called *Beauty*. She was lovely natured and wouldn't hurt a fly and she fell totally in love with Mother. Beauty was well overweight, this by the way is quite common for old Labradors. Their owners always seem to spoil them by giving them extra food and treats, which they could have done well without. When Labradors eat, most of them eat very quickly, almost turning themselves into doggy vacuum cleaners, sucking up the food so fast. And Beauty was a prime example.

Beauty was an ideal walk for Mother, as she was very slow, this was because she was so fat! (I mean Beauty, not my Mother!) Mother walked her every time and they became good friends. Beauty took to Mother like a duck to water, just as if she was her new owner and would always be nuzzling Mother as they walked around the wood.

One day at least twenty minutes must have gone by before I realised there was no Mother, and even worse, **NO** Beauty. Having experienced a few stressful moments with Mother, the staff always decided it was me who should search for her. So off I went to look for the dynamic pair. I thought, *This brings back memories. What will I find this time?*

Anyway, it wasn't long before I located both of them and will never forget the sight that beheld me.

There was Mother lying flat on her back, with big fat Beauty sitting proudly on Mother's chest! Now this is absolutely true and I just couldn't believe what I was seeing.

Mother was laughing and I could see Beauty thought it was some sort of game. Her tail was furiously wagging and she was trying desperately to lick Mother's face. With the weight of Beauty on her chest, Mother couldn't even move, let alone get up. Mother spotted me laughing at them. She half screamed and laughed at the same time, "Geoffrey! Get this damn dog off me now! She's crushing me to death!"

Have you noticed? Mothers always use your full name, especially when you are in trouble!

I shouted back to her, "You'll have to wait. I'm going to get the camera."

I wished I had got a camera with me at that moment in time to record what an extraordinary sight I was seeing.
Mother yelled back half laughing, "You dare, just you dare. GEOFFREY! GEOFFREY you come back here at once. Get this blasted dog off me."
As I turned to go away I said, "Oh, so you're daring me now. Are you?"
"GEOFFREY. Come back here this minute. I'll never ever forgive you," Mother shouted, still half laughing while struggling to get her breath.
I laughed and as I turned back toward Mother, I patted my thighs with the flat of my hands and called, "Here Beauty. Come on, good girl."

Beauty jumped off Mother's chest immediately and tried to come toward me, but came to an abrupt standstill, because Mother was still hanging on to Beauty's lead!
I jokingly said to her, "At least I have taught you to do something right."
Still lying on the woodland floor, Mother shouted to me in her most authoritative tone, "**GEOFFREY.** Don't just stand there gawping. Help me up, for Gods sake."
Mother was using the name *Geoffrey* a lot, I knew she really meant business. With that, I quickly went over and helped her to her feet.
I asked, "How on earth did you get yourself into this predicament?"
Mother spluttered out, "Beauty was fussing me then she got carried away. Before I knew what

was happening, she jumped up and knocked me onto my back. The next minute she was sitting on my chest! The more I shouted the more Beauty seemed to think it was a game. My face is all wet from where she kept licking me. I was shouting but no one came. I must have been lying here for over thirty minutes. I couldn't move."

Mother was always prone to just a little bit of exaggeration, like maybe double. With my brief calculations I estimated it would have been half that time. She would have been lying there with big fat Beauty on her chest for about fifteen minutes, and I have to admit that was still rather a long time to have a very fat, overweight Labrador pressing down on you. I asked Mother in a concerned tone, "Are you all right? You're not hurt are you?"
"Of course I'm all right. I'm just exhausted from laughing at Beauty," she replied.

Mother has always been a very good sport and of everyone I've ever known she was always the first to laugh and see the funny side of things. That particular instance was certainly no exception.

I think you now have the picture that Mother got herself into some unusual predicaments and she did love to exaggerate, ever so slightly. It was and still is part of her nature that everything is twice as big, or twice as small, or twice as disastrous as anything she had ever seen before.

It's Raining Cats and Dogs

In the early days Kathy and I didn't get too many chances to get away from the business, but whenever we were away, Mother stayed in our house. She often used to come with her best friend *Edna*, who was a lovely Welsh lady. She was very small and a few years older than my mother.

While we were on holiday I always used to phone home each evening to check how things were going. But to me it sounded quite horrendous with the disasters that were happening back there. The problems sounded mind-blowing according to Mother!

After a while, or should I say quite a few near nervous breakdowns, I used to get Kathy to speak to Mother first, to check out how the land lay or should I say how true things really were. If I went on the line first, there would have been so many disasters and catastrophes that you wouldn't believe. This led me to think we would be bankrupt before we even got home! After my phone call to Mother, it used to take Kathy at least an hour to calm me down and give me some de exaggeration counselling!

On one occasion I had phoned only to find Edna had been helping to walk the dogs from the kennels. God knows why. We had plenty of staff and Edna was getting on in years. Whilst walking a dog, Edna had apparently stepped into a rabbit hole and broken her leg! I was distraught. I knew broken legs could possibly kill old ladies. It turned out toward the end of the telephone conversation, Edna had only nearly broken her leg—yet another of Mother's exaggerations. Missing out the word, *'nearly',* was a very important part of that initial conversation. After all, there is a very big difference between breaking your leg and nearly breaking your leg!

All the dramatic phone conversations we had over the years with Mother, like twenty dogs dying in one week, slight exaggeration by Geoff this time, just didn't happen, as Mother could have led us to believe. There weren't any so-called disasters at all, just the normal day-to-day run-of-the-mill experiences, which occurred when running a busy cattery and kennels business.

Over the years when Mother stayed in our house, we all got wise to her elaborated stories, so the staff gave Mother very little information and only, and I emphasise *only,* what was absolutely necessary. I used to take some time off from skiing to phone in the day, to speak to the manageress and see if anything was really important that I needed to know about. In the evening I would then phone the business line, not the private line, to speak to Mother. She would always be cheerful on the business line, because she would be expecting a customer to be calling, rather than her son or daughter-in-law that she could give

all the 'doom and gloom' to, who were trying to enjoy themselves on holiday! Once I heard the cheerful voice of Mother, I knew I was on to a winner and would say, "Oh, you sound well and cheerful mum. I gather there are no problems at all and everything is going well."
So by then it would have been be too late. Mother wasn't able to use her dramatic private line voice with all the weight of the world on her shoulders. As the saying goes, "You live and learn."

Mother had lots of fun days dog walking and there are just too many stories to mention. I think I could write a book just on the trials and tribulations of Mother at the kennels. As I end with these stories of Mother, I would like to take this opportunity to thank my fantastic mum for being herself and of course all her help over the years. She will be eighty soon and still walks a dog, although not in the boarding kennels. And you will never believe what breed of dog it is, a massive Deerhound, named *Rusty*. He belongs to my sister Gail and he is almost as tall as Mother! Need I say anymore about this remarkable lady. My mother!

We are all so very proud of you, Mum. Just to let you readers know, she will read this story for the first time in Spain on the morning of her eightieth birthday.

Happy Eightieth Birthday Mum!

About the Author

The Author was born in the market town of Newport in county Shropshire, England, where he was involved in various businesses of his own until he took early retirement. They ranged from shop owner, restaurant owner, salesman, self employed gamekeeper, builder, followed by his very successful cattery and kennels business. Dealing with vast amounts of people over the years has given him a strong outgoing personality and he enjoys the fact that new acquaintances find him very likeable and humorous.

The boarding cattery and kennels was built from scratch—in fact he was the builder—it was situated in an idyllic spot near Newport. The market town of Newport, Shropshire is close to the Staffordshire border, therefore the business served those two counties, plus Cheshire and a large part of the Midlands. So as you can imagine he is very well known in those areas. Many of his customers travelled over a hundred miles to use the facilities and in the summertime the business averaged over a hundred cats and one hundred and fifty dogs per day, this obviously resulted in many pet owners coming and going. Hence a vast number of humorous situations arose.

Over the years he has travelled the world and spun many yarns about the hilarious adventures with animals and their owners, making people burst into tears of hysterical laughter. Many suggested he should write a book. This has given him the unique opportunity to share these stories and project his personal brand of humour.